WE'RE ALL A LITTLE BROKEN SOMETIMES

WHERE I'LL FIND YOU

J.A. OWENBY

WHERE I'LL FIND YOU

Copyright © 2018 by J.A. Owenby

This book is a work of fiction. Names, characters, places, and incidents either are products of the author's imagination or are used fictitiously. Any resemblance to actual persons, living or dead, business establishments, events, or locales is entirely coincidental.

Editing by **Wordsru**

Cover design by **Andrew Brown**

Book design by **Inkstain Design Studio**

Proofread by **Nadine Dekema, P. Salem, & Joy Editing Services**

First Edition

Text set in Adobe Devanagari.

Paperback ISBN-13: 978-1-7321510-0-0

Gain access to previews of J.A. Owenby's novels before they're released and to take part in exclusive giveaways. Sign up at: www.jaowenby.com

For Dad

ALSO BY
J.A. OWENBY

THE TRUTH SERIES

The Truth She Knew

Echoes Beneath

Whispers of Her

ACKNOWLEDGMENTS

This book almost didn't happen, and I'm so grateful for everyone who cheered me on.

Brett, thank you for all your love and support. I love you muches and muches.

A special thank you to Crystal Lynn, Aubrey Minear, Kara Long, Alexandra Keister, Posey Pie, Brittney Valencia, Sheri Kaye Hoff, and Shannon Barnard.

And to my sassy office kitty, Chloe, who still snores while I write.

WHERE I'LL
FIND YOU

CHAPTER

1

Life lay covered beneath a thick blanket of white, of death. My orange rubber boots stood out in stark contrast as I stared down at the snow-covered ground. The wind whipped through the leafless trees, yanking loose strands of my hair from beneath my knit cap.

"Stop your sniveling, Hadlee," Mom said, her tone sharp and stinging, much like the bitter air. She squeezed my hand tight, a reminder to behave or suffer the consequences.

But wasn't I supposed to cry? Wasn't my heart supposed to be broken? After all, there was no one around to hear.

I squinted up at her as she pulled her wool coat tighter around her slender waist. Her dark hair was pulled into a tight bun, makeup perfect to the last eyelash. No tears there.

"How did he die?" I whispered.

"He's not coming back. That's all you need to concern yourself with."

I wiped my runny nose. I didn't understand. Why wouldn't she tell me? I was eight years old—I had a right to know.

The snow crunched, breaking the silence. I turned to see who else was in the cemetery. Curiosity flooded me as I watched a boy approach us. He was a couple of inches taller than me—probably a few years older than me, too. He tugged on his Seattle Mariners baseball cap while he drew closer, his nose and eyes red. Was it the cold? Or had he lost someone, too?

He came to an abrupt halt a few feet away, and our eyes locked. Deep brown eyes held my stare. After a moment, his expression softened. A hint of sadness flickered across his face as he slowly raised his arm and offered me a single bright-red rose.

"Here—it needs a flower," he muttered, his eyes darting toward Daddy's headstone.

My eyebrows knitted together; my gaze flickered to Mom. She scowled but then nodded.

"Thank you," I said to him, taking the blossom from his gloved hand.

He nodded, turned, and walked away.

My heart pounded as I watched him trudge through the white powder. Why had he given me his flower?

Reluctantly, I turned toward Daddy's resting place and laid the single rose on his tombstone. The bright scarlet screamed against the gray granite.

"Let's go." Mom yanked me away.

I dug my heels into the ground, hot tears streaming down my icy cheeks. I wasn't leaving him.

But sharp agony shot through my wrist when Mom gave me a harder tug. I hated to admit defeat, yet it was futile to resist.

My throat tightened as we walked farther and farther away. This couldn't be real. I swallowed, choking back my tears, trying to pacify Mom by keeping quiet.

Sucking in the cold air to steady myself, I peered over my shoulder one last time.

I'd never feel his beard stubble against my cheek, his deep, rumbling chuckle when we watched cartoons together, or his strong arms as he carried me to bed.

Nothing. Ever. Again.

Sobs racked my body as I left my daddy in the frozen ground—and my heart with him.

THIRTEEN YEARS LATER

"Miss Jameson. Miss Hadlee Jameson!"

"Wha...?" I asked, jerking my head up off the desk. My eyes rebelled against the bright classroom lights; my hand swiped the drool from my mouth. "Yeah?" I leaned back in my seat and removed the small wad of hair that had managed to plaster itself against my cheek, refusing to acknowledge the seventy students who were most likely gaping at the entertainment.

"Late night?" Professor Maddock asked, his elbows perched on his podium as his bushy, gray eyebrow rose with impatience.

"Every night's a late night," I mumbled, shifting uncomfortably.

Snickers filled the room, but I ignored them and opened my textbook.

No wonder I had fallen asleep; this class could bore the dead. Or maybe it was the instructor? Truth be known, I hated history and found no real purpose for it in everyday life. I mean, was history going to do my homework? Work my job? Clean my room? Do my laundry? No. So why did I need it in order to be perceived as a productive member of society with a college degree?

"Miss Jameson, if you can't find it in your schedule to attend my class—while awake—then maybe you need to reconsider your options."

Was that his way of telling me not to come back? Was he going to fail me, making my junior year a complete waste? I'd never flunked a class before. I wasn't about to start now.

My eyes drilled holes in the book while my cheeks flamed red and my mind willed everyone to turn around and leave me alone. I sucked in a deep breath and held it until he began to speak again.

Professor Maddock's voice instantly drifted to the back of my mind. I glanced at my watch—only five minutes left. I'd gotten caught sleeping—right before the end of class. What crap luck!

The torture finally at an end, I closed my book, shoved everything into my navy-blue backpack, and slung it over my shoulder. Then I made a beeline for the exit before the professor could single me out to stay after.

I was at the door when my name left his lips.

There was nothing funny about the situation, but a laugh escaped me anyway. And then another as I scurried down the hall, pushed my way through the double doors of the building, and ducked outside. The cold late-October air slapped me, and the first flurries of the season drifted to the ground. The snow had come early this year—and I had stupidly opted for just my sweatshirt this morning. Hunching forward, with my hands shoved in the front pockets of my jeans, I hurried toward Whitworth's off-campus housing. There was no way I'd make it to my next class when I was this tired. I needed to sleep for a little bit, just an hour or two, before my shift started at work.

Ten minutes later, my feet shuffled across my front porch, the boards creaking beneath me. A cold burst of air bristled down my spine as I inserted the key, unlocked the deadbolt, and entered the house. College life should have been fun, but there I was, falling asleep in classes and sharing space with three smelly guys and my best friend—my housemates. But the real oddity? I'd lived there since the summer after my freshman year and still had never met two of them. Hell, I'd forgotten they even rented the space until the floor above my bedroom creaked with a few unfamiliar footsteps. According to Syd, they were football jocks, so I wasn't missing much, except the putrid stench after their workouts.

Lionel had lived there the longest, but I rarely saw him either. His major was computer science, and he was seriously one of the smartest people I'd ever talked to. But the kicker? He was a computer nerd with a great personality, which meant that he was popular and threw a lot of parties. Everyone loved him.

The front door was stuck, so I shoved it closed with my hip and leaned against it. I shivered and welcomed the warmth of the indoors, allowing it to seep into my chilled bones. My lips pursed, I scanned the cluttered living room, expecting to see a sleeping body on the couch beneath the pile of books and coats. For a change, though, no one was there.

Several beer bottles and an empty Cheetos bag littered the coffee table.

My nose wrinkled in disgust. How in the hell anyone could eat Cheetos and drink beer at the same time was beyond me, but I rarely hung out and drank with anyone, so I'd probably never find out.

Peanuts had rolled out of their package and were scattered across the end table beside a recliner that should really have been destroyed with a chainsaw. The only salvageable part of the chair? It was incredibly comfortable once it was reclined. I'd dozed off numerous times in it, studying, while Syd and her boyfriend, Marcus, used our bedroom.

I pushed myself off the door and proceeded quietly down the hall toward my room. My eyes narrowed and swept the kitchen as I walked by and saw the same stack of dirty dishes teetering in the sink. A sigh of relief escaped me. There were no signs of life.

The bedroom door was cracked open; I slowly poked my head through it, half expecting to see a leg hanging off the edge of Sydney's messy bed, but the room was empty.

Syd and I had first met in the school's student center, at a bulletin board covered in announcements. We had both pulled one of the phone number tags off the "Roomies Wanted" sign simultaneously. We stood there and stared at each other for a moment, then decided to look at the house together. When we arrived, there was only one room left, so we sat on the floor and talked. After an hour of Q & A, we decided we would share the room so neither of us would have to put up with dorm housing. The rest was history.

Although our schedules clashed, we always caught up at the end of the day, even if it was two o'clock in the morning and we were flopping into our beds. I loved my best friend and roomie, but a few hours alone would be a slice of heaven and a rare commodity.

The house felt empty. But I wasn't going upstairs to double-check. The silence spoke for itself.

My door clicked shut, and I groaned, dropping my backpack to the hardwood floor. I slipped my black Converse off and then sank into my rumpled bed. I tugged the blankets over me, then burrowed underneath the covers. My cold fingers fumbled for my cell phone in my back pocket. Before I could put it away, though, my head nestled into the feather pillow, my eyelids fluttered closed, and my hand relaxed. The phone clattered to the floor.

"Had-leeee!"

"Why is everyone yelling at me today?" I whined and scooted deeper into my bed, attempting to shut the world out again.

"Hadlee! Get up already. You're going to be late for work tonight."

"Shit! I just wanted some sleep after class this morning." I tossed the covers off and shot out of bed. Tripping over my shoes, I landed on the floor with a thud at Sydney's feet.

"Geez, Had, are you okay?" she asked, reaching down to help me up. "You're a mess. What's going on with you?" she asked, her large, sky-blue eyes studying me.

"Thanks for noticing," I muttered, reclaiming my dignity while I stood and smoothed my rumpled sweater.

"Where're my scrunchie and hat?" I asked, holding my hair in a ponytail with one hand and searching through the pile of shit on my nightstand with the other.

"Here." Sydney tugged the hair band from her jet-black hair. "I'll help you while you call and tell them you're on the way. Are you okay? This isn't like you. You're never late anywhere, much less for work." Her sculpted eyebrows furrowed, and worry pulled at her features.

I turned toward the mirror, my reflection glaring at me. My hand smoothed back a few strands of honey-colored hair that were tickling my face. Dark, sunken circles had settled in underneath my hazel eyes. No matter what, I couldn't seem to get enough sleep.

"Hey, look at me," she said, turning me to face her. "You haven't been yourself lately. Taking nineteen credits this term plus working is too much, Had."

"Tell me about it," I mumbled, embarrassed by her concern.

"You're burning out. Call in sick tonight and get some rest."

"I can't. I need the money; rent is due next week."

"I'll help you. Please," she pleaded, her hands steepled together.

Exhaustion seeped through every fiber of my being as I wilted and slumped forward. "I'm so tired, Syd. I don't know why," I confessed, laying my head on her slender shoulder.

"Ummm, hello, super brain. You need some rest. That's all." She patted the back of my head. "Call in, and I'll make you something to eat. Then call your mom and tell her you need some help this month. You can't keep going at this pace." She stepped back and slipped out of the room before I could reply.

"No!" I called after her.

Sydney returned, poked her head around the door frame, and batted her long eyelashes at me. "She loves you. Call her," she said, pointing to my cell on the floor.

My eyes automatically rolled at her. "She just pretends to love me so her reputation doesn't suffer. Don't you know having a kid is a burden?" I turned my back on Syd, unwilling to fall for any of her manipulation tactics.

"Fine!" she retorted, stomping off toward the kitchen and proceeding to bang pans against the stove and countertop.

I grinned at Syd's silliness while I sat on my bed and called Barkley's Bar & Grill. In my freshman year, I'd landed a job at the restaurant as a hostess. The day I'd turned twenty-one, I begged our manager, Richard, to let me become a server. That was where the money was: behind the bar and on the floor, serving alcohol. As the restaurant's phone line began to ring, I wondered if he were about to regret his decision to promote me.

Three minutes later, my thumb touched the *end call* button, and I took a deep breath. Richard had yelled at me for calling in right before my shift was starting, but he yelled at everyone. I imagined him frowning, running his hand over his short, brown hair, and then placing that same hand on his hip right before lighting into me. At least I wasn't fired.

I leaned back against the wall, stretched my legs, and allowed my thoughts to drift as I stared out the window and noted that the snow had begun falling faster. My nose wrinkled. I had hated the snow since I was eight, but for some unknown reason, I didn't have the heart to leave Washington.

"Come and eat!"

Syd had actually made me dinner? The girl could barely boil water, so any attempt at making food meant a lot.

I slid off the bed, slipped my feet into my Minion slippers, and then scuffed down the hall toward the kitchen. I expected to be assaulted by the aroma of Syd's cooking, but I didn't smell anything.

I slid my butt onto the wooden barstool at our counter and peered at the large round mug resting in front of me. "What's this?" I asked, sniffing the steaming liquid.

She snickered.

"What's so funny? I thought you were making dinner."

"That *is* dinner."

"What is it?" I frowned at her.

"A hot toddy," she giggled, releasing a snort at the same time.

I shook my head, pulled my sweater sleeves over my cold fingers, and laughed. "I seriously thought you were making something to eat."

"Alcohol is a main food group required for college survival, and it needs to be consumed on a regular basis," she explained, sounding way too much like Professor Maddock.

I shoved the mug toward her and wrinkled my nose. "I'm okay, thanks. I have a full day tomorrow."

She pushed it back in my direction and ordered, "Drink. It. You'll be asleep in no time, and then you'll wake up rejuvenated and ready to face the day. Besides, you know that when you get like this, you typically get sick, so bottoms up, toots."

I tucked a strand of hair behind my ear and stuck my tongue out at her before I picked it up and took a sip.

"Geez, Syd! Is it a cup of alcohol with a drop of honey?"

"Right? It's courtesy of our friend Jack." She held up the Jack Daniel's bottle while she leaned across the kitchen counter, her eyes flashing with mischief.

"How much did you have when you were making mine?" I asked. I took another taste, the warmth of the alcohol traveling down my throat and into my stomach. "I really should find something to eat."

"Wait," Syd said, holding up one hand and producing a box of crackers with the other. "Ritz, your favorite." She covered her mouth as she barked out a laugh.

"Nice." I took another swallow and then looked at her. We both burst into giggles.

My head tilted as she unscrewed the lid of the liquor bottle and poured a shot into an empty glass on the counter.

"Umm, is that yours?"

"No idea," she said, slamming it back.

My body shuddered. God only knew whose lips had touched that glass and where they had been beforehand. I shook my head as she grinned at me. I couldn't handle any alcohol straight. Like, none. It came right back up in five seconds flat. Unfortunately, I'd discovered that fact about myself at the first party Syd and I had thrown at the house. Thank God she'd been there and rushed me to the bathroom. I'd been MIA at parties ever since, and no amount of her pleading convinced me otherwise. I'm not sure anyone else remembered the incident since it'd happened at least two years ago. Now, when Syd and Lionel threw parties, I found something else to do; it sounded lame, but I'd typically pick up an extra shift at the restaurant. I needed the money anyway.

"What are you doing home tonight?" I asked.

"Taking care of you. And as soon as your noggin hits the pillow, I'm getting naked with Marcus," she said, wiggling her eyebrows.

"Ewwww, stop." I blocked my view of her with my hands. "I do not need to know your deets."

"Not only do you need to get some sleep, but you really need to get laid, too."

"I'd prefer a boyfriend first." I smirked at her.

"Puh-lease, that is a title that—" she started.

"Just boxes us into other people's perceptions," I finished for her.

She winked at me, poured herself another shot, and drained it.

"How's Marcus?"

"He's good, but I do have something to tell you," she admitted.

Syd and Marcus had been dating since before I'd met her. They were perfect for each other in every way: they were both fun, caring, and genuine. Marcus also provided a quiet strength when Syd was falling apart emotionally. He seemed to instinctively know how to handle her.

At one time, I'd secretly wished that I could be as lucky as she was with him. Then, I'd finally admitted that my mother was right. I was incapable of having a normal anything, much less a boyfriend.

"Hey, did you hear me? Where'd ya go there, Had?"

I blinked as Syd's hand waved in front of my face.

"Must be the alcohol," I said, my cheeks flaming.

"You're tired, so drink up, and I'll update you on Marcus another time." She leaned against the opposite kitchen counter and folded her arms across her chest. I'd upset her. Damn it. What was wrong with me? I couldn't even focus on my best friend for five minutes!

"Nope, I'm right here." My palm smacked against the countertop for emphasis. "I'm sorry. It won't happen again. You have my undivided attention."

She exhaled loudly, her hands dropping to her sides.

"I think he's going to propose to me," she said softly.

"What?" I scanned her face for a reaction. Was she happy? Sad? Scared?

"I'm not ready," she whispered. "I love him, but I can't."

"Can't ever or can't now?"

"Not sure," she said, twirling a strand of hair around her finger.

I rubbed my forehead, pondering the news. "Well, why do you think he's going to ask? Have you two talked about it?"

"No, but I overheard him on the phone," she said, her shoulders slouching with the confession.

"Oh hon," I said, slipping off the barstool and walking toward her. My hands gently squeezed her arms. "There's nothing wrong with wanting to wait. You're barely twenty-two; you have plenty of time to decide. And you're stressing yourself out—when he hasn't even asked you yet."

"Yeah. You're right, but until I have a plan, I'm not going to feel better."

"I know," I said, stepping back and grabbing the half-empty bottle of Jack from the counter. "Let's go sit and talk it out."

"You need sleep, though."

"Yes, I do, but neither one of us will get any until we have plans A, B, and C in place."

"You sure?" she asked, wincing. I knew it was painful for her to admit that she needed me.

"Yup. Let's go." I took her hand and led her back to our room.

Lionel waltzed into the house just then, his voice carrying down the hall. So much for any real privacy. My eyes rolled while I closed the door behind us and Syd muttered something about noisy buffoons under her breath.

We settled in on my bed, backs against the wall, our feet dangling over the side. I unscrewed the bottle and handed it to her.

"Start from the beginning."

CHAPTER

2

The morning sun cast a halo through the pine trees in our backyard. I stared out of the kitchen window, mindlessly munching on a stale bagel. Spokane had a ton of fir trees, more than I'd seen anywhere else, but I hadn't traveled much, so what did I know?

I swallowed the last of my lukewarm java, rinsed my mug, and loaded it into the dishwasher. Syd hadn't woken yet after our almost-all-nighter, so I tried to be quiet.

I located my keys and then scanned the living room for any bodies I might need to step over. Someone was always crashing on our floor, couch, or chair. As long as I got my sleep and they weren't serial killers, I didn't really care. I closed the front door softly behind me and locked the deadbolt.

The morning air was bitterly cold. I zipped my coat, pulled my bright-blue earmuffs into place, and slipped my leather gloves on. The grass glistened with a solid dusting of snow from the night before. My lungs filled with the crisp air as I took a deep breath. I loved my living situation, but sometimes dirty laundry, sweaty guys, and worn, holey socks were suffocating. My nose wrinkled at the thought. When a shiver shot through me, I hurried down the porch steps and started walking.

One of the reasons I'd wanted to live in this house was due to its proximity to school, work, and stores. It wasn't my day to grocery shop; it was Syd's turn, but she'd been snoring when I'd gotten up, and I hadn't wanted to wake her. Besides, my stealth skills were much better than hers when it came to sneaking out of the house and not waking everyone. No matter how hard she tried, she made a shit-ton of noise.

I almost ran through the grocery store doors. My teeth chattered as I sidestepped a mom and son who were discussing a school project. I opted to keep my coat and gloves on but removed my earmuffs and hurried toward the cereal aisle. My forehead wrinkled. The store was ridiculously busy. Who went grocery shopping at seven thirty in the morning? Slipping between parents with hangry children, I headed toward the Cocoa Puffs, picked out a box, and kept going in one smooth motion. I was on a mission.

Fifteen minutes later, I had cereal, fruit, and a half gallon of milk cradled in my arm. The high-pitched screams of a toddler split the air as I continued my quest.

What in the hell had I been thinking, trying to be nice and let Syd sleep while I shopped for her? She owed me. Big.

I zipped right past the coffee aisle and backtracked a few steps. The aroma tickled my nose, and I inhaled deeply, smiling. Nothing in this world smelled better than freshly ground beans. I turned down the row, eyed the shelves, and spotted one last bag of the Seattle's Best organic blend—the one brand of coffee that everyone in the house agreed on. White-and-blue sneakers caught the corner of my eye. My head snapped up. He was headed for the coffee. MY coffee. We were each about six feet away, and I'd have to hustle to grab it first. Apparently, he had the same idea. I made a mad dash for it. And a squeal escaped me as I snatched the package from the shelf. I'd intended to make an abrupt halt and hightail it in the opposite direction, but my shoes hit a slick spot of melted snow, and there was no stopping me.

His mouth fell open as I barreled toward him. My shoes scrambled to find traction, but I slammed right into his broad chest. My groceries flew up into the air, and we tumbled to the cold, hard tile floor.

"Shit!" I said, smacking my ass and elbow. My face flamed red when the milk carton burst open and a single apple rolled across the floor, wobbled, and stopped in front of him. I dared a glance in his direction to see if he was all right. I wasn't. That had hurt like hell.

He held up the coffee. Although I'd managed to drop him to the floor when we collided, he'd somehow won the coveted item.

"Seriously?" I groaned, staggering to my feet. I tugged my gloves off and shoved them into my coat pocket. He pushed himself off the floor and stood slowly. I mentally inventoried him, my eyes traveling up his legs and torso to a strong jaw that sported a hint of shadow. He cleared me by a solid six inches.

His dark-maroon sweater hugged his chest and arms as he ran a hand through dark hair that hung just above his shoulders. A crooked grin spread across his face.

"Nice play," he said, handing me the bag.

"You're giving it to me? Even after I made a run for it and took us both down?" I asked, shock rippling through my voice.

"That was pretty good, actually," he said with a hint of amusement. "The look on your face when you realized you weren't stopping made my entire day. No matter what else happens, I'm golden."

I snatched the bag out of his hand and glared at him. "If you'd been a decent guy, you would have let me have it to begin with."

He smiled, and my heart skipped a beat. "You have a little milk on your face."

"Gah! I do? Where?" I asked, horrified at the thought.

"Here," he said, gently touching my cheek.

I stepped backward at his touch and wiped my face. "Thank you," I muttered, irritated at myself for allowing him to get to me. My fingers clutching the package, I bent down to collect my cereal and other belongings. I'd report the mess I'd made when I paid for them.

"Are you okay?" he asked, picking up the bananas for me.

"Yeah," I complained, "other than my ass and ego being bruised, I'll be okay."

I maneuvered the cereal box, laying it flat, and used it as a tray. He balanced the fruit on top.

"You should have a basket." He frowned at the stack of food in my arms.

"Yeah. Well, a little late, but thanks. I gotta go." My brows knitted in frustration.

"Sure. Enjoy the coffee," he said, offering a small wave.

I limped down the aisle and snuck a quick peek over my shoulder. Our gazes locked briefly before I disappeared around the corner.

The pulse in my neck fluttered as I continued toward the register. My groceries dropped with a thud on the checkout counter, and I took a deep breath.

"Morning, Hadlee."

"Morning, Jim. I made a mess of aisle eight. Milk," I muttered. "I dropped a carton of milk."

While he called for a clean up, I placed my gloves on the counter and searched my pockets for my wallet.

"Oh my God. I didn't." I leaned my elbows on the counter next to the card reader and hung my head.

"What's the matter?" Jim asked, bagging the last orange.

"I thought I had my debit card with me this morning. I guess I left without it." My face reddened for the second time within ten minutes.

"I've got it."

My chin jutted up; I recognized that voice. Slowly, I turned toward my supposed savior. It was Coffee Guy.

"Nope," I said, holding my hand up to stop him from handing Jim his cash. I smiled at Jim. "I'll be back in just a little bit with some money. If you'd just hold my groceries for me, please?"

"It's only fifteen dollars. You can pay me back."

My gaze whipped toward him, my nostrils flaring. This morning had totally sucked, and this guy was really starting to piss me off—and I wasn't even sure why. I shoved my gloves back into my coat pocket.

Jim took his offering before I could form another rebuttal. "Hadlee, take the blessing and get your food home. Pay it forward. That's what I always say: pay it forward."

He handed me one of the bags, and I grimaced at the pain shooting from my elbow to my wrist.

"Let me help. You got hurt back there," Coffee Guy said, moving past me.

"I'm fine," I barked.

But he had already taken some of the bags off the counter.

"You're a good man, Kaisen Sinclair. Your pa taught you right." Jim nodded at him.

I glanced at my nemesis. "Kaisen? What kind of name is Kaisen?"

"It's *my* name. Where's your car?" he asked, ignoring my snarky comment.

"I don't have one." I walked through the sliding front doors and outside into the cold and then set my one grocery bag down on a nearby bench. Grabbing my gloves, I scowled at the harsh light of the sun.

"Listen, I appreciate the help, but I've got this."

"You sure?"

"Very." I collected my groceries from him and limped through the parking lot in the direction of my house.

"Have a good day!" he called after me.

I didn't even bother turning around.

My luck didn't get much better as the day progressed. The bar and grill was packed, and I wasn't sure what hurt more—my ass or my elbow. I even needed to use both hands to steady the full tray of food. I was an idiot. I never should have gone head-to-head with Coffee Guy.

"Hey, Had," Kara said as she stood next to the large kitchen window and loaded an order onto her tray. "I noticed you limping. Are you okay?"

I groaned. "A slight mishap this morning is all. I'm fine."

"What kind of mishap?" she asked while we walked toward our stations together.

"I'll tell you right after I get this food dropped off. I'll meet you at the computer station."

Somehow, I managed to deliver my four-top food without spilling anything on them or me.

"Can I get you anything else?" I asked.

"How 'bout your digits?" the towheaded guy asked.

"Sorry, I'd love to, but I have a boyfriend." I attempted the most charming smile I could muster. No way would I lose a tip over a phone number.

"Damn. Well, I gotta respect a girl who's committed and not a cheater," he said, winking as he popped a French fry in his mouth. The other guys laughed. I turned away and mentally rolled my eyes.

I steered my way down the aisle crowded with people who'd just filed in. Friday was always busy, especially in the winter. People were beginning to shop for the holidays, and college kids were burned out and seeking a break before finals. I made mad money during the weekends, which was why I signed up for any extra shifts that I could. Tonight's extra shift was perfect. Lionel was throwing a party, and I wasn't interested in hanging out with a bunch of rowdy people.

My stomach growled as I approached the wait staff station and scanned my section to make sure no one needed anything.

"All right, fill me in, gimpy." Kara smirked.

She and I had worked together for the last three years, and we'd become close friends. She and Syd were pretty much the only people I hung out with—they were also the only people I trusted. Although she was one of the few who could get away with teasing me about limping, I shot her a dirty look before I described my collision at the grocery store.

"Nice way to start your morning," she observed, tucking a stray brown curl back into her short ponytail. "Was he hot?"

I stopped in the middle of the food entry and stared at her. "Seriously? I almost broke my ass bone, and you want to know if he's gorgeous?"

Kara laughed. "'He was, huh? Lucky you!"

"Whatever," I replied with a half shrug. I tried to ignore her blatant stare and finish up on the computer.

"Deets. Now," she ordered, tapping her foot with impatience.

I didn't have to think too hard to recall the details. He might have irritated me, but there was no way I could have missed how attractive he was. "Around six-four, muscles, long legs, tight ass, and dreamy brown eyes. His dark hair was just shy of his broad shoulders, and it flipped out at the ends."

"Holy hell, Had. You paid attention, which means this guy is off the fucking charts. Did you get his digits?"

"What? Noooo. Nope." My head shook vigorously at her suggestion. "I had to pick myself up off the floor and limp away with what little dignity I had left. And, of course, that wasn't even the last of it."

"What do you mean?" Her big, green eyes glinted with eagerness.

"Nothing good." I groaned. "I forgot my wallet, and he ended up paying for my groceries," I muttered as my cheeks heated up. Again.

"Oh shit, you didn't!"

"Oh, yes. Yes, I did."

"That's hilarious. Did you get his number then?"

"Nope. I thanked him and then limped through the parking lot and back to the house."

"Maybe you'll run into him again," she said, making air quotes and giggling.

"I don't want to *run into* anyone again. It hurt like hell." I nodded to table five. "One of my customers is flagging me. Gotta run." My eyes cut toward her and narrowed. "Don't joke about me running either."

"You go make that money, Gimpy," Kara said, stepping up to the computer and snickering.

I covered my yawn and fixed my gaze on the astronomical clock that hung over the front door of the restaurant. Why would anyone choose such a gigantic clock? Maybe the decorator was hoping that it would be visible from any seat in the restaurant.

"At least we're getting out of here before 2 a.m. tonight. I bet that we won't tomorrow," Kara said, counting her tips.

"Yeah. I'm wiped out, too. I need to go home and put my earplugs in so I can get some sleep."

"Are you almost ready?"

"Give me a few," I replied, as I began to count my own tips. It'd been a good night, which meant that Syd didn't need to cover any of my rent. I loved her for it, but I hated owing anyone anything.

"I'm going to the bathroom. Then I'll find Richard and tell him we're leaving."

"Sounds good. I'll meet you out front; this won't take me long."

I wrapped up my tip report, cracked my neck, and leaned my head on the table, grateful that I could pay all of my bills. If I was careful, I could save a few extra dollars and buy Syd and Kara each a small Christmas gift, too. Not that they expected anything, and I certainly didn't expect anything from them, but they were important to me.

"Night!" I yelled and waved to our chef. Then I joined Kara at the front door and layered my winter outerwear. I looked like a blue Michelin tire by the time I was finished. And from the look on her face, Kara thought the same. She pushed through the door, and midteen temps greeted us. Our squeals ripped through the night as we raced to her car.

"Oh my God. I don't know what I'd do without you and your car," I said, slipping into the passenger seat of her green Toyota Camry and pulling my door closed. Teeth chattering, Kara started the engine; cold air blasted through the vents.

Once the car was warmed up, Kara pulled out of the parking lot. Neither one of us lived far from the bar and grill, but we never walked home at night. I tossed her gas money on the shifts we worked together, and she dropped me off. Half the time, she wouldn't take the money, but I discreetly tucked it into her cup holder or glove box. I couldn't have my friends thinking I was taking advantage of them. They were the only family I had.

I stared out the window while we passed the stores and then eased into the residential neighborhood I lived in.

"You okay?" Kara asked, pulling onto my street.

"Yeah. Just tired. Aww, shit," I murmured as my house came into view.

"What?"

"The party is still going on." I checked my Fitbit. "I can't believe they're still here! Do you want to come in?"

"Nah, I've gotta get started on a lit paper."

"Tonight? It's a little after two in the morning!"

"Yeah, I know. But I focus better in the wee hours of the morn."

I rolled my eyes at her and smiled before grabbing my purse, opening the car door, and stepping out onto the curb.

"Is it icy?" Kara asked, leaning across the passenger seat.

"No, it seems fine." I assessed the sidewalk for ice but only saw the remainder of the snow dusting from yesterday. "But be safe."

"It wasn't me I was thinking of," she said, giggling.

"I'm not interested in busting my ass twice in one day, so I'll keep that in mind."

I shut the car door, stared at the house for a second, and prepared myself for the smell of sweat and beer.

After Kara's car sped off down the street, the exhaust visible in the cold, I walked up the sidewalk, paying careful attention to any slick spots. The music thumped with Awolnation's "Miracle Man," and hoots and hollers carried out of the house and into the road. I was surprised no one had called the cops on them, but most of the people who lived in the neighborhood were most likely inside participating in the festivities anyway.

The front door swung open as I arrived on the porch.

"Dude!" someone yelled from inside.

A guy stepped out, doubled over, and proceeded to puke all over my feet.

"Are you fucking kidding me?" I screeched. My mouth dropped open in speechless fury while I tried to ignore the sensation of warm vomit seeping inside my work shoes.

"Oh, man. I'm so sorry," the guy slurred and attempted to straighten. "Shit, you're seriously hot," he added, offering a lopsided grin. Seconds later, he ran to the railing, leaned over, and graced the bushes with the remainder of his stomach's contents.

I hadn't moved. I was still staring at my feet and trying to decide what to do. Sticky, pink chunks covered my shoes and were splattered across the wooden boards. I had no choice but to go through the mess.

"Wait."

I peered into the doorway. And my fury came to a full boil. "What in the hell are you doing in my house? Damn it! All I wanted to do was come home and get some sleep. This entire day has been pure shit!" My fists clenched, attempting to keep my temper in check.

"Yup. Hang on." Kaisen took one giant step around the splatter of puke. I yelped as he swooped me into his arms and strode around the mess.

"What in the hell are you doing? Put me down!" Who did he think he was? My knight in shining fucking armor?

My heart thumped against my chest while he carried me. It had been longer than I cared to admit since I'd been this close to a guy—and I wasn't even sure I liked him.

He ignored me and continued into the living room, through the drunk dancers and people overflowing from the kitchen. He navigated his way down the hallway, past a couple practically having sex against the wall, and toward the bathroom. He nudged the door open with his elbow and gently lowered me onto the counter.

I gawked at him while he grabbed the towel from the rack, covered his hands, slipped off my shoes, and wrapped them up.

"You might want to take off your socks, too," he said, a crooked grin spreading across his face.

My nose wrinkled from the stench of vomit filling the small room.

"Uh, thanks," I said, grabbing some toilet tissue for my hands and slipping off my socks. "You didn't have to do that."

"I did, actually. I don't think you would have successfully stepped through the puke without sliding. I figured that busting your backside once today was enough."

"I'd have to agree with you." I reached for the stinky bundle that Kaisen was holding, placed it on the countertop, slowly lifted the corner of the towel, and peeked underneath. "I'll have to buy some new shoes."

"I figured."

"What are you doing here anyway? I've never seen you at one of our parties before."

He leaned against the wall, shoved his hands in the front pockets of his jeans, and studied my face. "Are you okay? I know damn well you got hurt this morning at the store. And from your uniform, it looks like you work at Barkley's, which means you've been limping around all night."

My face flushed from the reminder of my stupidity earlier in the day.

"Yeah. I guess I shouldn't have made a run for the coffee, huh? But you didn't answer my question. What are you doing in my house?"

"I've been to a lot of parties here. I've just never seen you."

"Probably because I avoid them if at all possible," I replied.

"Why? You don't like drunk people messing up your house and blowing chunks all over your shoes?" he asked, his voice dripping with sarcasm.

"Not to mention the party blunders that can be seen all over social media. Who in the world would want to miss that?" I shrugged. We shared a smile, and then my lips pursed together. "Um, sorry about earlier today. I really thought I could get that damned coffee."

"It's okay." He chuckled. "It was worth it."

"What do you mean?" I tilted my head and waited for his reply.

"Not many guys can say a gorgeous girl literally knocked them off their feet."

Gorgeous? I mentally swore while heat traveled up my cheeks. "Yeah, guess not. But I did get to it first."

"Competitive much?" He grinned.

"Sometimes. I ran track in high school and participated in chess tournaments."

"Wow, a brainy jockette."

"Seriously? You did not just say that."

He ran his hand across his chin. "Yeah, I think I just did. It's late, and I've had a few beers, so you can't hold me responsible for my big mouth."

"Sure I can." I paused. "But I need to take care of this," I said, motioning toward the disgusting towel next to me. "I'd better do something with it and get some sleep. Thanks for your help," I said. "It would probably have been disastrous if I'd tried to walk through that mess on the porch."

"No problem."

"Shit! I almost forgot that I owe you fifteen dollars. I can grab it for you."

"Don't worry about it. I think you need to take care of your shoes right now," he said, shoving himself off the wall. "I'll see ya around." He flashed me a smile and stepped out of the bathroom.

I tugged at my bottom lip with my teeth while I studied him in his sculpted jeans, waltzing down my hallway. Maybe he wasn't as bad as I had thought. I shook my head; I didn't have time to find out either way.

My fingers mindlessly tapped on the counter to the beat of the music, the party continuing at full blast. Exhaustion seeped through my body. I prayed I could find my earplugs.

"*Hads. Hadlee.*"

I rolled over in bed and wrestled to pull the covers up. Why wouldn't they move? I was freezing my ass off.

"Had, wake up."

A sharp jab to my ribs shot me into a sitting position. I blinked, trying to adjust my vision to the darkness, and pulled my earplug out. Apparently, the other had fallen out somewhere.

"Oh, didn't realize you had those in," Syd said, frowning. "Sorry for poking you so hard."

"You okay?" I asked, rubbing my face and collapsing backward into my oversized pillow. Syd had crawled into my bed, pinning the blankets in place, and was now lying on her side, her head perched on her hand. No wonder I was cold.

"Yup, I'm awesome," she said, snickering.

"You're drunk."

"Maybe just a little." She held her fingers an inch apart.

"If you're okay, then why in the hell did you wake me up?"

"I had to know who the hottie was."

"No clue," I mumbled.

"Bullshit. He carried you through the party. Where did you go?" she asked, wiggling her eyebrows at me.

"The bathroom."

"Oh my God, Marcus and I had sex in there tonight, too!" she squealed.

"No!" I said, pulling the pillow over my head. "You did not just tell me that. Syd, you do understand what TMI is, right? I do not need to hear about you and Marcus in *our* bathroom. Did you sanitize the counter at least?"

"It wasn't the counter. He held me against the wall. I think I have wall burn on my ass."

"What am I going to do with you?" I asked.

"You love me, and you know it." She yanked my pillow away and tossed it aside. "Now, tell me about getting laid tonight. I'm so proud of you. How long has it been?"

"Three years. I was eighteen, and nothing has changed. I didn't sleep with anyone tonight."

"Then why did he carry you through the house?"

"Vomit."

"You got sick?" she asked, gasping. "I knew you were pushing yourself too hard!"

I covered my face with my hands and groaned. She wasn't going to let me go back to sleep until I told her about Kaisen.

"I'm fine, Syd." Rolling onto my side, I propped my head on my hand and stared at her. She signaled for me to continue. "Some guy puked on the porch and all over my feet. Kaisen just helped me get through the house and into the bathroom without leaving a nasty trail. We chatted for a minute, I thanked him, and that was it. Nothing happened except my shoes were ruined."

Syd's lips formed a pout. "Damn. I thought your drought was over."

"It's not a drought if I choose not to have sex."

"Why would anyone want to avoid getting laid? I don't get it."

I rubbed my face and took a deep breath. She was definitely drunk and not thinking things through.

"My mother says I have daddy issues, remember?" Sarcasm laced my words.

Sadness flickered across her face. "I'm sorry," she whispered. "I didn't mean to bring it up."

"I know. It's okay."

"For the record, I don't agree with her. You're dedicated to school and work; that doesn't mean you have problems."

"Well, she's been attacking me lately because I refuse to date anyone. She says I have commitment phobia. Whatever. If she weren't bitching about my love life, she'd find some other reason to put me down."

Syd snorted. "What the hell does she know?"

"Nothing. She knows nothing about me." My eyebrows pinched together as I thought about how little my mother actually knew me. She only lived twenty minutes away, but we were a million miles apart.

"Well, did you get a phone number?" she asked, changing the subject.

"Man, what's up with you and Kara? Both of you wanted to know if I got his info."

"He's gorgeous and considerate, and we both want you to be happy. You need someone to help you release all of your pent-up stress," she said, patting my hip.

I couldn't stop myself from grinning. "Sex can be complicated and emotional, though. I don't have time for it, and I certainly don't have time to date. It's just a distraction."

"Aww, man. Just when we were starting to talk about the good stuff, I gotta pee," she said, slurring her words. She rolled off my bed and landed on the floor with a loud *thunk*.

"Shit! Are you okay?" I peeked over the edge at her.

"Yup. It's all good. I got this." She groaned as she pulled herself up and hung onto my headboard for balance. Then she straightened her top and teetered across the room.

I snuggled back under my blankets and laughed. She was going to feel like total and complete shit tomorrow.

One thing I enjoyed about working at Barkley's was the music they played. It kept me going during my shifts, especially when I was really tired, like today. "Chain Smoking" by Jacob Banks belted through the speakers while I approached my newest customers and placed cocktail napkins in front of everyone.

"I'm Hadlee, and I'll be taking care of you this evening. Can I start you off with some beverages?"

"Excuse me." The voice came from behind me.

I stepped out of the way and allowed my gaze to drift toward the voice. Kaisen slid into the booth and joined the other guys. My jaw clenched as I shot him a withering look.

"Stalk people much?" I sneered, unable to hide my irritation.

"Dude, you're stalking her?" one of the guys asked.

"Bud on draft, please," another chimed in.

"No," Kaisen said, chuckling. "We just ran into each other at the grocery store yesterday. I barely know her."

"So, you're not following me around? You just happen to show up everywhere I go lately? Are you some kind of weirdo?" Panic gripped me while scenarios played through my head of him crouching in the darkness of my bedroom with a butcher knife.

"I'm just joining my friends for some food. That's it. I didn't even make the plans for us to meet here, so you'll need to talk to Michael about it," he said, nodding toward a sandy blond.

"Yup, he had no idea until I texted him to join us," Michael said.

I didn't believe a word they said. Bending over, I whispered in his ear, "If you're following me, it will be your last mistake."

His brows arched. "Hey," he said, tossing his hands up in surrender. "You've got it all wrong. I've been here tons of times; we just never noticed each other. I swear I'm just here hanging with my friends."

"Are you always such a ballbuster?" one of the guys asked me. "I mean, aren't you supposed to be getting our food and shit instead of harassing your customers? Zero tip from me tonight, honey. Maybe I should talk to your boss and he can adjust your attitude for ya." He leaned back in his seat, his gaze growing more intense with each word.

"Shut up, Tim," Kaisen said, then turning to me, "Ignore him. He's already been drinking, and he can be an asshole sometimes."

My body had tensed with Tim's words, though. He was right. I should always put my tips first. I grabbed my pen and pad and shoved my irritation aside.

"What can I get you guys?" I asked, beaming at them.

"There ya go." Tim nodded in approval. What an asshole. "Cheeseburger, fries, and a Jack and Coke."

"You?" I directed my question at Kaisen.

"Reuben and fries, please."

"To drink?"

"Water. I'll be driving everyone home tonight."

"Soda is on the house for designated drivers. What would you like?"

"Root beer."

"Sure thing."

I finished taking the others' orders and then stormed to my workstation to enter the information. Kara joined me.

"What was that all about? Was that guy being a douchebag?" she asked, crossing her arms.

"Majorly. I can't believe he's here!"

"Who?" Kara asked, her forehead creasing in confusion.

"Kaisen. All of a sudden, he's everywhere I go."

"Who?"

"Coffee Guy. He's here."

"What?"

"Kaisen is here, at that booth." I pointed with a flick of my wrist, trying not to be obvious. "He's some kind of weirdo, and he's freaking me out." I folded my arms across my chest.

"Explain it to me. What's going on? Do I need to let management know? Richard can ask him to leave if it'll make you more comfortable."

"No, it's okay. It's just that after I saw him at the grocery store, he showed up at my house last night."

"What? He was at your house when I dropped you off?" Her brows shot up.

"Not like that. He was at the party. And now he's here."

"That does sound creepy. I'll talk to him." She walked off before I could argue with her.

"Kara!" I hissed. She ignored me.

Oh my God. What was she going to do? I peeked around the edge of the computer station while she spoke to Kaisen and the other guys at the table. I watched her toss her head back and laugh. Was she flirting with him? What the hell? I chewed my bottom lip, my heart pounding until she turned away and headed back in my direction.

"And that's how it's done," she said, grinning.

"What's done?" I asked, trying to control the pitch of my voice.

"A phone number."

I waited for her to explain what I'd just seen while she stepped in front of the computer and checked an order. But she was holding back.

"Kara, spit it out. Quit messing with me. What happened?"

"Michael asked if he could text me," she said nonchalantly.

"I thought you were going over there to talk to Kaisen."

"I did talk to him for a second, Had, and I'm sure he's a nice guy. Michael, on the other hand, is hot, so we exchanged digits. When he messages me, I'll ask him about Kaisen. Come to think of it, I've seen them in here several times. Maybe you're just now noticing him because you ran into him yesterday?"

"Really? You think that's all it is?" I asked, peeking over at Kaisen.

"I think he's okay. Try not to read too much into it. As I said, those guys have been in here before. I've just never waited on them, so I didn't pay much attention."

"I hope you're right."

"I promise to let you know if I see any red flags," she said, patting my back. "Looks like Jamie just gave you a six-top."

"Maybe I won't blow this tip," I muttered, rubbing my neck. "I'm sorry I wigged out on you. It's just the third time I've seen him in forty-eight hours."

"Maybe we can double date."

"When hell freezes," I replied, shooting her a disapproving frown.

"We'll see," she said, a broad smile easing across her face before she sauntered off.

I clutched my tray and introduced myself to my new customers. And as hard as I tried to restrain myself, my eyes continued to wander back toward Kaisen and his friends. He seemed to just be having fun and talking. Guilt flooded me. I'd basically threatened him. What was wrong with me? Was the simple thought of having a guy friend in my life that scary?

My chin tilted in the air while I finished taking the order. I knew how to fix this.

I shoved my pen and pad into my apron pocket and approached the bar. "Hey, Hank. I need two Buds on draft, one Heineken, a Jack and Coke, and a root beer."

"Comin' right up," he said, tossing the glasses into the air before filling them.

I couldn't help but grin. He was a damn good bartender, and the ladies loved him. I suspected that his tips were terrific with all the entertainment he provided—not to mention he was panty-dropping gorgeous.

He slid the bottles toward me and placed the drafts on the counter.

"You're the best. Thanks." I loaded the beverages on my tray and delivered the drinks. "On the house, guys."

"Really?" Tim asked.

"Yup, this round's on me." I turned and muttered to Kaisen, "Sorry for thinking you were a creeper. A girl can't be too careful these days."

"No, I'm sorry. I really didn't mean to scare you."

I flashed a quick smile. "I'll be back with your food shortly."

An hour later, the guys stood to leave. Kaisen smiled and, giving me a wave, waltzed out the door with his friends.

"Everything good?" Kara asked from behind me.

"Yeah. I comped them a round of drinks since I was a jerk. Thanks for calling me on my shit."

"It's over. No biggie. Honestly, that would probably have freaked me out, too."

I gave her a quick hug and then checked on my other customers. On the way back to the kitchen, I stopped by Kaisen's table and opened the check holder. My mouth dropped. Two twenty-dollar bills were tucked neatly beneath the receipt. They'd tipped me forty dollars? Even after I was a total ass?

I flipped the book closed, wiped everything clean, and practically ran across the room to the front kitchen window. "Oh my God, Kara, you won't believe it."

"What?" she asked, mirroring my excitement.

"Forty dollars! They tipped me forty dollars off a fifty-eight-dollar check," I squealed.

"Awww, that's so sweet. I think someone might like you."

"All I did was bring them a free round."

"That's my point. No one tips like that because of one free drink. Someone is trying to get your attention."

I smacked her on the arm. "Be serious."

She gave a lopsided grin and laughed. "Mark my words, Hadlee. Kaisen is interested in you."

"No. He can't be. He doesn't even know me; he doesn't know anything about me except that I like coffee and I work here."

"Why is it so hard for you to believe that a gorgeous and nice guy could want to get to know you?"

I blinked at her. She couldn't be right. "Well, I'll just have to keep my distance, then."

"Ugh, you can be so frustrating sometimes. When is the last time you even went on a date?"

"I don't know. I stopped keeping track after a year."

"Hadlee! You're twenty-one, gorgeous, super smart, and, most of the time, a lot of fun to be around. Loosen up, have some fun, get drunk, get laid—live a little."

"Most of the time?" I asked.

"Yes, unlike this very moment, when you're being difficult. Get his phone number and ask him out."

I shook my head.

"Is something wrong with you I don't know about? Do you have three boobs or something?" She motioned toward my chest.

"No," I said, frowning at her. "Three boobs? Really? That's the best you could come up with?"

"Pretty bad, I know." She shrugged. "Just think about it. Maybe you'll warm up to the idea."

My eyes narrowed as she walked off. I didn't want to think about Kaisen or any other guy. I was lucky to be hanging on to my two best friends. They were the most important people in my life. But someday, I'd probably lose them, too.

spent the next three weeks peeking around every corner. Somehow, I managed to avoid Kaisen. When he came back to the bar with his friends, I asked Jamie to seat them in Kara's section. She welcomed them with a big grin and a hug for Michael. They'd gone out three times now, and things were going well.

After the guys left, she made a point of showing me the ten-dollar tip they'd left.

"At least you know Kaisen isn't cheap," she mumbled as she shoved it into her pocket.

"Maybe Michael is trying to save money to take you out for a nice dinner," I suggested, nudging her with my elbow.

"He'd better be," she said. She shot me a look and then broke into a wide smile. "I think I might really like him."

"As long as he's good to you."

"Very good," she said, her eyes sparkling.

I raised my hands. "Please, don't pull a Sydney and share the details of your intimate life. I'm glad it's working out for you guys."

"I'll do my best," she said, bumping my hip with hers before she strolled away toward her next customers.

Although I'd managed to stay awake in Professor Maddock's class, I was still struggling to maintain my heavy class load and work schedule. Somedays, I barely had time to breathe, but whenever I thought I couldn't do it anymore, I remembered why I was doing it in the first place. I refused to be a failure; I would not prove my mother right. That thought alone rekindled the fire inside me and kept me from asking her for anything.

I'd been self-sufficient since I'd turned seventeen, and I wasn't going to stop now. She could keep her perfectly manicured nails, uptight clothes, Prada, and Louie Vuitton bags to herself. I was better off without her continually following me around and telling me what I was doing wrong. Or that I'd never amount to anything. I didn't need to hear her yelling at me about being anything other than a daddy's girl. Although, to be honest, I secretly enjoyed hearing her say it because she was right. And I'd still have been one today if he were alive.

I hated her. One summer, when I'd finally reached my limit, I'd left for college and never returned. I had made a commitment to myself. I would work as many jobs as I had to if it kept me from showing up on the doorstep of her mansion and begging for help.

My classes had wrapped up for the day, and I was almost skipping as I left the campus and headed toward the bar and grill. Since my shift started at three o' clock today, I jogged straight to work. Ten blocks was an easy jaunt, and it helped me stay in shape.

The Wednesday before Thanksgiving was usually so slow the staff did nothing but hang out and talk. Richard was actually pretty cool about it but insisted that we took care of the customers first. Lately, it seemed like he'd stopped yelling so much, too. According to Hank, Richard had a new girlfriend, so maybe getting laid on a regular basis was improving his mood.

The warm air of the grill welcomed me as I stepped inside. I hurried to the bathroom, changed clothes, and brushed my teeth. There would be no tips at all tonight if my breath reeked.

Ten minutes later, I tucked my backpack behind Hank's bar and clocked in. The restaurant was nearly empty, which meant the grocery stores were most likely packed. Hank, Kara, and Jamie were scheduled to arrive at four. I'd watch the restaurant and take the first few tables until we had additional staff. At least Richard was in his office if I needed help.

I hummed along to a few bars of Jeffrey James's "Carry You" and meandered behind the bar.

For the first time since I'd worked there, I had four days off in a row. My heart sang with the idea of no work or school. Of course, Sydney and I had plans, but it was fun stuff, not adult drudgery.

I stocked the bar for Hank and kept myself busy. Kara traipsed in at a quarter to four and waved.

"Man, am I glad to see someone," I told her. "I nearly passed out from boredom."

"Yeah? Nothing going on yet, huh?"

I nodded toward the single table with a lonely customer.

She stuffed her purse behind the bar and grabbed a soda. "Are you ready?"

"For?" I asked, my eyebrow lifting in question.

"The four-day weekend! Hello!"

"Ha, ha. I thought you were going to tell me something exciting. I have to depend on you for a social life, you know. Speaking of which," I studied her, "you've been really quiet about Michael. 'Sup?"

Kara couldn't have hidden that grin even if she'd tried.

"Say no more," I told her. "I just wanted to make sure you guys were doing okay, and by the smile on your face, you're doing really well."

"Four weeks today." She beamed.

"Wow, really?"

"Yeah," she said, a hint of dreaminess hanging on her reply.

"That good, huh?" I didn't have to explain that I was referring to the sex. She knew me well enough; I wouldn't come out and ask.

"Off. The. Charts."

I giggled as she continued to fill me in on their relationship. She was so happy. And I loved that she was, but I couldn't ignore the pang of loneliness that ripped through me when she and Sydney talked about their guys. I didn't want to be one of those friends who was a downer, though, the kind who refused to listen to the great things that were happening with them. And I had to remember the last three years had been my choice. No one had made me take so many classes and work all those long hours.

A few minutes later, Hank, Jamie, and the other team members strode in the front door. We had more than enough staff to cover everything. I don't know if Richard thought the tide would turn and we'd end up with a full house, but at least he was pretty good about letting people leave early if it was slow.

Our heads turned as Richard and a few of the kitchen crew brought out a big turkey, potatoes, dressing, cranberry sauce, rolls, pumpkin pie, and apple pie. At his gesture, we followed them, and our mouths hung open when they placed the food on the long table in our meeting room. He'd never fed us dinner before! Everyone's attention fell on Richard as the double doors rolled closed behind him.

"I can tell by the look on your faces that you're surprised by the food. I just wanted to take a minute and tell you all I have the best staff I've ever had in the eight years I've managed this place. You guys are always on time, and you take amazing care of our customers. I don't have to babysit and deal with a lot of drama either. With that said, this dinner is my way of showing I appreciate you." He paused, checking his watch. "You've all got thirty minutes to sit down and eat. I'm going to cover the few customers we have, and if I need help, I'll come get someone. Happy Thanksgiving, team."

The room broke out into applause and cheers.

"Wow! That's the coolest thing I've ever had a boss do," Kara said as we got into line.

"Right? Oh my God, my mouth is watering." I grabbed a couple of plates and handed one to her.

We all dished up our food and, for the first time, sat down together to eat and chat.

Thirty minutes flew by; we soon were cleaning up our mess and returning to the restaurant with full bellies.

"Ugh, now I need a nap," I said, rubbing my tummy.

"Well, good luck. Jamie just gave you a five-top."

"Excellent! I'll take it." I began loading my tray with waters.

Saint Motel's "My Type" floated through the speakers and drove me to pick up my pace a bit. I really wanted to crawl into a booth in a dark corner and fall asleep, but money called.

By eight o'clock, the grill was completely quiet. Richard had let a few people go home already. He'd asked me if I wanted to leave first since I'd been there the longest, but I didn't have a family to go home to, so I stuck around. Besides, Kara was closing, so if I didn't want to pay for an Uber, I would have to stay and help her clean up. However, as the time wore on, I began to regret my decision.

The seconds ticked by agonizingly slow. Completely bored, Kara and I sat at the bar and observed the cute elderly couple who had wandered in for dinner.

"Do you think we'll be lucky enough to grow old with someone like that?" She tilted her head as she watched the gentleman assist his wife with her coat.

"You will. I'm not sure I will, though. Maybe I'll just be your third wheel for the rest of my life." A crooked grin pulled at the corner of my mouth.

"You'll find someone," she assured me.

I cracked my neck and stifled a yawn. There were only a few other staff on the floor, and they were rotating any customers who came in.

"Why don't you ask Richard if you can go? Just get an Uber."

"I'm thinking about it…"

"You've been here since three, Hadlee. Go home and get some sleep."

I left her sitting at the bar. Richard's laughter floated down the hall. I wondered if he was talking to his new girlfriend. I tapped on his office door, not really wanting to interrupt him.

"Still slow?" he asked after I hesitantly entered.

"Yeah. Do you care if I go?"

"Nope. Happy Thanksgiving, and try to do something fun on your days off. You're one of the best employees I've got. Take care of yourself."

"Thanks," I said, glancing down at the floor and attempting to hide my embarrassment. Accepting compliments didn't come easily for me. "Happy Thanksgiving to you, too."

I passed the kitchen and approached Kara at the bar.

"He said yes?" she asked.

"Yup. I'm going to change."

I grabbed my backpack and hurried toward the bathroom. I was free for four days. Four glorious days with no homework, no classes, and no customers. What was I going to do with myself? A stupid grin spread across my face while I considered. First, I would shut off the alarm clock. Then, I would eat a ton of food and visit Syd's parents. I would also make it a priority to watch a bunch of movies and lounge around in my pajamas. Life was good.

I stripped out of my uniform, exchanged it for my comfy sweater and jeans, and tapped the Uber app on my phone.

"Hey," Kara said, poking her head in the bathroom. "You might not want to get that Uber yet."

"Why?"

"You'll see. Trust me. Wait a minute before calling for your ride."

Curiosity piqued my interest as I followed her out of the bathroom. She nodded toward the corner booth I'd wanted to take a nap in earlier.

I followed her gaze, then froze.

"Kara?" I asked, hesitating.

"Go. Don't you even think about giving me any sass either. Get your ass over there."

"I…"

"Nope. Not one word. Go. Now," she demanded with her hands on her hips.

"Damn it." I groaned while trudging toward the table, my pulse racing in my ears with each step. I didn't want to do this. At. All.

"Hey," I said, approaching him.

"Hey," Kaisen responded with a small wave.

"You look all serious," I said. *And why are you here?*

"Can you sit down for a few minutes? Kara said that you're done working and I caught you just in time."

I stared at the vacant seat for a moment and then back at him. His eyes lit up, anticipation written across his face. Did I want to talk to him? Could it hurt anything? I chewed my bottom lip, placed my bag on the seat, and slid into the booth. He looked good. Really good. Butterflies fluttered in my stomach, and I attempted to calm myself without being obvious about it. Shit, maybe I needed some alcohol to steady my nerves.

A flicker of sadness clenched my heart, and I realized I might have missed seeing him a little over the last several weeks. Sometimes ignoring people was more work than facing them, but he scared me too much. And besides, everyone I cared about eventually left or turned on me. So, what was the point in starting a relationship?

"How are you?" he asked.

I frowned. "Fine. You?"

"Not really sure. You've been avoiding me."

"No, no," I stuttered. "I've just been really busy, but that's normal for me. Nineteen-credit class load and work shifts don't leave time for anything else."

"Hadlee, I've seen you duck around corners when our group walks into the restaurant. Why?"

"What? Nooo." I shook my head emphatically.

He simply stared at me.

My nose wrinkled. He'd caught me, and I could no longer deny it. "Fine. I've been ignoring you."

"Have I offended you? Was I rude? An asshat?"

"No. The opposite, really."

"So, you're ignoring me because I'm *not* an asshat?" he asked, confusion clouding his face.

I heaved out a sigh of exasperation. He was making me feel like an idiot. "It's a long story, Kaisen. I'm sure you're a nice guy, but when Kara said you were interested in me, I panicked. You already know I have a full schedule; I can't fit anyone in my life right now. I just didn't want to have a conversation like—well, like this," I said, my finger pointing at him and then myself for emphasis.

He leaned forward, folding his hands on top of the table. My anxiety stepped up a notch as I searched his face for some type of reaction.

"I'll tell you what—you're off work, and tomorrow is Thanksgiving, so you don't have to get up early. Spend a few hours with me. Let's hang out, and after tonight, if you aren't interested, then I'll never bother you again."

"Why? Why do you want to get to know me? There are a million beautiful girls out there."

"I'm not interested in the other million, just the one sitting in front of me—the one who swept me off my feet almost a month ago in the grocery store."

My gaze dropped to my lap, and my cheeks flushed.

"Sorry, but I'm not sure I can ever let you live that one down."

I covered my face with my hands. Our first meeting at the store definitely wasn't one of my best moments. "Fine," I said, finally looking at him and leaning back in my seat. "Since I'm off the clock and have a ride home, I think I'd like something to drink."

"It's on me, and Kara's our waitress."

"Oh, she must have taken over my section. Well, I'll tip her well." I grinned and raised my finger toward her. She'd already been watching us, so it wasn't difficult to get her attention.

She hurried over to us, not even trying to hide her excitement. "What can I get you two?" she asked, beaming.

"I'm starving, so a hamburger, fries, and root beer would be awesome," Kaisen said.

"Had?"

"White Russian."

Kara's pen dropped to the floor. "Really?"

"I don't have to work or go to class tomorrow. And I'll either take an Uber or catch a ride home with you tonight, if that's still okay." I brushed a stray hair back from my face and smiled.

"Puh-lease. I'll bring all the alcohol you want. You'll have a ride home. Just relax." She winked at me before leaving to put our order in.

"White Russian, huh?"

I shrugged. "I don't indulge very often."

His deep chuckle sent chills through my body. I hoped Kara would hurry up with my drink, before I passed out from nerves. Other than my best friend in high school, David, I hadn't hung out with many guys, not even casually, at a restaurant.

"It is nice to just stop and take a breath sometimes," I admitted. "No school tomorrow and no job to go to. Do you work?"

"Yeah. I manage my dad's construction business, and I'm doing some on-site building during the summer. After I graduate, he'll teach me everything else I need to know so I can take over full time."

"Oh, wow! I'm guessing you're a business major, then?"

"Yeah. I've been around it since I was young, and it's home. I love everything about it—bidding on projects, talking to clients, and seeing the project grow from ground zero to completion."

I chewed my lip while it dawned on me why he was so strong and muscular. I'd have bet he tanned beautifully during the summer, too. My face reddened just from thinking about him shirtless and muscular with sun-kissed skin.

"Here ya go. Bottoms up. Hank said it's on the house, and he and I will keep an eye on you."

She placed the root beer and water in front of Kaisen. "Did you hear that?" she asked him, offering a smile that said she'd kick his ass if he hurt me. "Say *hi* to Hank." She nodded toward our bartender. I stifled my giggle as Kaisen turned and offered him a tight wave.

"Okay, then. Your food will be done soon." She hummed while she sauntered away.

"Sorry," I said, my nose scrunching. "But I wouldn't want to mess with Hank. He trained in karate for years. Like, hardcore. His hair is short now, but a few years ago, it was long, like, down-to-his-ass long. He'd braid it and run a thin piece of barbed wire through it in case anyone got any big ideas, jumped him, and pulled his hair."

Kaisen's brows shot upward. "Are you serious?"

"Yeah. He's a big teddy bear and will give you the shirt off his back if you're in his circle, but God help you if you cross him or anyone he cares about."

"Thanks for the heads-up," he said, pausing for a moment. "Not to change this pleasant subject, but . . . when do you graduate? What are you majoring in?" he asked, playing with the straw in his soda.

"I'm a junior this year, and I'm majoring in psychology with a minor in criminal justice."

"Are you planning on taking nineteen credits every term?"

"Yup. If all goes according to plan, I'll graduate halfway through my senior year."

Kaisen slipped the straw into his mouth and took a pull of his root beer. I took a big swallow of my White Russian. And then another.

"Is it good?" he asked, cracking a grin.

"My favorite." I released a soft sigh of contentment as the alcohol tingled through me, my shoulders releasing the pent-up stress.

"Bottoms up," Kara said, setting another one in front of me. She placed Kaisen's plate of food in front of him and waited while I tipped up my first drink and drained it. I handed it to her, but my focus was on Kaisen. She took the glass and quietly slipped away.

"Why psychology?" he asked.

A beat of silence hung in the air between us. I took one last unladylike gulp of my alcohol and then moved it away from me. It had been several hours since I'd had any food, and it was hitting me fast.

"My mother."

Kaisen bit into his burger and chewed as he waited for me to continue.

"My dad died when I was eight, and she turned into a cold, heartless shell of a woman."

He hesitated and then placed his food down on his plate. Confusion clouded his face, and something else I didn't recognize flickered across his handsome features. Maybe I'd shared with him too soon and it was a little TMI for our first time hanging out.

"Your dad's dead?" he asked softly. After an uncomfortable pause, "I'm sorry." His deep voice filled with compassion.

There was something different about Kaisen's condolences. Everyone else said the words, but really had no idea what it was like to have a parent there one minute and gone the next. It left a hole inside you, no matter what you did to stitch it up.

"Yeah," I replied. "I was eight." Oh jeez, now I was repeating myself. Tears threatened to spill over, so I quickly glanced up at the ceiling.

"Anyway, my mom turned into a different person afterwards. I'm an adult now, I can understand, in a way, but her behavior was so extreme. She used to be happy, warm, and gentle, even when I got into trouble. But after he died . . . you'd think she would have gotten depressed or drunk herself to sleep every night, but she didn't. She started a business, became a workaholic, and developed a mean streak. She criticized everything I did."

Kaisen remained quiet while I chattered. The alcohol must have been affecting me, because I never talked about my mother to people—other than Syd and Kara. I picked up my glass and took another sip of liquid courage.

"I remember that day so well. It had snowed, and Mom took me to his grave. She didn't even cry. When I asked her what had happened, she refused to tell me, and to this day, she still hasn't. But when I was ten, I found his death notice announcement tucked away in Mom's closet." I took a deep breath. "He was killed in a car accident on his way home from a business trip. I guess it was just too painful for her to talk about.

"I do remember he traveled a lot, but when he was home, it was the best. After he passed away, when Mom got mad at me, she'd tell me I was just like him, that I was a daddy's girl. And then she'd remind me he wasn't there to take care of me anymore. She'd smirk and tell me I'd have to deal with it. But, how was I supposed to deal with it when I was only eight years old?" I grabbed my glass, lifted it to my mouth, and let the alcohol wash the memories away. The anger bubbled up briefly, and I accidentally clanked the glass against the table top. I grimaced.

"My mother's a pain, but her behavior drove me toward psychology. I guess what I really want to know is why people keep big secrets. What motivates them to do different things in crazy situations? Maybe I'm trying to understand myself, too. Mom says I have daddy issues. I think she needs to shut the hell up and leave me alone."

With a loud groan, I dropped my face into my palms. After a pause, I swallowed my frustration, lifted my chin, and met his gaze. "I'm so sorry. This is why I shouldn't consume alcohol. I'm making an ass out of myself. I should go." I began to scoot across the seat.

His hand gently grasped mine.

"You're not making an ass out of yourself. Stay. Please," he said.

"Really?" I asked, surprised. "We can talk about something else." I moved the alcohol away from me and snatched Kaisen's water. "Can I have it? I think I need it. And some coffee."

"Yeah, go ahead. I'll get Kara." He slid out of the booth and strode across the room. My God, he looked good. My focus remained on his broad shoulders and tight ass while he chatted with my best friend. He returned with the cup of coffee.

"Here ya go," he said. "Kara already made it the way you like it." His forehead furrowed as he handed me the cup. "Are you okay? I think you feel like you overshared. You didn't. You're fine."

I sucked in a sharp breath. "I did tell you too much. It took me almost a year to talk to Sydney about it, and I provided you with even more detail. Kara knows too but just bits and pieces. And it makes me an awful person to hate my mother. I shouldn't hate anyone." I winced. I should really have stopped talking. I blew on the steaming liquid and sipped at it while I tried to contain the ongoing thoughts that had been unleashed and were now running rampant in my mind.

"No, you're not an awful person at all. In fact," he said, pausing to pop a french fry into his mouth. "I'll share, too."

CHAPTER

5

My anxiety calmed to a dull roar once I realized I hadn't scared Kaisen off. I don't know what the hell I had been thinking of, drinking with a stranger. And not just any drinks—White Russians on top of it! Apparently, I'd unleashed the beast I'd kept tucked tightly away. My focus dropped to my lap as I attempted to regain some composure.

"I lost my mom," he said, quietly.

My head snapped up at his words.

"Oh." I knew I had recognized something about him when I'd shared about my dad. It was almost as though he'd reached his hand out and touched my heart. I'd felt an electric spark that had connected us in ways other people couldn't understand, from a place of grief and darkness.

"Suicide," he said, leaning back and putting his burger down.

A heaviness settled between us, and we sat quietly, without speaking. Sometimes silence said what words couldn't.

I resisted the urge to reach out and touch his hand, let him know I understood and, even though I couldn't fix it, I supported him.

"My dad hasn't ever fully recovered. That's one reason I'm taking over the business. My mom left us when I was eleven. For a while, I had to get him out of bed, clean the house, do the laundry, and make sure we ate, even if some nights it was a bowl of cereal. Eventually, he started to function again, and then it was my turn to fall apart. I had some rough teen years, played around with drugs for a while, and fell behind in school. Eventually, I realized shit like that would get me nowhere fast, so I gave myself a hard kick in the ass and graduated on time. I dedicated myself to my dad's business and my future. I wanted my mom to be proud of me."

I nodded. He'd been kind enough to let me talk, and whether or not he realized it, he probably needed me as much as I needed him right now.

"Schizophrenia."

I titled my head and frowned. I couldn't even begin to understand what it had been like for his family.

"She was diagnosed when I was six, so I didn't understand what was happening or where she went mentally. It was like she was present one minute and then someone else showed up in her place. I remember finding her in a corner, all balled up and covering her head. She rocked back and forth, crying, and telling herself to stop. I thought she was playing since there was no one else around. Later, when Dad came home, I told him what'd happened. She was diagnosed shortly after," he said, his voice thick with sadness.

We both fell silent. He ran his fingers across the back of his neck and then rested his hands on top of the table. Maybe it was the alcohol or the fact we shared the same type of loss in our lives, but my hand crept toward his, and I took his fingers in mine. His thumb gently traced the back of my hand. The heat from his skin sent tingles through me, but as much as I wanted to just sit there with him, touching him, I gave his hand a brief squeeze and then pulled mine away.

"My dad said she had tried meds, but nothing seemed to work. She finally gave up. I can't say I blame her, but a part of me still does. I can't help it. I'm angry with her, but now that I'm an adult and reading information about the illness, man . . . I don't know if I could have lived like that either."

"I'm sorry," I whispered. "I can't imagine what you went through."

"Yeah. You can."

Stillness lingered in the space between us as we crawled our way out of the past and back to each other.

"So, what about now? With your mom? Will you see her tomorrow?" he asked, redirecting the conversation.

"No. She's the head of a makeup company and works nonstop, even on the holidays. I go to my friend Sydney's for Thanksgiving and Christmas. I love her parents, and they've taken me under their wing. They're good people. What about you?"

"Dad and I will drive to Portland for a few days to see family. We'll be back on Saturday. It's a quick trip, so it works."

Kara approached us. "You two have been sitting here all night. We're closing in half an hour."

"Seriously?" I checked the time on my Fitbit. "I forgot we were closing early tonight."

"I'm going to get my crap done, and then I'll be ready to go. You good with that?" she asked, giving a discreet nod toward Kaisen, her eyebrow arching.

"Yup. I'll be ready."

"Damn," she muttered, walking away.

"She seemed disappointed. You'd think she'd be ready to leave," Kaisen remarked.

I shook my head. "She was hoping you'd offered to take me home."

"You should let me. It's not like I haven't been there before."

I paused. I'd already shared way too much with him. "I appreciate it, but I'm going to ride with Kara."

He nodded. "Those walls you toss up so easily . . . at least I understand why now."

What exactly was he implying? "What do you mean?"

"The next time you talk to your mom, tell her you don't have daddy issues. You're fine."

My eyes flashed. "Why would I tell her something like that?"

"Because it's true. You are fine; you've just had a lot of loss and grief which would make anyone shy away from getting too close to other people."

"I thought I was the one majoring in psychology," I said, my tone sharp. "Just because we shared a brief moment doesn't mean you know me or get to analyze my life. You don't. Happy Thanksgiving," I said, grabbing my backpack and flying out of the booth.

"Hadlee, I'm sorry! Hey, I didn't mean to upset you. Please, sit back down," he said, reaching for my hand.

"It's late, and you need to go. We're closing," I huffed. I stormed off without looking back, and left Kaisen sitting in the booth by himself.

"That guy has balls, and I do *not* mean in a good way," I said to Kara while I shivered in the passenger seat.

"Are you sure you didn't overreact? I mean, seriously, Had . . . you guys shared some deep shit. And I know you're not used to telling people about your family, but he doesn't know that. So, are you sure you're not really mad at yourself for drinking and telling him about it in the first place?"

My annoyance flared while I listened to her, but I refused to say anything. Normally, I was reserved about the information I shared. But not tonight. The alcohol had stripped me of my walls, and I had stood naked in front of him.

I frowned, a nagging thought beginning to form. "Wait, I get I'm a lightweight, but how strong did Hank make those White Russians? I had two, and my brain turned to mush. Then, all of a sudden, everything gushed out."

Kara grimaced. "Well, we might have put a little extra in there to help while you were talking to Kaisen."

"Oh my God, you didn't!" Exasperation sharpened my voice.

"I'm sorry." She winced. "We weren't thinking; we were just trying to help, and apparently, we gave you too much. You have like zero tolerance, by the way."

"Shit." I covered my face with my hands and slid down in the seat.

"I'm so sorry. Don't be mad at us, please," Kara pleaded.

My hands dropped away from my face while I gaped at her.

"What the hell am I going to do now? I mean, do you think I just got drunk and flustered? I couldn't shut the hell up. And when he made a comment about why I don't allow people to get close to me, it was like he slammed me into a brick wall—and I was furious."

She stopped at a light and turned toward me. "Well, it wasn't the smartest thing he could have said, but I don't think he was trying to hurt you or piss you off. And alcohol can make people more emotional than they would be sober. So, yeah, I think that's what it was. I don't think he meant to be an ass." Her voice suddenly turned playful. "But maybe you should get drunk again and let Kaisen take care of all that angst you've got pent up inside."

"Kara!"

She giggled into her gloved hand and started driving again. "Okay, seriously. Why don't you text him and see if you two can get on the same page?"

"I don't have his phone number because I got mad and left, remember? This is way too much drama in my life. Just forget it. I'm done."

"Hadlee Jameson, knock it off right now," she demanded, her tone booming through the car.

I shrank even deeper into the seat.

"This is a misunderstanding and the result of too much alcohol, not drama. Getting to know someone takes a little effort, and he's really trying. You guys have some things in common that even Syd and I don't have with you. If nothing else, be friends with the guy. Give him a chance—before I pull that pretty blond hair out of your head."

My head tilted, and my arms folded over my chest. I almost challenged her to try to, but deep down, I knew she was right. I'd lost control of the night by hiding behind liquor.

"Fine. But I don't know how to get in touch with him."

"I do." Kara grinned as she pulled up to my house. "I'll send it to you." She put the car in park and, within seconds, had pulled her iPhone out of her purse.

"What are you doing?"

"Hang on." She tapped her screen a few times, and then my phone buzzed.

I pulled it out of my back pocket and laughed. "Are you serious? You have Kaisen's number?"

"Well, yes, but only because of Michael."

"I don't understand. Why would Michael give you Kaisen's information?"

"It's for emergency purposes only, but we were hoping, eventually, you'd want it." She bit her lip while she waited for me to respond.

I wasn't sure if I should laugh or yell, but I'd already done enough yelling tonight. So, I did the next best thing. I saved his contact information, rolled my eyes, and hugged her. "I love you. Be safe and tell your family Happy Thanksgiving."

"Love you, too," she said, returning my hug.

I stepped onto the sidewalk, closed the door, and waved goodbye. A glance at my phone revealed that it was a little after eleven. The cold, crisp air filled my lungs as I took in a deep breath and tapped my screen. I needed to text him before I chickened out.

I'm sorry I got so mad.

I stood with my feet glued to the walkway, the wind whipping around me while the three little dots began to blink.

Who is this?

I took a few steps toward the porch. I was still safe. I didn't have to respond. I could just act like none of this had happened and return to my busy life without him. But something inside me wouldn't allow it.

Hadlee.

No dots appeared. He was mad, and I couldn't blame him. I shoved my phone back in my pocket and ran up the steps. It vibrated as I walked into the house.

It was a big night for both of us, and I'm sorry I stuck my foot in my mouth again.

A stupid grin lit my face. How was this guy getting to me? I closed and locked the door behind me and then texted back.

Kara and Hank made my drinks too strong. They did it on purpose but didn't realize I'd sit there and tell you my darkest secrets.

Those were your darkest secrets?

I stared at the message. Were they? Had I told him the worst? And he hadn't run out of the restaurant, pulling his hair and screaming?

Maybe.

I can handle that if you can.

Could I? Was I ready to let someone else in other than my two best friends? My pulse sped up at the thought. I reached for the light switch and flicked it on. My thumbs danced across the screen as I tapped a message and walked toward my room, completely oblivious to everything except Kaisen.

My fingers found the doorknob, and I flung the bedroom door open. A scream ripped through me. My phone clattered across the hardwood floor while I covered my eyes and flattened myself against the hallway wall.

"You're fucking kidding me, right?" I snarled. "Why didn't you leave the blue ribbon on the door handle?" Squeezing my eyes closed, I hugged the wall and inched away from the room.

I could hear Marcus and Syd shuffling around while I tried to remove the mental images that had rooted themselves deeply in my mind—both of them, one hundred percent naked. I'd just witnessed Marcus's junk firsthand—and Syd's, too.

"Sorry," she hollered. "I forgot."

I don't think she was apologizing for herself. We dressed and undressed in front of each other all the time, but Marcus was a different story.

I plopped into the recliner in the living room and released a heavy sigh. I'd have Marcus's naked body imprinted on my brain for life. Syd wasn't joking about his sculpted abs, but I wished it was all I'd seen.

"We're covered," Syd said as they entered the room. "We weren't expecting anyone for a few more hours."

"Obviously," I said.

"Sorry, Hadlee," Marcus said, his fair skin reddening while he gripped Sydney's waist with his hands. I stared at them and once again realized what a breathtakingly exotic couple they were. Marcus's reddish-brown hair and light complexion were noticeable on their own, but when he stood next to Syd, the couple lit up the room. Maybe it was the contrast of his features with her black hair and tan skin, but they had something special. Something rare.

"Yup. Me, too," I said, shooting her a nasty look. "I guess I saw a whole new side of you tonight, huh?"

For the first time since I'd known Syd, she blushed.

"Well, I'll leave you two alone. I'm going to bed."

"Have a good night and Happy Thanksgiving," Marcus said.

"You, too."

I grabbed my phone off my bedroom floor, my conversation with Kaisen forgotten. But once I was in the safety of my own four walls, I noticed the phone lighting up again, showing me six messages.

I kicked my way through the pile of dirty clothes on the floor and sank down on my bed to read them.

Can I save your number?

Maybe text you while I'm in Portland?

Would that be okay?

Hadlee?

You there?

Guess not.

My head dropped into my hands. Marcus and Syd had shit timing; Kaisen probably thought I was ignoring him.

I'm here. I texted, waiting for the dots to flicker with his response.

Thought I'd scared you off again.

My thumbs danced across the keyboard. *No, just a small situation at home.*

Everything okay?

If he meant was I okay after seeing Marcus in his full glory, the answer would be no, but I couldn't tell him that.

Sometimes having roommates sucks.

I leaned back in bed, the little dots flickering back to life. I kicked off my shoes and slipped underneath the covers. Sleep seductively whispered my name as my head nestled into the pillow. The dots continued to flash steadily across my screen. I yawned. My eyes fluttered closed with the realization that I didn't have to set my alarm tomorrow. Syd and I weren't due to volunteer at the shelter until noon, and we didn't have to be at her parents' house until three. I'd definitely wake up before then.

Sleep tugged at me, and I gave in.

We *always received a lot* of snow in the winter, but the sunshine was never far behind. The golden rays frequently filtered into our bedroom window and woke me earlier than necessary.

But that wasn't the case this morning. My brain jerked awake, and my eyes slammed open to find Syd sitting on the side of my bed, shaking my own phone at me.

"What are you going to say?" she asked, bouncing up and down.

"Huh?"

"He asked you out! Oh my God, say yes. You have to say yes."

"No, he didn't," I said, pulling myself into a sitting position.

"Oh, yes he did," she said, shoving the phone closer to my face. "Read it. The poor guy asked you last night, and you never replied."

I grabbed the phone and scanned the messages, my finger hovering over the last one.

Can I take you out Saturday when I get home?

"Shit. I fell asleep on him."

"Well, hurry up and tell him yes," she squealed, clapping her hands together.

"I can't, Syd. He's really nice, but I'm not."

"What?" She froze, waiting for my explanation.

The truth was that any relationship would just be a disappointment waiting to happen. But I said, "I'm jumpy and overly anxious around him. I attack him with little cause. I am always suspicious, and I do and say stupid shit. He doesn't bring out the best in me."

"Stop making excuses and go out with him," she ordered, folding her arms over her chest.

I yawned. "Isn't this *my* decision?"

"No. That's where you're wrong. Kara, Marcus, and I have already discussed this, and you're going out."

"Wait, you talked to Kara and Marcus about me going on a date? When?"

"About an hour ago. You were still asleep."

A pang of frustration filled me, and I flopped back on my pillow. "What time is it anyway?"

"Stop changing the subject. We have plenty of time to go volunteer and then get to my parents' house."

"Good. I need to shower. I smell like hamburgers and alcohol."

"Answer him, please. Go out. You have all three of us supporting you, Had. I think he might be good for you."

Damn. She was pulling the support card. When she reminded me they were there for me, she meant business.

I held up my phone and reread the messages. He'd asked me out. I could feel the weight of Syd's gaze growing more intense, and I tried to calm the pounding in my chest. I typed my message, then tugged at my lower lip as I stared at it. Releasing the breath I hadn't realized I'd been holding, I tapped Send.

"What did you say?" she asked, leaning over to try to read my phone.

I hugged it to my chest. "Wait."

She chewed on her thumbnail as we both waited for my phone to vibrate with a response. It seemed like forever, but it only took a minute for him to reply. I held up the phone and grinned.

"I said yes," I said softly.

Syd jumped off the bed and bounced around in the middle of our room. Her long hair covered her face while she danced in her Christmas pajamas. I couldn't help but laugh. You would have thought this was her date!

"Hey, it's Thanksgiving today. Aren't you a little early to be wearing Santa and his reindeer?" I asked, pointing at her clothes.

"Hadlee, where have you been? I've been wearing these since July!"

She pulled me out of bed and hugged me. "I'm really proud of you."

"Thanks," I whispered. I could only hope I hadn't just made the biggest mistake of my life.

After years of Thanksgivings, you'd think it wouldn't bother me anymore, but I still looked at my messages, hoping for a *Happy Thanksgiving!* from my mother.

"Nothing?" Syd asked.

"Nope. Stupid to think she could take a few minutes out of her busy schedule to text me."

"She's probably working and getting ready for the insane shopping crowds tonight."

I nodded and stared out of Syd's car window. Her parents had leased her a BMW sedan last year. As long as her grades were good and she stayed out of trouble, they paid for her car, rent, gas, and food. Even though she loved the car, she'd have made good grades regardless because that was who she was.

She pulled into the long circular drive of her parents' house and parked in front of the five-car garage. We grabbed our purses and ran up the front stairs. She rang the doorbell once, opened the front door, and yelled hello.

My phone vibrated as we stepped inside.

Your belly full yet?

"Anyone good?" Syd asked.

"Just Kaisen."

She smiled while we hung our coats up in the closet.

"Just Kaisen?" she asked, her eyebrows wiggling as she laughed.

Not yet. Just got to Syd's house. Text you later?

Sounds good. Have fun.

I followed Syd into the kitchen, inhaling the aroma of turkey and stuffing.

"Rosa," I said, bending down and hugging their housekeeper and chef. "Happy Thanksgiving and thank you for cooking."

Rosa was a plump, friendly woman, and it was obvious how much she loved working for Syd's family. She'd been with them since Syd was ten, and they treated her like one of their own.

"My Hadlee," Rosa said, patting my cheek. "Always so glad to see you."

"Hi, Rosa," Syd said, hugging her next.

"My girls are all grown," she said, smiling proudly and pulling the turkey out of the oven. "Everyone is already sitting down. Go on now so I can serve everyone before the food gets cold."

I followed Syd into the formal dining room. The table was set with beautiful blue-and-white china, white cloth napkins folded into turkeys, and a few expensive bottles of wine.

"Hadlee, honey, come here!"

"Hi, Camille. Thank you again for having me."

Syd's mom wrapped her arms around me and pulled me in for a long hug. I blinked my tears away as she hung onto me. After a moment, she stepped away, scanning me up and down. "How's my girl?" She beamed at me. "You're looking well."

Her large, dark eyes sparkled against her red blouse. Sydney had been adopted at birth by Camille and Jonathon, an African-American couple. Unfortunately, it had caused a lot of issues for all of them, but Sydney knew, although there was a racial difference, they were truly her parents.

"Starving," I said, smiling. "Hi, Jonathon," I stood on my tiptoes and hugged Syd's dad.

"So good to see you," he said, patting me on the back.

I sat next to Syd while Rosa served the food. I gained five pounds merely by smelling it.

"Let's say grace," Jonathon said, and we joined hands. I used to tell Syd her dad had the right voice to be a pastor. We'd laughed and agreed that he'd never leave his position as CEO with the technology company he worked for. Jonathon was one of the most intelligent people I'd ever met and a phenomenal conversationalist.

When I first began spending time with them, we'd sit in the library for hours discussing history, religion, politics, and any other topic we could think of. He was so patient when he challenged me to research the facts and form my own opinions. He never grew angry when I expressed my thoughts or when I disagreed with him. But he did want me to explain *why* I disagreed with him, and he refused to accept regurgitated information; only the cold, hard facts would appease him.

Camille was gentle and funny, but she could snap her head around when she was mad faster than anyone I'd seen. The first time I saw her do it, I'd quietly backed out of the room and hidden in the library.

Syd teased me about it for years. Now, I'm just one of the family. We've laughed until we cried, witnessed Jonathon and Camille yelling at each other, and heard Jonathon cussing a blue streak when the kitchen faucet broke and caused damage to the kitchen. They were the only normal family I'd ever experienced, and I would love them forever.

We spent the next several hours stuffing our faces with fantastic food and catching up with each other.

"I have no clue how you didn't end up weighing three hundred pounds with Rosa cooking for you during your childhood," I said as we pulled into our empty driveway.

"I know, right?" she asked, scanning the house. "I think all our roomies have left to visit their families and we have the place to ourselves."

"Ohhh," I said, "now that calls for some strong alcohol and a good action flick."

"Oh, yeah? A few hot toddies for Hadlee?"

"We might as well. It's not like Kaisen is here; I don't have to worry about saying a bunch of shit I shouldn't."

"Don't be so hard on yourself. He seemed okay with what you told him, and he shared with you in return."

"I guess," I said. My phone started vibrating. I dug my phone out of my purse and attempted to hide my smile.

"That's Kaisen. I can tell by the look on your face," Syd said.

"Maybe, maybe not," I replied, tapping my screen.

We came back early. Dad has to be at a site at six tomorrow morning. How are you?

You mean you drove down to Portland, ate, and came right back? That sucks, I replied.

Pretty much, but I was hoping to see you tomorrow instead of Saturday?

I paused. I had the day off, so there wasn't any harm in moving up the plans.

Okay. Where are we going? I waited while the dots flickered across my phone.

It's a surprise. I'll pick you up at 7.

Not sure I like surprises. Is it a good one? I hit Send and groaned. Shit. Is it a good one? What a stupid thing to say.

"Are you coming?" Syd said, grinning at me before shutting her car door.

I sure as hell hope it's a good surprise. If not, then you'll probably refuse to see me again.

We have to get through the first one. One date at a time...

I finally got out of the car and caught up to Syd on the porch. What was he up to? A surprise?

My phone buzzed again as I followed her inside, removed my shoes, and switched on the lamp. The soft glow barely provided enough light to see ten feet in front of me, but no one had bothered to purchase a stronger bulb.

See you tomorrow.

Okay.

I glanced up.

Something was wrong. I clutched Syd's arm before she could take another step.

"What?" she asked.

I held my finger to my lips and pointed toward the kitchen. A light was on. No one in the house ever left one on, even though we should have.

"No one should be here, right?" I asked in a hushed tone.

She nodded, frowning as she realized what was going on.

"Get behind me," I mouthed to her. I reached for the baseball bat we kept tucked away in the corner and then handed Syd my phone.

"Dial 911 but don't call yet," I whispered.

Her brows shot up, but she did as I asked, and we slowly crept toward the room together. I stopped short of the entryway and peered around the corner.

"Are you fucking kidding me?" I muttered. I sucked in a deep breath, straightened my shoulders, and walked in, tugging Syd behind me.

"What are you doing here?" I snapped.

"Is that any way to speak to your mother?"

Syd handed me my phone. I placed it on the counter and then removed my coat. She must have come straight from work because there wasn't a dark hair out of place. Her red, manicured nails flashed in the dim light as she adjusted her diamond pendant around her slender neck.

"How did you get in?" I asked, leaning the bat against the lower cabinets.

"Some young man named Lionel let me in and said I could stay. He said you were with Sydney and thought you'd be back soon. So, I thought I'd make myself some tea, but your kitchen is disgusting, so I just wiped off a barstool and sat here."

"Hi, Ms. Jameson," Syd piped up and stepped out from behind me.

"Sydney, darling!" Mom said as she stood and hugged her. "Thank you so much for calling me. You're such an amazing young woman. I'll bet your parents are so proud."

I rubbed my forehead and shot Syd a venomous look. "You called her?" I asked, my voice rising an octave.

Her face paled as she nodded. Mom strolled back to her seat and folded her hands in her lap. No greeting for me. No surprise.

"And by the way, Mom, Sydney cleaned the kitchen before we left," I said, smirking. "If you don't like it, take it up with her."

"Such an attitude, Hadlee. I just don't understand you sometimes."

I squeezed my eyes closed and willed her to disappear, but apparently, my magic skills weren't up to par. I turned to Syd. "Why?" I asked. I didn't even try to subdue my searing tone.

"It was a few weeks ago . . . you know, the night I made you dinner."

My head snapped back toward my mother. "She called you, and it took you a *month* to find out why? When does Sydney ever call you?"

"When you've made a mess of things."

"And how often is that, Mom?"

"Well, in the three years you've been in school, she's called once—and that was one too many. Not that I mind you calling me, Sydney dear."

My stomach churned, and I swallowed, attempting to force her words out of my mind.

"Do you even remember that I'm obtaining my bachelor's degree early? And that I work and support myself?"

"Well, apparently, it's not enough, which is typical for you."

I turned to glare at Syd, to thank her so much for her sneaky, backhanded intrusion into my life. But she'd already gotten the picture. Syd's mouth had dropped open.

"Ms. Jameson, I'm sorry I called." Her words tumbled over each other. "Hadlee is doing great. She just got exhausted and stressed out about her classes and work. She was super tired, and I had hoped you might be able to help her with the rent. I didn't mean to cause any problems."

"You're never a problem, Sydney. Hadlee, on the other hand, has a habit of screwing up everything she touches. She rarely gets anything right."

My nostrils flared, and my throat tightened. She'd been saying this shit to my face for years, but to say it to my best friend? To act as though I weren't even standing in front of her? My vision clouded, and I blinked, trying to gain control of my temper, but something inside me snapped.

"Get out," I flared, outrage hanging off each syllable.

"I'm sorry. Were you saying something?"

"Get out of my house!" My body shook as I pointed toward the front door. "And don't come back. I don't ever want to see you again."

"What?" Her eyebrows arched in surprise. I'd never spoken to anyone like that in my life, much less her. "You have no right to speak to me like that," she huffed and stood.

"I have every right when you waltz into my home and tell me I'm worthless. I do not need that—or you—in my life. There's the door. Get. Out. Do not, under any circumstances, come back. I've put up with you for years, and I am officially done."

My neck and cheeks burned hot with anger. Nausea rolled in my stomach as she collected her Prada bag from the counter and let herself out. The door slammed behind her.

I collapsed onto the barstool and laid my head on the cold counter. It felt good, solid, calming.

"Well, fuck me runnin' sideways," Syd mumbled, lowering herself onto the stool across the island counter from me. "I've never heard you lose your shit like that."

"Don't talk to me right now. I'm furious with you, too. I need a minute before I say something I don't mean."

Her barstool scraped across the hardwood floor, and I heard glasses clinking. After a few minutes, my breathing began to steady, and my brain fog subsided. I'd never been so furious before; I'd actually scared myself. The pounding in my ears was still intense enough that my head was beginning to ache.

"Sydney," I said, sitting up and eyeing the drinks she'd made us. Bottles of Jim Beam and Coke were on the counter, along with two glasses filled two-thirds full. She pushed one toward me, apprehension written all over her face.

"Do not call her again unless I'm on the brink of death. And, come to think about it, spare me the anguish and call her *after* I'm dead."

"Had . . . I'm so sorry. I had no clue that's how she treated you," she said, her eyes brimming with tears.

"That is how she treats me on a good day," I said, exhaling in relief that she was gone. "Holy hell, did I just kick my mother out of our house?" I grabbed my tumbler and took a big gulp. It burned my throat, making me wince. "Do you know how to *not* make a drink that gets me drunk in two swallows?" I asked, frustration filling my voice.

She pinched the bridge of her nose. "I'm sorry," she said again, her tone heavy with regret. "I was just trying to help. You've been so tired, and you never do anything for fun. I was worried. I know what you told me about her, but . . . the only reason I called her was because I thought she would want to help her daughter when she learned you were working so hard."

"No, that's what your parents would want to do." My chest ached. I took another sip. "I know you didn't mean to hurt me, Syd. I'm sorry I got so pissed at you."

She jumped off her seat, ran over to my side of the counter, and wrapped her arms around me. I leaned my head against her shoulder and, for the first time in years, allowed the tears to spill down my face.

"Oh, Had. I just didn't understand," she murmured, patting my back while I cried. "You're breaking my heart."

Syd had never seen me get a single tear in my eye, much less have a full-on crying jag. We were the opposite in that way. She cried over romantic comedies and action flicks. The last time tears had fallen from me? I was eight.

My body shook as I gave myself permission and let it all out. The anger, frustration, sadness, and finally, a wave of acceptance flowed over me. There was nothing in the world that would ever change my relationship with my mom. I had to stop trying; I was just hurting myself in the process.

I lifted my head, and Syd handed me a tissue. I dabbed my eyes, took a shaky breath, and rubbed my forehead. My head pounded, the result of residual emotions I'd stuffed deep down for years.

"Now you know why I love your parents so much."

"I should have believed you," she said, patting my back.

"It's hard for people to understand until they see it, and I do everything possible to not let that happen. And, as I said, she wasn't bad tonight. Something inside me just broke. I've had it, Syd. If someone can't be kind and respectful, then they have no room in my life. I have you, Kara, and your parents. You guys are my real family."

"I love ya." She hugged me again.

"Love you right back," I said.

She stepped around the counter and took a long pull of her drink.

"Well, let's get everyone over here to help cheer you up."

"Ugh, I don't know if I want to be around people right now."

"It's not people, just family," she said, smiling gently as she grabbed her phone and began texting. "Okay. Just chill, and we'll have your mind off everything in no time."

I frowned at her. What was she up to?

Ten minutes later, Kara walked through the door.

"Hey," she said, hugging me and pulling up a barstool to join us at the kitchen counter.

"Thanks for coming over," I said.

Syd made her a drink and slid it to her.

"She's staying over tonight," Syd told me.

"Slumber party?" I couldn't remember the last time I'd stayed up until the early hours of the morning because I was having fun.

"Yup, you're stuck with me." Kara winked at me and took a sip. "Damn, Syd, that's strong."

I covered my face with my hand and laughed.

"To real family," Syd toasted, holding up her glass.

We clinked them together and drank up.

I started to relax after a while; the alcohol began to loosen the muscles in my neck. It seemed as though it loosened my tongue, too, so I'd have to try to curtail the desire to say whatever I was thinking tonight. Maybe practice made it more manageable?

The front door opened; I peered into the living room. "Hey, Marcus," I said, waving. "Glad you could join us with your clothes on this time." Hmm. Maybe I needed more practice.

Kara's brows pulled together, so I updated her on the X-rated episode from last night.

"He's staying the night, too," Syd said, planting a kiss on his mouth.

The doorbell rang. I frowned. Wasn't everyone who mattered already here?

Syd shot me a look, then ran out of the kitchen, to the front door. Voices floated into the room, but I couldn't make out what they were saying. As Syd approached the kitchen, there was no way she could continue to hide Kaisen.

"Look who's here, Had," she said. Nerves tightened her features. Considering my reaction to the last unexpected visitor, her anxiety was understandable.

My head tilted, and I shot her a dirty look.

"Don't," she said, holding her hands up in front of her to ward off any further nasty looks or harsh words. "We're all here because we love you. Well, three of us love you, and one of us likes you a lot."

"Hey, Hadlee," Kaisen said, stepping out from behind Syd. A pang of frustration jabbed my chest; I folded my arms in front of me. Why had she invited him? How could I possibly relax with him here?

Although my emotions were fully charged tonight, I couldn't stop my gaze from scanning his face and traveling down his chest to the jeans that fit him in all the right places. I wasn't sure how a guy could make a sweatshirt look good either, but he did.

"Don't be upset with her. She said you'd had a rough night and invited me to hang out with everyone. That's all. If you'd rather wait to see me tomorrow night, I can leave."

Silence hung in the air, and everyone waited for my response. I glared at Syd one more time for extra effect, and then my expression softened. I'd had just enough alcohol to be honest with myself. I wanted him to stay.

"I've been hanging out with Jim Beam, so fair warning."

"Warning heeded," he said, smiling as he approached me. "Can I give you a hug?"

I nodded and stood. He wrapped his arms around me, and I leaned against his chest. My arms slipped around his lower back, and my eyes closed as I listened to the steady beat of his heart. For a split second, everything that had happened with my mom slipped away, and the warmth of his body and my friends surrounding us melted my heart a little. Or maybe it was the strong-ass drinks traveling through my system.

Kaisen stepped back and smoothed my hair.

"Beer? Jack? Jim?" Syd offered. "You're staying the night, too, so no limits. We've got more alcohol in this house than a liquor store."

"Wait. What? He can't stay the night!" I squealed.

"Hon, calm down. He can have the couch or the chair in the living room. We're not offering him your bed with you in it. Although, none of us think it's a bad idea," Kara said, laughing.

My face flushed at the thought.

"A beer is great, thanks. It's okay, Had," Kaisen said, gently rubbing my shoulder. "No one is rushing anything."

"Damn straight. You're welcome to stay on the couch, and I'll just lock my bedroom door." A smile tugged at the corner of my mouth when I glanced at him.

"Not a problem. Whatever you need," he reassured me.

"All right, everyone, let's refill and move into the living room," Syd suggested. "Marcus, can you grab us all some water, please?"

"Good idea. Especially since we have a lightweight with us tonight."

He chuckled.

"Hey, you have no room to tease me. All those great things Syd said to me about your naked body . . . they're not true," I said, snickering.

"Hadlee!" Syd and Kara shouted simultaneously.

"Point taken," Marcus said. "I'll probably never live that down, so I might as well get used to it," he said, grinning as he filled the glasses.

"Those two think it's okay to not put the ribbon on the bedroom door when they're occupying it even though we share the room. But that didn't seem to be in the forefront of their minds while they were rolling around naked on the floor," I explained to Kaisen.

He laughed, sending chills through my body. I grabbed my drink and handed his to him. As I peered up at him, his gaze grew more intense, causing my body to tingle with possibility. Or maybe it was the alcohol, because I hadn't felt a hormone tickle me and create this kind of ache in a long time.

His expression softening, he leaned down, his forehead a mere inch from mine, and tucked my hair behind my ear.

"Are you okay? Syd told me what happened," he whispered. A sweet and spicy fragrance filled my nose, and I allowed his presence to surround me.

Why did he have such an effect on me? Unable to find my voice, I nodded and resisted the urge to pull him to me and taste his lips. I needed some space between us before I did something stupid.

As I stepped back, my foot tangled around the barstool leg. My tumbler flew across the kitchen, and I flew backward. "Shit!" I yelped.

Kara, Syd, Marcus, and Kaisen all scrambled toward me, but Kaisen caught me a split second before my ass smacked the floor, and he pulled me to my feet. The glass wasn't so lucky; it lay shattered across the tan tiles, leaving a dark, sticky mess in its wake.

"Are you okay?" Kara asked, gathering the broom and dustpan from the closet to sweep up everything.

"Too much alcohol, too fast?" Syd asked, cringing.

I was still struggling to regain my footing. "No, I'm okay. I just got hung up on the stool."

Kaisen picked me up with one smooth move before I could protest. He carried me as though I weighed nothing, strolled into the living room, and placed me on the couch.

My brows knitted together. "Why did you carry me in here? Although it doesn't seem like it, I really am capable of walking."

"You don't have any shoes on. I didn't want you to cut your feet."

I looked down and wiggled my toes. I hadn't even thought of that. "Oh. Thanks," I muttered while silently scolding myself for being so clumsy.

"I'll get you a new drink and some water. Be right back," Kaisen said.

I watched him as he proceeded back to the kitchen and helped everyone clean up. My mother's earlier comment rang in my ears, reminding me that I was continually creating situations for everyone else to mop up. My eyes squeezed closed, and I tried to block her from my mind.

CHAPTER

7

Ten minutes later, everyone was in the living room, and Syd turned on some music. Charlie Puth's "How Long" floated through the speakers. I leaned my head back on the couch and softly sang along.

"You sing?" Kaisen asked.

"A little bit. I'm not that good, so I don't ever sing very loud," I said, smiling. "What were you like in high school?"

"I played football, but I didn't allow myself to have much of a social life after I got off the drugs. I figured hitting other guys on the field would help me deal with my anger issues and remain focused on graduating. It kept me too busy to get in any more trouble."

"Hmmm."

"You?"

"As I've mentioned before: track, chess, and all nerdy activities. I kept to myself except for one or two close friends. Not much has changed," I said with a nod toward Kara and Syd.

"There's nothing wrong with that. I'd rather have a few people I can trust with my life than twenty fair-weather friends."

"Right?" I gazed up at him through my eyelashes. Even though there were a few inches between us on the couch, I could feel the heat of his body. I wanted to scoot closer to him, but instead, I took another sip of my drink.

"I had a best friend in high school named David. We were really close." My cheeks warmed with the recollection of how close. "We had a bet." I stopped short, chewing my lip before I spilled more about myself than I was ready to.

"Yeah?"

"I really shouldn't tell you this." I shook my head. "Are you going to hold anything against me tonight?" I asked, my voice barely more than a whisper.

"Unless you're harming children or killing animals, I think we're good; you don't have to worry about it. I know you had a shit day with your mom. So, tonight, anything we say is chalked up to a night of alcohol. It will officially be forgotten tomorrow."

"Really? It can work like that?"

Kaisen laughed. "It can work any way we want it to. Tonight, you create the rules."

My focus dropped to my lap. What would it be like to have that kind of control, even for one night?

I mindlessly took another sip and faced him more fully.

"David. Uh, well . . . our bet. How do I say this?" I asked, frowning.

Kaisen waited patiently while my mind scrambled through its tipsy fog for the right words.

"When we were in middle school, we made a bet that, if we were still virgins when we both turned eighteen, we'd get it over with and sleep together."

"And?"

"I lost my virginity when I was eighteen," I said, giggling even though it wasn't funny.

"With David?"

"Mm-hmm. It was okay. I mean, ya know, I think he enjoyed it more than I did."

"Did you guys get together after that? I mean, did you two date?"

"No. It wasn't like that at all. I just wanted my first time to be with someone I trusted, and David and I had practically grown up together. Some of the girls I knew had been date- or gang-raped at parties, and I . . . at least I can say I don't regret the one time I've had sex." My mouth dropped open when I realized what I'd said. "Damn it. I didn't mean to share that with you."

Kaisen frowned, and then his eyes widened. "Oh, wow, so you . . ." His voice trailed off.

"It's okay. Yes, I've only been with one guy, and it wasn't because I was in love with him. We loved each other as friends, but that was it. And after we were together, he found a perfect girl for him. They're engaged now."

"You still talk to him?"

"Not much anymore," I said, sadness tugging at me. "She didn't like me, and I suspect he told her we'd slept together. Which was soooooo stupid. I mean, what the hell was he thinking?" My nose wrinkled. "Shit, I just did the same thing, didn't I?" I gently smacked the palm of my hand against my forehead.

Kaisen attempted to hide his chuckle. "Yeah, you did. No worries. And guys say stupid shit on a pretty regular basis. I can attest to that."

"Yup, you can," I said, smiling. I took a deep breath and struggled to pull myself out of the funk that had settled over me.

"Thanks."

"For what?" I asked.

"For sharing. I mean, I suspect the alcohol had something to do with it, but we typically do things we want to anyway. The alcohol just makes us braver," he said.

I sat up straighter, staring at him. "So, you're telling me somewhere in my subconscious, I wanted to share that with you, and the alcohol just gave me a swift kick in the ass to do it?"

"Basically, yeah."

"Are you sure you're majoring in business? Because I'd swear you're getting a degree in psych."

A smile eased across his face while he gently touched my cheek. "I'm majoring in business, but I have studied mental illness and psychology a lot." Sadness flickered across his face, and then he dropped his hand.

"I'm sorry. I didn't mean to bring it up, and you're right. If I'd gone through all that, I'd have a vested interest, too."

"One thing that helps me, when the pain and grief threaten to take me over, is to take a minute to look at my life, really look, and realize how many great things I have. My dad and I are super close, I have great friends, and a solid future is ahead of me when I graduate. I'm comfortable financially, and I'll be debt free when I get my degree. Plus, I have one hell of a beautiful girl sitting in front of me, giving me her undivided attention."

Heat flooded my body, and I resisted the urge to straddle him and run my hands through his hair.

"Shit," I said, shaking my head. "Kaisen, you *cannot* say things to me like that."

"What?" he asked, worry lines creasing his forehead. "What's wrong?"

"Nothing, but that's the problem."

He frowned as I stood up and put some distance between us. I was afraid I would lose what little good sense I had left and take him to my bedroom.

"Gotta pee," I explained, setting my tumbler down.

Safe in the bathroom, behind the locked door, I released a heavy sigh. "It's just the alcohol," I muttered to myself, turning on the cold water and splashing my face.

"Had? You okay? Are you sick?" Kara asked through the door.

I opened it and peered through the crack, making sure no one else was with her.

"I'm okay. Come in."

"I was worried you might be sick when I saw you go into the bathroom," she said, closing the door behind her.

"I'm fine. I just needed a minute. I'm spiraling with everything that's happened today."

Kara hopped up onto the counter. I slid my back down the wall and sat on the cold laminate floor.

"Sometimes alcohol doesn't help; it makes things worse. I'm sorry about your mom."

I shook my head and closed my eyes as the earlier events replayed through my mind.

"She's been that way forever."

"You shouldn't have to deal with her. Even though you might feel guilty for losing your temper, it doesn't mean you weren't right."

"You think kicking her out of the house was the right thing to do?"

Kara's lips pursed together, and she waited before replying. "I do, and I would have done the same thing. There comes a time when a person realizes she doesn't deserve to be treated poorly. You might not recognize it yet, but something inside you stood up and said, 'No more. I don't give a rat's ass who you are. I deserve better.'"

"You got all of that out of me telling my mom to leave?" I asked, surprised.

"Hell yeah. And you will, too. Right now, you're processing." She grinned. "And you've had a lot to drink."

Why were my friends better at this psychology stuff than I was? Why weren't things as clear to me? My thoughts floated from Mom back to Kaisen. "He's so fucking hot."

Kara covered her mouth and giggled. "You're definitely drunk. But yes, Kaisen is super hot, and is head over heels for you."

"No, he isn't. He just wants to get laid. And, hey, maybe it's not a bad idea." I peeked up shyly at Kara.

She clamped her gaping mouth shut and stared at me for a moment. "Hadlee, listen to me. I highly recommend you get laid but not tonight. I take back what I said earlier about him being in your bed."

"What? Why?"

"First, you're not even close to sober, but more importantly, you're emotional. Drunk sex with someone you're not committed to isn't going to make anything better. In fact, it will make it worse, and I can't watch you do that to yourself. So, unless you can promise me you won't sleep with him tonight, I'm going to ask him to leave."

"You're fucking serious, aren't you?" I snapped, stunned that she thought this was her decision to make.

"Promise me, Hadlee. I am not playing with you. I love you, and you're my best friend. You deserve more than to be a sloppy one-night stand."

Something inside me wanted to high-five her, but I was miffed at the same time. When it came down to it, though, this was why she was one of my best friends. I never doubted where I stood with her. I never doubted I was important.

"Promise?" she asked, her tone firm.

I nodded.

"Nope, not good enough. You've gotta say it."

I watched Kara as she slid off the counter and joined me on the floor.

"Look me in the eyes and promise me—no sex tonight with Kaisen or anyone else."

I snorted, realizing that the only other guy here was Marcus. "You have my word," I said.

"Okay. Tomorrow, have all the sex you want—just be sober."

"All right," I said, giggling.

"Let's get back in there. I think we're keeping Kaisen waiting. And he's smart enough to know you haven't been peeing for ten minutes." She stood and held her hand out to me.

I inched myself up the wall to a standing position. "What if I don't have any more alcohol tonight? Can I jump him then?"

Kara laughed as she opened the door. Then she swatted me on the butt and followed me back to the living room.

"Everything okay?" Kaisen asked, his face filling with concern.

"Yup. Just girl talk. I'm good." I glanced at Kara, who plopped down in the recliner and began chatting with Syd and Marcus. "I just needed to take a timeout and remember all the good people I have in my life."

He nodded and stood. "Good tune," he said, gesturing to Bluetooth speaker in the corner. He extended his hand. "Dance with me?"

Syd turned up Maroon 5's "Lips on You," and he guided me to the center of the living room, took both my hands, and wrapped them around his neck.

"Step on my feet," he whispered in my ear.

"Huh?" I said, shivers traveling through me.

"I don't want to step on your bare feet, so you can stand on mine."

My heart melted, and my shell cracked wide open. I looked down and placed each foot on his. His muscular arms pulled me against him, and I gasped, my body molding itself to his.

"You good?" he asked, swaying gently to the beat.

I nodded. I didn't trust my voice to respond. If he hadn't been holding me up, I might have been a puddle on the floor. His hand traveled gently up my back, the other remaining around my waist. I leaned my forehead against his chest while longing spread through me. Biting my lip, I remembered my promise to Kara. I was silently arguing with the part of me that wanted to drag him to my bedroom.

He continued to move us to the music, and I finally dared a glance up at him. My breath caught in my throat as I watched his eyes fill with need. His gaze dropped to my lips, and my fingers danced through the soft curls at the back of his neck.

"How much have you had to drink?" I asked him.

"Not much. Just one."

"So, you're sober?"

"Yeah," he mumbled, his eyes never leaving my mouth. He continued to rub my back, and I arched into him, moaning softly. His hips shifted slightly, and I realized he wanted me as much as I did him.

I took a deep breath and realized that Marcus and Syd were dancing next to us, kissing, unaware of anyone around them. I scanned the room for Kara but didn't see her. Had she stepped away to call Michael? It was probably hard for her to see everyone together and not have him here.

My attention returned to Kaisen while the song repeated for the third time. Fuck it. I stood on my tiptoes and jumped. Kaisen caught me as my legs wrapped around his waist and my gaze held his. His hands grabbed my ass, and he held me in place. I slid my hand through his hair and cupped the back of his neck.

"My room," I whispered in his ear. "Please."

Without a word, he carried me down the hallway.

"Second door on the left," I said, nipping his ear. His moan rumbled through his chest. He pushed the door open, turned around, and leaned me against it. I fumbled for the doorknob and turned the lock.

His hands traveled up my sides, and I curved into him. "Kaisen," I whispered.

His lips hovered above mine. "I've wanted to do this since the first time I met you," he said, his soft mouth gently brushing my lips.

He leaned into me, and I moaned. I tightened my legs around his waist while my mouth parted and his tongue swept over mine.

"I'm in trouble," I whispered, our kiss growing more intense. For the first time in three years, I was allowing someone to touch and kiss me. "Bed." I pointed.

Kaisen gently placed me on my back and lay down on his side, facing me.

I rolled and slid my arm around his waist. He lowered his head, his lips soft against mine. I placed my leg over his hip and scooted into him, my desire building from the heat between us.

His head dipped down to my throat, and I threaded my fingers through his hair, pulling gently on his curls while he claimed every tender place on my throat and ear.

I shifted onto my back.

He hovered over me, balancing on his arms.

"What's wrong?" I asked shyly.

Worry lines pulled at his handsome features. He leaned back and studied me for a long moment.

"Nothing's wrong." He rubbed his face with his hands.

"But?" Knowing what was coming next, I sat up slowly.

"My dad," he started and then paused.

"Kind of an odd time to talk about your father, isn't it?" I asked.

"Yeah." He blew out a breath. "But my dad told me the only time I had business sleeping with a girl was, first, if I had every intention of engaging her emotionally and not just physically; second, if I could see myself having a future with her; and third, if—and only if—she were sober. He said if those three things weren't in place, I'd better keep my damn pants zipped."

"Wow, seriously?" I asked, leaning back on my elbows.

"Very." He smiled sadly.

I scooted up against the headboard so he could sit and lean against the wall. "So, which one is it?" I asked, afraid to hear the answer. Tonight, when he'd kissed me, it felt as though he were taking the part of me that had died when I was eight and breathing life back into it.

He leaned his head back and looked at me, his eyes dropping to my swollen lips. My pulse raced as I waited for his answer. Our gazes locked, and he took a slow, steady breath.

"You're not sober," he whispered.

Through our brief make-out session, the alcohol had begun to simmer down, and the drunken brain fog had lifted enough for me to realize what Kaisen had just said. He pulled my feet onto his lap and closed his eyes.

"Kaisen?" I asked, my voice shaking slightly. "What about the other two?"

He melted me with his gaze. "Those aren't a problem."

I blinked. "You? We?" My finger darted back and forth in the space between us.

"I hope so, but it's up to you. We can take this as slow or as fast as you want to. Just say the word, and I'm there."

"Word," I said softly, without hesitation.

With a groan of longing, Kaisen pulled me down onto the bed and kissed me.

"Word," I said again, breathlessly.

I melted into him as his strong hands caressed my neck and our bodies molded themselves against each other.

He gently pulled back and smoothed my hair out of my face.

"I'm going to get up now, before I can't walk away. I'm going to get us some water, and I'll be back." He scooted to the edge of my bed and ran his hand through his hair. His broad shoulders straightened as he stood.

"Don't leave," I said, moving to the edge of the bed and grabbing his hand.

"Hadlee, you in there?" Kara asked, tapping on the door.

"Shit, unlock it really quick and then go sit on the other bed." I pointed toward the doorknob. "I promised her I wouldn't attack you tonight," I said, stifling my giggle.

"You can't attack the willing," he muttered.

Kaisen took four long steps, unlocked the door, and then leapt onto Syd's bed on the other side of the room. I wiped my swollen lips, adjusted my shirt, and smoothed my hair.

"Yeah? It's open. Come on in."

The door cracked open, and Kara poked her head into the room.

"You okay?"

"Yeah. I had too much to drink, so we were just talking. We wanted to hear each other over the music."

Her attention gravitated toward Kaisen. She issued a one-word warning: "Hank."

"Kara," I chided her but laughed anyway.

"I remember Hank and his badassness. You have my word that no clothes have come off."

"Keep the door open," she directed, pushing it all the way open herself.

"Yes, Mommm," I said, sarcasm dripping from my words.

"You'll thank me when you're sober."

"No, I won't."

Her brow rose, and she tossed me a questioning look.

"I'm thanking you now," I said, smiling at her. "I love you."

"You, too," she replied, winking and then backing out of the room.

I bit my bottom lip and tried not to burst into laughter. I shot Kaisen a look across the room. "I feel like a teenager who just got busted."

He chuckled. "You and me both. It's been awhile."

"What do you mean?"

"Since I got caught making out. I've had my own place for a few years, so I don't deal with roommates or parents."

"Wait, what?" I stood and closed the door. "You're telling me that you have your own place and we're here? With a million other people?" Before he could reply, I was straddling him. "Why aren't we there?" I whispered. Then I gently kissed him.

"Because we'd be naked right now." He growled the words.

I slipped my hand underneath his sweatshirt. His abs tightened wherever my fingers brushed against his hot skin. His palms slid from my waist down to my ass, and he pulled me into him, shifting his hips upward. My breath hitched when I felt his arousal through his jeans.

"Okay, okay," I panted and gently pushed him away. "I'm getting up now. In fact, I'm pretty sure that kiss just sobered me up."

"Is that a good thing?" he asked, his gaze never leaving me as I stood.

I proceeded toward my bed, plopped down, and brushed my hair away from my face. "Yeah, but I know myself well enough to know that I don't want to move too fast. This," I said, motioning between us, "whatever this is . . . it's more than I've had in a long time, so I need to try not to screw it up, like I do everything else."

"I understand. But, Hadlee, you do so many amazing things. You support yourself, you're graduating early, and you're surrounded by good people who care about you. Sometimes taking a leap of faith is worth it, and you need to trust yourself."

"Maybe that's what scares me—leaping," I whispered. "I've lost everyone I've loved—my dad, my mom, and even myself. I can't afford to lose anyone else."

The door burst open, and Marcus, Kara, and Syd filed in.

"Oh, no. I like you, Kaisen, and I think you're just what Hadlee needs, but ya gotta get that ass off my bed. Hers is over there." Syd pointed toward me. "The bed you're on belongs to us," she added, winking at Marcus.

Kaisen stood, shook his head slightly, and strolled toward me. "Sorry, it was just a place to sit down. I didn't mean to invade your space."

"Syd, do you really want him in her bed while she's drunk?" Kara asked.

Syd frowned and stared at me. "Yeah, no. No, you're right, Kara. Kaisen, it's the floor for you."

Everyone broke into laughter, but Kaisen remained standing. The tension in the air was undeniable. "How about I find everyone something to eat?" he asked, shuffling from one foot to the other.

"Yup, I'll help you," Kara said.

As soon as they left the room, I skewered Sydney with my gaze.

Poor Kaisen probably didn't know how to handle being chaperoned, but I did. "What the hell was that?" I asked, frustration sharpening my voice. "He was trying to respect my space since I'd been drinking. What the hell is wrong with all of you?" I rubbed my forehead with the back of my hand. Why was everyone hovering over me?

"We were just looking out for you. That's it, so don't get mad."

Several beats of dead silence filled the space between us while we glared at each other. I never treated her and Marcus that way—as long as they weren't naked in the middle of the living room. But I didn't need to be mothered. I was an adult, damn it, and everyone needed to stop treating me like I was incapable of taking care of myself.

Syd broke the tense moment by grasping Marcus's hand and marching out. I hated it when we argued. It rarely happened, so I always felt like shit afterward. But she had to respect my space if I was going to be dating Kaisen.

Butterflies danced in my belly as I realized that Kaisen and I might be a thing. Maybe even a good thing? I flopped down on my bed and listened to everyone in the kitchen. The aftereffect of the alcohol had drained me. It'd been a long day. I glanced around for my phone and realized it was most likely in the living room. The glowing red numbers on my alarm clock blared at me. Surprised, I realized it was already after 2 a.m.

My mind raced as I thought about Kaisen's kiss and the three things his father had taught him about sleeping with a girl. Was the only thing that had kept us out of bed tonight the fact I'd been drunk? Did he care that much about me to wait?

I rolled over on my stomach and willed my thoughts to quiet while the laughter in the kitchen grew louder. Was I doing the right thing? Was Kaisen the right guy for me? I wasn't sure if I really had a choice anymore.

If I was honest with myself, it was too late. I'd already fallen for him, but I couldn't admit it quite yet.

The aroma of bacon and eggs tickled my nose, and I peeled my eyes open. My brows knitted together at the wretched aftertaste in my mouth. I swallowed, my throat scratchy and raw from my bout of sobbing the night before.

My arm hung off the bed, and I attempted to move it, but it resisted. Heavy with sleep, I peered over the edge. Panic rose inside me. Kaisen was sleeping in a sleeping bag on the floor, our fingers intertwined. His chest rose and fell with the rhythm of his breathing. He'd stayed the night even though he hadn't really been drinking. I pried our fingers apart and gently laid his arm down. Had I made an ass out of myself last night? I mentally scrolled through the events of the evening; other than practically jumping him, I'd done okay.

I quietly sat up and scanned the room, realizing Syd was already up. A heaviness settled over me. We'd argued, and I felt like I owed her an apology, but we needed to figure some things out if I was going to be with Kaisen. I scooted toward the end of my mattress and placed my feet on the cold floor. Hopefully, he was warm enough in the sleeping bag. A smile eased across my face as I stood, walked backward, and closed the bedroom door quietly behind me.

I hurried to the bathroom and showered. Today was yet another day that I was grateful for my stockpile of clean clothes behind the towels. I never wanted to wake Syd after work while rifling through my dresser but didn't want to fall asleep to the smell of hamburgers either. By the time I'd dressed and dried my hair, Kaisen had woken up.

"Hey," I said, entering the kitchen.

"Morning." He stood and kissed the top of my head. "How are you feeling?"

"Fine. You?" I asked, pulling out the barstool next to him.

"Good." He slipped his hand into mine and gently squeezed it. My attention was so focused on him that I forgot to say hi to Syd and Marcus.

"Morning, and I'm sorry." I held Syd's gaze for a moment, then released Kaisen's hand and made myself a cup of coffee. "I'm sorry," I said again, turning to face her. "We can talk about the rest later, but I needed to at least say that."

She nodded, and a smile pulled at the corner of her mouth. "It's over, but yeah, I think getting on the same page would be a good thing."

I returned to my seat next to Kaisen. He wrapped his arm around me and pulled me toward him, stool and all. Syd and Marcus smiled, watching us.

"Good grief, already. I need to go see Michael," Kara remarked, laughing. She waltzed into the kitchen and headed straight for the coffee. "How ya doin', Had?"

"I'm okay. Thank you all for coming over last night. Sorry I got a little drunk and feisty."

"Nah, it's good to be feisty sometimes," Kara said. She stared at Kaisen's arm around me and then at him. "Hank," she said, raising an eyebrow at him. She laughed and blew on her steaming mug.

"Kara," I said, laughing, "it's all good."

"Why would Hank have anything to do with Hadlee and Kaisen?" Marcus asked, pulling Syd into him for a hug.

Kara described Hank's attempt to ensure that Kaisen treated me well at the restaurant. We all laughed and chatted as we ate breakfast. I couldn't remember the last time I'd had everyone here at the same time, just us. What I'd have given to keep it like this for a little longer.

An hour later, Kara headed out, and Syd and Marcus weren't far behind. After the late night and the drinking, Syd and I decided we'd shop for Christmas gifts later so I could have some time with Kaisen.

"Look," Kaisen said, pointing out of the kitchen window.

I paused in the act of drying a plate and focused on the snowflakes silently falling and covering the world in white. There was something so eerily quiet about it, almost as though life could sneak up on you and you'd never hear it coming. A hollow ache pulsed through me with the memory of my dad and the snow that refused to stop falling on his grave, burying him deeper and deeper.

"Hey, where'd you go?" Kaisen asked, shaking the extra water from his hands and grabbing another dish towel.

"It was snowing the day I buried my dad," I whispered.

Kaisen placed his hands on my shoulders and turned me to face him.

"I know what that's like," he said quietly. "Come here." He pulled me into him. I laid my head against his chest and continued to watch the snow fall. It was such a sharp reminder of what I had to lose.

I pulled my hair up in a ponytail and grimaced in the mirror. My makeup was scattered across the small, antique vanity that Syd and I shared. We'd found it at a garage sale together and brought it home. It was the first piece of furniture we'd purchased for our room.

"Wear it down," Syd said, striding into the room. "Your hair should be down."

"You think?" I asked, my nose wrinkling with indecision. "Nothing seems to work tonight."

"That's because it's your first official date in, like, well, forever." She smiled, standing behind me. "Let me do your hair. Is the curling iron on? And the flat iron?"

"The flat iron is. I'll dig out the curling iron," I said, rummaging through the drawer and pulling it out.

"You nervous?" Syd asked, scrolling through her iPhone and turning on Spotify. She placed it on the docking station, and seconds later, Halsey sang to us through the small speaker.

"I don't think that's the right word for it. I'm trying to keep my lunch down."

"Oh, Had. No, don't be scared. You know he likes you. You've already kissed him. And he's carried you through puke and broken glass. I mean, Marcus hasn't even done that for me!" she exclaimed.

"Really? You think it'll be okay?" I asked, attempting to calm my nerves.

"He's seen you drunk, too, so if he can handle that, then it's all good from here on out."

I focused on Syd while she gathered my brush and the flat iron.

"How are you and Marcus?"

"Fine," she said, gently pushing my head down to work on my hair in the back.

"Hmm. You don't typically say you're fine. You run off at the mouth about your sexcapades."

She laughed. "Yeah, well, if you and Kaisen keep going, you'll be talking about your own sexcapades."

My eyes widened, and I realized she might be right. I forced my thoughts away from Kaisen and back to Syd. "Has he asked you? Marcus?"

"No. He hasn't proposed yet," she replied.

"Are you still worried?"

Syd set the flat iron on the vanity and remained silent. She didn't want to talk about it.

"Okay, I'm here when you're ready."

"I know. And we're good, really." She smiled, but I knew her well enough to realize it was forced. Whatever they were going through, she wasn't feeling okay about it.

"I'm a little jealous," she muttered, picking up the flat iron again and grabbing a hank of my hair.

"Jealous of what? Ow! Shit!" I screeched, rubbing my neck where the flat iron got too close.

"I'm sorry! Are you okay?"

"Yeah, but remember—I'm. Your. *Friend*. We don't hurt our friends." I frowned and then laughed.

"You're such a nerd. You realize that was a total nerd joke, right?"

"Don't ignore me. What are you jealous of?"

"You."

"Whaat?" I asked, shooing the flat iron away. "Have you been eating pot brownies again?"

"No. But Hadlee, look at you."

"What about me? Have you seen my life lately?" I turned around in the seat and took her free hand. "Talk to me. What's going on?"

"It's just you and Kaisen, seeing you two fall in love, how he—"

"Wait. Stop. First of all, we are not falling in love."

"You tell yourself whatever you need to, but the rest of us are watching from the sidelines. The way he looks at you, Had." She exhaled slowly and sank onto the side of her bed, still holding the flat iron.

"He looks at me a certain way?"

"You don't see it? I just wish Marcus still looked at me like that. We've been together for so long I feel like it's just another day. There's nothing special about it anymore."

"Oh, no. Syd, he's crazy about you. Maybe you guys just need a fancy date. Do something different. Put some spice back into things?" I couldn't believe I was giving Syd relationship advice. I could barely hold myself together. But sometimes, it was easier to help someone else than to focus on my own shit.

"You're probably right. And about last night," she said.

I realized she was referring to our argument. "I guess we should figure some things out now that I'm seeing him?" I asked.

Syd paused. "It's going to be a change. I promise not to treat you like a little kid; I'll give you some space. It's just that I'm used to having you to myself, and I don't want to lose you." Her words were so faint I could barely hear them.

"You're my family, Syd. You can't lose me. Yes, things will change but not that much. Kaisen has his own place, so you and Marcus can use the room if things progress for me. But, we will deal with it later. I just don't want everyone freaking out and thinking I can't handle myself. That's not fair."

"I know. I'm sorry about everything, too—about barging in on you guys."

I walked to her bed and hugged her, careful to avoid the flat iron. "Thank you for caring."

"You're my sister, Had. I'd do anything for you," she said, her voice heavy with emotion. Silence hung in the air as we exchanged reassuring smiles. "I should finish your hair and makeup before he gets here." She rose from her seat, and I sat down and faced the mirror again. We'd said everything we needed to, and our disagreement was over. "I'm really happy for you, Had. But more than that, I'm proud of you for giving someone a chance."

My heart pounded against my chest, and I glanced over my shoulder at her. "I just hope I'm giving the right person a chance."

"**W**here are they?" **I said,** tossing out all the shoes in my closet. "Syd, have you seen my boots?"

"Nope," she said from behind me, picking up all the rejects.

"Found them!" I yelled from the back corner of the closet, tugging them out from underneath another pile of Syd's sandals. "Good God, who needs this many? You only have two feet. You know that, right?" I asked, shaking my head and crawling backward on my hands and knees.

"Umm, I do," she said, piling more pairs onto the stack in her arms.

Syd could have supplied an army with her inventory. I reached for the towel in the dirty clothes pile. I'd stopped throwing my clothes all over my side of the room since Kaisen had spent time in here. At least they were now in a pile in the corner. Syd didn't care, but I was trying to keep things a bit more organized.

I wiped the dust off my boots, unzipped them, and shook them upside down in case any creepy critters had nested in them over the last year. Satisfied, I slipped them on and tucked in my skinny jeans.

The doorbell rang at precisely seven o'clock. I liked a guy who was on time. I made the final adjustments to my hair and smoothed down my teal sweater.

"Come on. He's here," Syd squealed. "Go, go, go!" She swatted my butt as I ran past her, giggling. I rounded the corner and flung the door open with a big smile.

"Wow," Kaisen breathed, the weight of his gaze traveling over me. "You look beautiful. I haven't seen your hair down before," he said softly.

"You like it?" I asked, trying to control the Jell-O effect in my knees. Kaisen's muscular chest filled out a dark-gray button-down shirt that was tucked into his jeans. I wasn't sure where he'd bought them, but he certainly knew which brands would showcase every muscle in his body.

"Do you have your coat?" he asked, pulling me from my thoughts. "It's started snowing; I need you layered up," he said, unable to hide the grin on his face.

"Yeah, right here," I said, grabbing it off the coat rack by the door. "Bye, Syd! Don't wait up!" I laughed.

"Bye! Be safe and use protection," she ordered, poking her head around the corner of the hallway into the living room.

I shot her a withering look. I'd kill her when I got back home.

"Love you," she sang.

"Ignore her," I said, closing the door and then zipping up my coat.

"I'm getting the feeling Syd's a bit on the ornery side," he observed with a chuckle. "The truck's warm, but stay bundled up," he recommended. He took my hand, guided me down the sidewalk, and opened the door for me. Snowflakes landed in his hair as he waited for me to get settled in my seat. "Thanks," I said, buckling up.

He hurried to the other side of the pickup and got in. Heat blasted through the vents when he pulled the Silverado away from the curb.

Kaisen reached for my hand. "You ready?"

"I hope so since I'm not sure where we're going." I batted my eyelashes at him for added emphasis. Maybe he'd tell me since we were on the way.

"Nice try, Had, but my lips are sealed." He released my hand and turned the radio on—just loud enough to be heard. "It doesn't seem like I just saw you this morning."

"I know. It seems like it's been a long time. Syd and I didn't even go shopping today, which is fine; we have plenty of time before Christmas."

"You go to Syd's for Christmas, right?" he asked, pulling onto Division Street.

"Yeah. I spend all of my holidays there."

He nodded. "We're not going to Portland, so I'll be around," he said, his voice trailing off. "You know, in case . . . in case you want to spend some time with me."

I squeezed his fingers. "I'll keep that in mind." Holy hell, he'd just offered to see me on Christmas. That was a month away! I guessed he really was serious about dating me.

Minutes later, Kaisen parked in Downtown Spokane. He opened the passenger door for me and helped me out.

"Ready?" He checked my coat zipper and adjusted the scarf around my neck. "Did you bring a hat?"

"No, did you?" I asked, staring up at the sky. The snowflakes were growing larger and larger as they descended.

"Nah, I'll be fine. Let's go."

We rounded the corner of Wall Street, and I gasped.

"Hey, Mr. Randall," Kaisen said, approaching an older gentleman. "Thanks for doing this for me. I appreciate your giving us a ride before the season starts."

"How could I not help you out, Kaisen? And who is this beautiful young lady?"

"Hi, I'm Hadlee." I shook his hand.

"Nah. If you're Kaisen's girl, you get a hug." He laughed and pulled me in for an embrace. My cheeks flushed at the mention of being Kaisen's girlfriend, but it would have been awkward to correct him.

"Get on in. It's all yours."

Mr. Randall helped me into the horse drawn carriage, and Kaisen hopped up on the other side, settling in next to me.

"What did he mean about the season?" I asked quietly.

"The carriage rides don't start for a few more days, but I hired him just for you tonight."

Guilt gnawed at me. I'd feel bad if Mr. Randall was in the cold because of me.

"He's been friends with my dad for a long time. We hired his grandson to work on a few projects, too, and got to know them. Mr. Randall raised his grandson after he lost his parents in a car accident."

"Wow. He seems like a nice guy, especially to do this tonight," I said, chewing on my bottom lip, deciding to release the guilt. Maybe I'd have to get used to someone doing nice things for me. It was such a change since I'd been on my own for a while.

"Is this okay?" he asked, his brows knitting together in concern.

"Yeah, thank you! I was just surprised that you'd hired him for me."

The snow fell, covering downtown in a white dusting. Kaisen pulled out a thick blanket and tucked us in. A smile lit up my face as I glanced up at him.

"I can't tell you how beautiful you look with the snow falling around you," he said. He tilted my chin up and gently kissed me.

Although it was thirty degrees outside, my body grew hot from his touch.

"Thank you," I whispered. "I've never taken one of these carriage rides before."

"Really? Why not?"

My focus flickered down to my lap and then back up to his. "The day we buried my dad . . . he was going to take me on a carriage ride."

Sadness clouded Kaisen's face. Shit, I shouldn't have told him that. I'd just ruined the night. Damn it, why had I opened my mouth?

I looked away from him, embarrassed I'd shared that detail on our first date.

"Hadlee, look at me."

I slowly turned to face him again.

"The hardest thing I've had to do was take the memories that hurt so damn bad and create new ones after my mom died. Everything reminded me of her. Her laugh, the way she frowned when I'd gotten into trouble, her voice as she read to me at night. My heart ached nonstop, and I couldn't seem to put the pieces back together. I was broken."

He paused, brushing my cheek with his fingertips.

"Please, let me be a part of the new memories you create—the new ones that make you happy," he whispered.

His gaze rested on my lips, and I nodded. I wanted that so much. New memories.

"Okay. I can do that."

He kissed the top of my head as his fingers threaded gently through my hair and massaged my neck. I sighed softly, and then he pulled me tight underneath the blanket. Maybe I really could look at life differently with him next to me.

Oh my God, that was fun!" We got into the truck, and Kaisen turned the heat on. "Your hair is all wet from the snow," I told him.

"It'll dry," he said, a mischievous grin spreading across his face. He shook his head, and droplets of water flew at me, making me squeal. He leaned across the seat and pulled me to him. "Did I make you all wet?" he asked, his voice husky.

"You have no idea," I whispered, covering his mouth with mine. My lips parted, and his tongue swept over mine. Heat coursed through me, our kiss deepening.

He lifted me off the seat and onto his lap. I moaned softly as I felt his arousal. His fingers dug into my hips, and he arched his upward.

Goosebumps dotted my skin when he slid his hand beneath my sweater and up my spine. His touch consumed me; my entire world consisted of Kaisen and his sweet, slow kisses.

"Hey Mom, is she getting pregnant?"

My eyes popped open, and I looked out the window. A van had parked next to us, and a little boy was standing outside, ogling us.

"Damn it!" I hopped off Kaisen and back into my seat.

"You should be ashamed of yourselves! Get a room," the mother roared, banging on Kaisen's window. She then grabbed her son's hand and dragged him out of the parking lot.

"That did not just happen," I said, covering my face with my hands.

Kaisen ran his hand through his wet hair and grinned. "Sorry."

I slipped further down into the seat and peered up at him. "Are they gone yet?"

He nodded. "Yeah. Man, I am so sorry." He shook his head and grinned sheepishly.

Pursing my lips together, I straightened in my seat and buckled up.

"Have you ever gotten caught like that before? That little boy thought I was getting pregnant!" As hard as I tried, I couldn't control the giggles that bubbled up. "I've never had anything like that happen before. What are you doing to me?" I laughed and smacked his arm.

"Well, you're certainly not helping me think clearly," he said, chuckling. With a smile lighting up his face, he shifted into reverse and pulled out of the parking lot.

Our laughs filled the pickup while he drove. Every time I thought I'd settled down, I'd start up again, and so did he.

"My stomach hurts from laughing so hard," I said, grabbing my sides.

"I guess that's a good thing, huh?"

"Wait until I tell Syd and Kara."

Kaisen snickered, and then he pulled into the grocery store parking lot.

My hands flew to my mouth while I glanced around. "You didn't!" I said between fits of laughter.

"I thought we'd stop and grab some coffee," he joked, unable to hide his grin.

I undid my seat belt and shook my head. "You're ornery, Kaisen Sinclair."

"You have no idea," he said, hopping out, strolling around to my side, and opening the door for me. "Ma'am," he said, lifting me from my seat and slowly lowering me to the ground.

"Thank you," I replied breathlessly.

A snowflake landed on my nose. He kissed the tip of it and then closed and locked the door.

"Why are we really here?" I asked, as we hurried across the parking lot, hand in hand.

"We're returning to the scene of the crime," he said, smiling. The front doors of the grocery store whooshed open, and the warm air welcomed us. He paused, looked around for a second, and then pulled me toward an aisle.

"I can't believe that, almost six weeks ago, I literally ran into you here. Never in a million years would I have thought I'd be back here on a date with you," I said.

We rounded a corner, and then he stopped and turned to face me. He pulled me to him and smoothed my hair, his expression growing serious.

"You stole more than the coffee right out from under me that day, Hadlee. I haven't been the same since I met you, and I wouldn't have it any other way."

His expression softened. Tilting my chin up, he kissed me tenderly. I wanted to stay there forever, forgetting everything and everyone else.

"Me neither," I said, peering up at him through my eyelashes.

His gaze traveled over my face, and he smiled. "You're so beautiful."

My cheeks flushed with embarrassment, my pulse quickening with his words.

He stepped away, and then we continued down the aisle.

"There," he said, grabbing a package of marshmallows. "Graham crackers are next."

"S'mores?" I asked, unable to hide the excitement in my voice.

"Yup."

"But it's snowing outside," I reminded him.

"I noticed," he replied, locating a box of graham crackers. "You'll see." He guided me down the coffee aisle next and stopped in front of the wide selection of bags. I inhaled deeply, and then a broad grin spread across my face.

He bent down and took a bag of coffee—the same brand we'd fought over. "This is special, just for you," he said and winked.

Minutes later, we were crossing the parking lot, and my Fitbit clock started flashing at me. I realized this night would eventually have to end, but I didn't want it to. I couldn't remember the last time I'd laughed so hard or when I hadn't been worried about classes or making it through a shift at work without falling on my face from exhaustion. Everything that had seemed so important slipped away when I was with him.

"You okay?" Kaisen asked.

"Yeah. I'm good." I opened the pickup door and slid into the seat. Kaisen didn't join me. I glanced at him and frowned. He was still outside, shaking his head. His mouth was hanging wide open, and his eyes were widening.

"What's the matter? Aren't you coming?"

"Umm, Hadlee, that's not my truck."

"Huh? What are you talking about?" I asked, staring at him with growing intensity.

"This isn't mine. You just opened the door and sat in a stranger's pickup."

I looked around and spotted the sunglasses on the dashboard and a pair of baby-blue fuzzy dice hanging from the rearview mirror.

"Shit! Seriously, oh my God, I'm so embarrassed," I squealed and hopped out. "Why did you let me do that?" I smacked him on the shoulder.

"Hey! What are you doing?" a man's voice called from across the parking lot. We both turned to see a round, bald man shuffling toward us. "Hey! That's my truck! Get the hell away from it before I call the cops!"

"Damn it," Kaisen said, shutting the door and grabbing my hand. Our laughter rang through the night while we ran a few rows over. As Kaisen unlocked his doors, I shot a glance backward. The guy was picking up speed and running for us.

"Hurry, Kaisen!" I yelled between giggles. "He's coming."

"Saw that," he hollered as he ran to his side, hopped in, and started the truck. The engine revved, and he shifted into drive, peeling out of the parking lot.

"Your face," I said, laughing so hard I was gasping for air. "Holy

Hannah, I can't believe I did that. Why didn't you say something before I got in it?" I asked, grabbing hold of my aching belly.

Desperation crossed his face, and he barked out a laugh. "It took me a minute to realize it wasn't mine. It looked just like mine from the outside, but the look on *my* face? I thought I was going to lose my shit when you realized you'd just gotten into someone else's car!"

"Who the fuck doesn't lock their doors? I mean, really?"

"I know, but I bet he won't ever do that again," he said, shooting me a look out of the corner of his eye.

"Right?" The last few giggles escaped me, and then I drew in a deep breath, attempting to settle down. "I've got a headache from laughing so hard. I'm never going to live this down, am I?"

"Nope. No way in hell," he said, chuckling.

"I think I need a moment to . . . to calm down before I toss my cookies in your floorboard from laughing so much."

"Please, don't do that. I just cleaned her."

"Her?" I asked, tilting my head.

"Yup."

"And does said beautiful blue vehicle have a name?" I asked, running my hand across the dashboard. "Does she purr under your touch?" I wiggled my eyebrows at him.

"Martha," he said softly.

"Martha? What kind of name is Martha?"

"After my mom. She always wanted a pickup."

How quickly the mood can shift.

"Sorry. I didn't mean to bring it up."

"It's okay. I suspect we'll have a lot of those conversations." He reached for my hand, and my fingers intertwined with his.

Silence filled the space between us as he headed north on Highway 2. The plump snowflakes bounced off the windshield while he picked up speed and headed out of town.

"Before we go too much further, I should ask—are you okay with going to my place for a while?"

"Oh. Really?" I was surprised. It was only our first date . . .

"Yeah, but only if you want to. We can grab some dinner in town if you'd be more comfortable."

I paused and searched his face. It wasn't like an I-just-met-him first date; it was more like an I've-known-him-for-a-while first date. And for whatever reason, everything about him felt right—it felt safe.

"I'd love to," I said, smiling shyly. Nerves kicked in as I wondered what that meant for us, if I'd wake up the next morning sore and naked.

"I'm about half an hour out of town. I didn't want you to think I was kidnapping you or anything. Although, it's actually a good idea," he said, grinning.

"Ha, ha. I'm pretty sure Hank would come find you if you did. And honestly, I'm not sure if Syd, Kara, or Hank would be the worst to deal with."

"Not something I want to find out."

"Does the drive bother you?" I asked. "You're always in town. At least, I've been seeing you in town a lot."

"Nah, I've lived outside of Spokane most of my life. I enjoy the city, but when it comes down to it, I love the quiet of the country. There's nothing better than sitting out on the deck and watching the deer and moose wander across my property."

"It sounds beautiful. I can't wait to see it," I said quietly.

I leaned my head back against the seat and noticed that the trees were growing thicker with every passing mile. Minutes later, Kaisen turned left off Highway 2.

"Are you kidding me?" I asked, snapping to attention. "You live off of Fertile Valley Road?"

He covered his mouth with his hand and tried to hide his grin.

"You're fucking with me, right?"

"Well, I would like to, but we should wait. This is only our first date."

"Kaisen!" I huffed and smacked his arm. "I've never been up here before. Wow, the snow is really coming down." I sat up straighter and peered out the window.

"We always get more up here. I won't see my grass again until April once it really starts."

I white-knuckled the door handle while we continued to climb. I'd grown up with snow, but the thought of being all the way out here—with him, alone—had just become a stark reality. My lips pursed together while I chided myself for being silly. This guy had walked through puke for me. I was safe.

The truck jostled as he turned off Fertile Valley Road and onto a single wide dirt lane already covered with snow.

"Sorry, it's a little bumpy right now. I've got some work to do on it after winter."

I nodded, my breath hitching when I realized how isolated we were. Shit, what had I agreed to?

He pulled into a long driveway and then stopped in front of a two-car garage.

"Here we are," he said, shifting into park and turning the engine off. "You okay? You look a little freaked out. I tried to ask, but it's different once you get out here. If you're uncomfortable, we can go back into town right now." Kaisen inserted the key back into the ignition, waiting for my response.

My forehead creased, I viewed the area as much as the darkness allowed. The log house rested on top of the hill under the wide-open sky. Fir and pine trees lined the hill, creating a boundary around him. I opened the door and slid out of the seat, my face turning up toward the falling snow. I inhaled slowly and released my breath, absorbing the scent of the trees and the clean country air. A calm washed over me.

"It's beautiful," I said, joining him on the other side of the truck. He took my hand and guided me up the walkway and onto the porch.

After he opened the door, I gasped at the tall wall of windows in the living room that opened to a stunning view of the mountains. A black leather sectional, resting on an oyster-colored carpet, filled the room. The scent of the woodstove lingered. I looked past the living room, at the small, clean kitchen and dining room, and then spied the back deck.

"Can I be nosey?" I asked.

"Go for it."

I strolled through the dining area, opened the sliding glass door, and stepped outside. My eyes scanned the surroundings easily once the motion lights around the house sliced through the night. Kaisen tugged the door closed behind him, his attention on me as I proceeded to the railing and absorbed a wonderland.

"This is my place, Hadlee," he said, quietly. "Dad purchased the acreage after Mom died so we could hunt and have somewhere to go besides the house where she . . . where she took her life. A few years later, Dad and I began to build this home. We even felled the logs off the land. Building this place, being out in nature, it all helped me piece my life back together. Something about it here . . ."

"It's breathtaking," I said, turning toward him.

Taking my hand, he gave me a smile of thanks. "Are you cold?"

"A little, but it's so beautiful out here; I don't want to go in."

A small smile pulled at the corners of his mouth. "Come with me," he said, grabbing a towel from the BBQ grill in the corner.

He led me across the deck and down the stairs toward the backyard.

"Here," he said, using the towel and brushing the snow off a couple of bright green plastic chairs next to the fire pit.

I sank into my seat while he opened the door to a large brown shed and disappeared inside. A minute later, he emerged with a load of firewood in his arms. He propped his foot against the stones that circled the firepit and strategically placed the pieces of wood inside of it.

"Smores! I almost forgot," I said, my excitement growing again.

"I have some hotdogs in the fridge, too, if you're interested. I'll get the bonfire going, and you'll warm up in no time."

I settled in and waited while he brought the fire to life. By the time he finished, the snow had slowed down.

Kaisen rubbed his hands together and held them toward the flames. "I'll go get everything. Be right back."

The blaze lit up the night, the wood crackling and popping. My thoughts drifted toward my dad. I remembered the times we'd gone camping, the aroma of freshly brewed coffee in the morning, and the kayaking. Sadness hung over me, but I pushed it away and remembered Kaisen's words from earlier. It was time to make new memories.

"Here ya go," he said, placing the food on the extra chair.

I tore open the bag of marshmallows.

"Hungry?" he asked on a laugh.

"Yes, starving." I beamed at him. I loaded my skewer, stood, and held the white, creamy puffs of sugar over the fire. "This is really toasty. The front of me is about to start sweating, but my ass is freezing." I giggled.

"I'll help," he said, approaching me from behind. He moved the chair, wrapped one arm around my waist, and pulled me into him.

"Better?" he whispered in my ear.

"Much," I said, leaning back into him and absorbing the warmth of his body.

A comfortable silence hung in the air while I continued to roast the marshmallows, hyperaware of Kaisen's body against mine. A spark of desire stirred inside me.

Within another minute, we'd made our first set of smores and were sitting in the chairs, enjoying our culinary success. Heat radiated off the glowing red-and-orange flames, and the snow picked back up again.

"Do you do this for girls a lot?" I asked, peeking over at him. I wasn't sure I really wanted an honest answer.

"No. You're the first."

"Uh-huh. I bet you bring girls up here all the time."

"I'm serious. I've never brought a girl up here before."

"Why? I mean, it's the perfect romantic place to—" My voice hitched, and I stopped myself from finishing my sentence.

"I've never met anyone I wanted to bring here until now," he said softly.

Was I really that special to him? My gaze dropped, and I focused on the sticky goodness that had oozed out of the side of the graham cracker. I poked it back in and then licked it off my finger.

"Shit," he muttered. He stood awkwardly and attended to the logs in the bonfire.

"What's wrong?"

He bent down in front of me and whispered, "You shouldn't lick your finger like that."

"Oh." My cheeks reddened.

He began to straighten, but I grasped the front of his coat with one hand and held him in place.

I placed my half-eaten s'more on the little table next to me.

"You want to taste it yourself?" I pulled his mouth down to mine. Our lips grew sticky from the marshmallow remnants on my lips. His hands wrapped around my waist, and he pulled me out of the chair, flush against him. Our kiss deepened, and his desire grew. Shivers of anticipation shot through me. Then, I allowed myself to get lost in him.

"You're cold; let's get you into the living room, and I'll put out the fire."

I smiled, unwilling to correct him. Five minutes later, we were settled on the couch in the living room, and he drew me to him, his soft lips brushing mine. I lay back on the couch, pulling him with me. He gently lowered himself on top of me.

His light kisses feathered down my throat and my collarbone. My back curved when he continued down the V of my sweater. His fingertips grazed my skin as he moved the material to the side, exposing the white, lace bra I'd selected for tonight.

His lips brushed against the exposed swell of my breast, and my body ached for more.

My hands traveled down, and I pulled his shirt free from his jeans. My fingers splayed across his lower back and then slipped beneath his waistband. The heat from his skin was intoxicating. He caressed me through my bra, and then he slid it out of his way. A moan escaped me as his tongue massaged my nipple. I dug my fingernails into his skin, his ass muscles tightening beneath my touch.

Kaisen's movements were slow and deliberate, and my core throbbed with anticipation. I lifted my hips. I needed him. I wanted him. My breath came in short gasps as his mouth continued to tease me. He paused for a minute and glanced up at me, his eyes heavy with need.

"We can take a break," he murmured.

I cupped the back of his head and started to lower his mouth to my breast again.

"Wait," I said suddenly.

He abruptly leaned back, raising his hands in the air. "Okay. We can stop."

"No, that's not what I meant." I slipped my sweater off. "This is what I meant." I unfastened my bra and slipped the straps off my shoulders one at a time. My nipples hardened as the cool air brushed over them. "Your turn," I said.

His fingers flicked open the buttons on his shirt, and my attention remained glued to him while he removed it, revealing his muscular chest and shoulders. His abs rippled as he tossed his shirt on the floor.

"Keep going," I whispered.

"Hadlee, we don't have to."

"Hush."

He nodded and stood, flicking open the button on his jeans and then sliding them slowly down his hips. His jeans and boxer briefs dropped to the floor, and he stood in front of me, long, lean, and hard. Everything about him was hard, from his arms to every beautiful muscle that rippled through his body.

Now I stood, and my eyes remained on his face as I unbuttoned and unzipped my jeans. I could feel my pulse quicken as my jeans and panties dropped to the floor. I'd never been more aware of my nakedness. His expression softened; his gaze swept over me.

"It's been a long time," I said softly.

He nodded and reached for my hand, leading me to his bedroom. The glow from a small lamp on the nightstand filled the room. His king-sized bed was perfectly made with a black comforter. A variety of black and white pillows were propped up against the headboard.

"You okay?" he asked, tilting my chin up so he could search my face.

"I am," I said, trying to reassure myself as much as him.

His mouth crashed down on mine, and he walked me backward toward his bed. When my knees met the mattress, I lowered myself down on it. His hot gaze rolled over my naked body.

"Hadlee," he said, his voice raw and husky. "We can still stop, but I'm not going to lie. If we keep going—"

"I know. I'm fine. I want to be with you, Kaisen."

He slowly lowered himself on top of me, and I sighed as the weight of his body covered me. He kissed me softly, his fingers brushing the hair from my face.

He leaned to one side and ran his hand down my stomach and the inside of my thigh. I inhaled sharply when his thumb brushed across my core.

"You okay?"

I nodded, unable to take my eyes off his face.

His fingers stroked me, and I moaned when he slid a finger inside me.

"You're so damn wet," he whispered, grazing his tongue over my nipple.

My fingers wrapped themselves tightly in his curls when he eased another finger inside me, his thumb massaging my clit.

"Kaisen," I whispered, my breathing heavy. "Why did this take me so long?"

He merely smiled, and I arched against his hand.

He trailed hot kisses down my stomach and inside my thigh, his breath brushing across my center. His hand continued a steady rhythm while his tongue danced against my overly sensitive skin. He moaned, his head dipping lower and awakening a part of me that I never knew existed.

My legs widened, welcoming him. "Oh. My. God," I said, my back arcing off the bed. He gently pulled his fingers out of me and slipped his hands underneath my ass, bringing me off the bed. His mouth sucked me as a warm sensation began to swirl deep inside. My hips bucked, my fingers digging into the soft material of the comforter.

"Kaisen," I whimpered. "I can't—"

Sweet ecstasy teased my senses as he continued, and seconds later, I exploded. I'd never experienced anything like this. Everything inside me submitted to him.

I struggled to slow my breathing as he moved up my body, his hardness throbbing against the inside of my leg. I kissed him, tasting myself on his lips. My hands wandered across his shoulders and slowly traveled down his muscles and over his ass. I tilted my hips upward and rubbed against him.

"I'm not going to last long if you keep doing that," he said. "You ready?" he asked gently.

He waited for me to nod, then reached into the nightstand and pulled out a condom. He leaned back, and my eyes widened as it dawned on me how large he was. I wasn't sure he was even going to fit inside me.

He rolled the condom on, and I took a shaky breath.

"Three conditions," he said. His expression calmed. "First, if I want to be with her emotionally and physically. Second, if I want a future with her. Third, if she's sober."

My body relaxed as I realized what he was saying. This was way more than sex to him.

I straightened up, touched his cheek with my fingertips, and pulled him toward me. He positioned himself over me and paused. My fingers wrapped around him and gently guided him to my entrance. I gasped as he slowly filled me.

"Did I hurt you?" he whispered.

"A little, but I'm okay."

"You sure?"

"Yeah."

He moved in and out of me, taking his time, my body adjusting to him with each stroke, deeper and deeper. My legs tightened around his waist, and I timidly moved with him—one motion, one body, one soul. He gripped my hands and moved them above my head, our fingers intertwining, our gazes locking, rocking against each other. My eyes fluttered shut, and I surrendered to him. Everything I had, and everything I was, now belonged to him.

Our breathing came in short bursts as his pace quickened, my nails digging into his skin, the sensation building inside me again. And with every thrust of his hips, he claimed another piece of my heart.

"Hadlee," he whispered as he kissed me. "Come with me."

I gasped as every fiber of my being came alive. "You're so beautiful," he whispered, his breath hot against my skin.

He pulled out and slid inside me with one final stroke that sent me over the edge. My body molded against him when I released again. "Kaisen," I cried out, my body shuddering as we finished together.

Our bodies fell limp against each other, and my arms wrapped around him. His head rested on my chest as I played with his curls and we took a moment to just be.

Eventually, he looked up at me, his expression soft and gentle. I smiled, placing a light kiss on his forehead.

What had he just done to me? I'd never felt so safe in my entire life. I never wanted to leave him. I closed my eyes, realizing what I was thinking. Was I falling in love?

"What are you thinking?" he asked as he sat up and disposed of the condom. "Did we move too fast? Do you regret it?" A hint of worry clung to his words.

"No," I said, smiling at him. "I don't regret a thing."

"**I** **need to check and make** sure the fire went out. Don't move."

I snuggled underneath the covers and watched him rustle through his drawers before pulling on a pair of jeans. A calm washed over me while I nestled into his pillows, recognizing his sweet-and-spicy scent. After he left the room, I scanned his dresser and noticed his pile of textbooks. I wondered what it would be like to have your life already planned out. Uncertainty nagged at me, and I considered my options with a psych degree. In a lot of ways, Kaisen was ahead of the rest of us who were just struggling to graduate and keep food on the table. But maybe our biggest struggles led us to our biggest successes?

"Hey," he said, smiling and leaning against the doorframe. "You hungry? I can make an omelet."

"That sounds great. I could use some food."

He remained there, unmoving.

"What?" I asked, pulling the covers over me. I still didn't have a stitch of clothing on, and suddenly, I found myself too shy to stand in front of him naked. My nose wrinkled as I realized that my clothes were on the floor of his living room. "I don't have any clothes in here," I said sheepishly. "But you already realized that, didn't you?"

"I'll bring them to you," he gallantly offered, backing out of the room with a grin.

Relief washed over me when he brought me my jeans and sweater and then left for the kitchen. I joined him a few minutes later.

"Wow, is it really after eleven already?" I asked, eyeing the stove clock.

"I was surprised, too. It's almost like we're in a time warp together. But I could stay here forever with you." He glanced at me, then quickly away.

The pulse in my throat fluttered with his confession.

I studied his every move as he whipped our omelet together. Could life get any better than this? Good sex and a gorgeous man in the kitchen. I couldn't have stopped my smile even if I'd wanted to.

"Can I help with anything?" I asked, leaning over the counter and peering at the vegetables he was chopping.

"Nope, just sit there and look beautiful."

My cheeks warmed as I stood out of his way and allowed him to cook for me.

"Who would have thought this weekend would have turned out like this? I mean, I love having the time off for the holidays, but they aren't my favorite. And yesterday, with my mom. That was shit," I said in a hushed tone. "But I guess it was time."

He poured the egg mixture into the pan and reached for the spatula.

"It's difficult when family won't recognize their behavior isn't appropriate and we're forced to put those boundaries in place. It's not easy, and a lot of people can't do it, even if it's harming them."

"You sound like you've been through this."

He nodded while he continued to cook. "Yeah. I've had my share of learning about boundaries."

Silence hung in the air. I waited for him to elaborate, but he never did. Whatever had happened, maybe he'd trust me with it soon.

Kaisen moved in his kitchen like he was born to cook. He pulled a few plates out of the cabinet and halved the finished omelet.

"Here ya go," he said, grabbing some forks out of the drawer. "Salt and pepper are on the table."

"Thank you," I said, sitting down. Kaisen sat in the chair across from me.

"How long have you lived here?"

"I finished the house almost two years ago, and I've been here ever since," he replied, pausing to take a bite of his food.

"Oh. My. God. What the hell? You're a fabulous cook!" My eyes rolled in ecstasy, and I covered my mouth with my hand while I chewed. "Is there anything you're not good at?" I paused and savored the combination of vegetables and seasoning.

"It's the fresh eggs. My neighbor sells them to me, and the flavor is so rich. I don't know what he does, but it's a winner."

"No shit. You can cook for me anytime," I said, laughing.

"I love that sound."

"What sound?" I asked as I placed my elbow on the table and leaned toward him.

"Your laugh. I love your laugh," he said. "I love that you're sitting across from me and I had the opportunity to make you breakfast. I love that you got in the wrong truck tonight and we laughed so hard we couldn't breathe. I feel alive when I'm with you, Hadlee. It's like, all of a sudden, there's more to life than work, school, and the future I've so carefully planned out." He paused as he searched my face.

I swallowed and placed my fork down on the side of my plate.

"I've done all of this, but there's been no one to share it with." Sadness flickered across his face, and his eyes dropped to the table.

"Kaisen," I said, standing. I settled into the chair next to him and took his hand in mine. My pulse raced as he looked at me again.

With his free hand, he lightly stroked my cheek. "I might love you a little," he said softly.

My lower lip trembled slightly. His words rushed through me and breathed life into parts of my heart I'd thought were lost forever. "And I might love you a lot," I whispered.

"Hadlee." His gentle kiss pulsed through me, making my body ache for him again.

I'd done it. I'd admitted it to him and myself.

I. Loved. Kaisen Sinclair.

My arms wrapped around his neck, and I lost myself in his touch. His hands slipped underneath my sweater and pulled it over my head. I grinned as he moved our plates and silverware to the side.

"Tell me again," he said, picking me up out of the chair and laying me down on the table. My bare skin touched the cold surface, and I squealed and shivered.

Kaisen unfastened my jeans and slid them and my panties down my legs, tossing them on the floor. I leaned forward, flipped open the button, and tugged his jeans and boxer briefs down his hips. I wrapped my hand around his erection, slid off the table to my knees, and glanced at him.

"Oh shit," he said.

I eased the tip of him inside my mouth and ran my tongue along his sensitive head. His fingers threaded through my hair. My hand stroked him while I took him in, inch by inch, his hips moving in sync with me. I peered up at him through my eyelashes; his eyes were closed and his mouth slightly parted. Every part of me craved him.

"It breaks my heart to say this, but you gotta stop," he said, gently pushing me away. I smiled and sat on the edge of the table, leaning back slightly.

"I need you inside me." I said.

His heated gaze drifted down my body, and then he reached into his pocket and grabbed a condom. He ripped the packet open, and within seconds, he was at my entrance. I gasped as he filled me, and his mouth came crashing down on mine. The silverware clinked, the table rocked beneath my weight, and for a fleeting moment, I prayed it wouldn't collapse beneath us.

He thrust inside me as we clung to each other. I focused on how good he felt while he moved inside me. Nothing had prepared me for this. For him. For how I felt about him.

He moved his fingers between my legs and massaged my swollen clit as he continued. The other hand grasped my hip for leverage, his pace quickening.

"Tell me again, Kaisen," I pleaded, my breathing heavy.

His eyes opened, and his pace slowed. He pulled out of me and then buried himself deep inside me—again and again and again.

"I love you. You're what I've been missing my entire life," he said, his voice raw with emotion.

His expression tightened, and pure ecstasy swirled through me. My muscles clenched around him as he filled me, and moments later we released together.

Our breathing came in short bursts as our heartbeats slowed. He brushed the hair from my face. "I love you," he whispered.

"I love you, too," I replied.

He kissed my nose and then eased out of me. He tossed the condom in the trash, took my hand, and guided me into the master bath. My mouth dropped as I took it all in: a soaker tub with jets, dual countertops, and a shower with three heads.

"How about a shower?" he asked, a lazy grin spreading across his face.

"Oh my God, yes. This is amazing." I studied the collection of cologne on his cabinet while he turned the water on for us.

"It'll take a minute to warm up," he said, wrapping his arms around me. He placed a kiss on my shoulder, and his lips slowly traveled up my neck.

"I love everything about you," he said, whispering in my ear. Goosebumps pricked my skin as he hardened again. He lifted me up, and I wrapped my legs around him. I didn't let go even when he opened the shower door and closed it behind us.

Not in a million years had I ever imagined I'd have sex three times in one night.

Soreness had settled into my body, but I wouldn't have traded it for anything. I slipped into my bedroom and spotted Syd and Marcus snuggled up together in her bed. I crept toward mine, taking extra care not to wake them. I was glad they were already sleeping; I needed some quiet time to process everything. In the past two months, I'd met an amazing guy, had mind-blowing sex, and fallen in love. I almost laughed at how my life had taken a sharp one-eighty.

A soft sigh escaped me, and I drifted off to sleep, remembering the feel of Kaisen next to me.

"Wake up. You've got some details to share," Sydney said, nudging me.

"Damn. What time is it?" I asked, peering at her through one eye.

"I don't know, seven, eight, nine—who cares? How was your date? I don't even know what time you came home last night. You could text a girl next time, ya know, so I don't think he's kidnapped and taken advantage of you."

A small smile pulled at the corners of my mouth. "Well, there was no kidnapping. And I'm not exactly sure who took advantage of whom," I said, laughing.

"Ohhhhh. Ohhh!" Syd pointed at me. "You slept with him?" she asked in a hushed voice.

I frowned at her, wondering why she was trying to be quiet.

"Marcus is still asleep," she explained, nodding toward her bed.

"What time is it, Syd? It's still dark." I sat up, focusing on my clock. "Jeez, you couldn't even wait until everyone got up? It's only a little after three!"

"Shh!" She patted my arm. "I needed to know," she said, bouncing on the side of my bed. "Was it good? Was *he* good? Did it hurt? Are you okay?"

A smile pulled at the corners of my mouth. Multiple expressions danced across her face with all of the questions. I filled her in on the majority of the evening, neglecting to mention he'd told me he loved me. That secret I'd keep to myself for a little bit longer.

"Maybe we can all go to his place and have a big bonfire. Do you think he'll cook for us?"

I stifled a laugh. Syd was more excited about him owning a home and cooking than she was about my breaking a three-year dry spell.

"Slow down, Syd. Let me get my feet on the ground with all of this. He's different, and . . ." I glanced away from her, unwilling to finish the sentence. Too late.

"Oh, shit," she whispered. "You're in love with him. How did I miss that?"

My spine went rigid with her words. "How would you even know something like that?"

"Did he say it first?" she asked, motioning for me to give her details.

"Yes." I leaned back against the headboard.

"Did you melt a little?"

"A lot," I said, wrinkling my nose at her.

She quietly squealed and hugged me.

"I'm so happy for you two. Marcus will be excited, too. In fact, he owes me fifty now. I'll have to collect in the morning."

My gaze narrowed. "Tell me you don't mean what I think you mean."

She cringed and then confessed, "We had a bet about whether you would fall into bed with Kaisen tonight."

"What?" I hissed. "Sydney, some things are private and not to be discussed with boyfriends! What am I going to do with you?" I covered my face with my hands and struggled to regain my composure instead of smacking her.

The sound of Marcus snoring startled us. I'd forgotten he was in the room. We peered at him as he lay sprawled across the bed, his feet dangling off the edge.

"I guess you're sleeping on the floor now," I said, smirking at her. "Serves you right."

"Don't be mad. It was his idea," she said, pointing at her boyfriend.

"That makes it worse. Your middle name should be 'Ornery as shit.'"

"That won't work. Middle names are normally one word. That's three," she argued, defiantly tilting her chin in the air.

"Scoot over." She nudged me and slipped under the blankets. "What was it like? It's been so long since my first time with Marcus; I don't really remember."

"It was scary and exciting all at the same time. I totally freaked when I saw him naked. I had no idea how in the hell he was going to—well, how I was going to accommodate him," I gushed, my cheeks burning bright red.

"I do remember that concern. I mean, you saw Marcus."

"Ewww, Syd, stop. I don't want to think about him naked right now. That's wrong in so many ways."

"Well, at least you now have a good reference when I'm talking about him," she said, snorting.

I lay back on my pillow as I stifled a yawn.

"Were you scared?"

"Shitless," I replied.

Syd reached for my hand. "It's scary, falling in love. You just have to grab on tight and hold on. Emotions are crazy, and everything gets tied up into one beautiful mess."

I frowned at her choice of words. "It's a mess?" I asked, whispering.

"Sometimes, but you learn to talk things through. You and Kaisen are going to be great. Don't worry." She patted my arm and then rolled onto her side, pulling the covers up underneath her chin.

"Guess you're stuck with me since Marcus is hogging the bed."

I smiled. "It's okay. That's what sisters are for."

Unfortunately, I had to return to the real world. As the weeks flew by, Kaisen filled every spare minute that I wasn't in class, studying, or working. It never seemed like it was enough time, though.

He and Michael came into the grill several times a week to see Kara and me. No matter what we told them, they always left us a big tip. I suspected it was more Kaisen than Michael just because I knew about Kaisen's financial situation.

"Can you believe it's Christmas Eve eve?" Kara asked, gathering waters for our new customers.

"It's nuts! The time has rushed by. The only good thing is Kaisen will graduate soon and have a little more free time on his hands."

"Is he excited?"

"Shit yeah. Hell, I'm excited, and I'm not even graduating yet. It'll feel weird when we're done though, huh?"

"Yeah, and then we'll be off to get real jobs."

"At least we've got this one while we look for work in our field," I mentioned wistfully. It was a bittersweet detail.

"Man, I hope it works out like that."

"Me, too," I muttered, a knot forming in the pit of my stomach. "Do you wonder if sometimes . . ."—I was almost afraid to voice my thoughts—"if sometimes things are too perfect and you're just waiting for something to go wrong?"

"Paranoid much?" Kara asked on a laugh. Her cheerfulness abruptly vanished when she realized I was serious.

"It's nothing," I said, waving it off. I smiled when I heard Kaisen and Michael laughing at Kara's table. They alternated between my station and Kara's when they came in. Everyone who worked there knew they belonged to us.

"You okay?" she asked, patting my back.

"Yeah." I shook my head to clear it. "It's just the holidays. Sometimes I get a bit moody."

"You're not the only one. Syd's been really moody lately."

I looked up from my tray and nodded. "You've noticed that, too?"

"Mm-hmm."

"I know she's stressed about school, especially this next term. As far as I can tell, she and Marcus are doing well. So, I don't know. I'll talk to her tonight, though."

"We'd better get to our customers before we piss them off and lose our tips," Kara muttered. She threw her shoulders back, balanced her tray on one hand, and plastered a smile on her face. I laughed as she waltzed away, and then I did the exact same thing.

Although I tried, I couldn't shake the nagging feeling that something wasn't right—but I had no clue what it was. Deciding to chalk it up to the holiday blues, I focused on all the good things in my life.

"Are you sure you don't mind my borrowing your car tonight?" I asked Syd.

"I offered, silly," she said, handing me the keys to her BMW. "Daddy had the studded tires put on already, too, so you should be all set."

"You're the best." I sank down on the edge of her bed, where she was reading *Someone Like You* by Brittney Sahin. "How's the book? Any good?"

"Soooo good." She put a bookmark inside the pages and closed it.

"Holy hell, look at the guy on that cover. Do you think he's real?"

"Of course he's real," Syd said, laughing. "And I'm pretty sure I drool every time I look at him."

We burst into giggles. I missed Syd. Her prediction had been right—things had changed between us. It wasn't bad; it was just different.

"Are you sure you'll be okay tonight? I know we typically hang out on Christmas Eve and Christmas Day."

"Go," she said, shooing me away with the book. "Have fun, get laid, and don't wreck my car."

I grimaced at the thought of messing up her BMW. "I'll be extra, extra careful," I reassured her.

A sad smile crossed her face. I leaned in and hugged her. "See you in the morning."

"By the way, that navy-blue top looks amazing on you. I think sex agrees with you, Had. Be safe, and would you just text me a few times to let me know how it's going?"

"Of course." I stood, collected my purse, and headed out. I wasn't sure how my heart could be so happy and sad at the same time. It was harder than I'd expected to leave her.

I unlocked the car and tossed the key fob in my bag. I was stunned when Syd had offered me the car so I could spend the night at Kaisen's. He'd offered to drive me home, but Syd said that she wasn't going anywhere and she would call Marcus if she needed anything. She figured it'd save Kaisen a trip into Spokane, not to mention some gas. I thought she was trying to show her support even though we missed each other.

The car purred to life, and I shifted into drive. I could feel the studded tires gripping the asphalt as I pulled out of the driveway and headed toward Kaisen's.

A thick layer of snow covered the ground as I headed north. I pushed the power button on the stereo and turned on some Christmas tunes while I drove. Luckily, traffic was minimal as I drove out of town.

Twenty-five minutes later, I turned onto Fertile Valley Road. I smiled, my belly filling with butterflies and excitement. I hadn't spent Christmas

Eve with anyone other than Syd since I'd started college. As a little kid, I'd been stuck with Mom and her side of the family.

I flipped the headlights onto bright as I made the steady climb. Syd was right—this car handled like a dream. The moonlight bounced off the snow; the sky glistened with stars. I took a deep breath, pulling onto his road and then into his driveway. I opened the door and placed one foot on the pavement. I tested the slickness with my foot, but there was no need; Kaisen always had it cleared and salted for me.

He opened the door for me before I could even knock.

"Hey," he said, picking me up and twirling me around on the porch.

I giggled as he kissed me, and then I followed him inside.

"Is it illegal to be this happy?" I asked, hanging up my coat and smoothing my hair.

He chuckled and kissed the top of my head.

"I'm going to use the bathroom. I'll join you shortly."

He nodded, and I proceeded down the hall.

A minute later, I strolled into the kitchen and inhaled deeply, the scent of prime rib and fresh bread tickling my nose. "It smells amazing."

Kaisen turned and smiled. His mouth dropped open. "Shit." The knife clattered to the floor while he stared at me.

"What? Do I have something on my shirt?" I asked, trying to hide my smile.

"You're not wearing one. Or anything, for that matter," he said, unable to remove his eyes from me. He finally grabbed a dish towel and wiped his hands off.

"Yes, I am." I patted the bright red bow I'd placed on the top of my head.

"I love the bow. I love you, Hadlee Jameson," he said as he wrapped me in his arms and drew me in for a kiss.

I caressed him through his jeans as he removed his Maroon Five concert T-shirt and tossed it on the floor.

"Are you ready for me?" I asked, fluttering my eyelashes at him.

"Always." He slipped out of the rest of his clothes, attempting to kiss me in the process. I laughed, tripping over his jeans and almost falling. He steadied me and then walked me backward into his bedroom.

"Mr. Sinclair, are you trying to take advantage of me?" I asked, wiggling my eyebrows at him as I lay down and propped myself up on my elbows. "If you are, then let me help you," I said, parting my legs for him. His tongue darted across his lips, moistening them. "Merry Christmas to me," he said, smiling. He lowered his head between my legs and kissed the inside of my thigh.

My head fell back as his tongue grazed my skin, and I grew wetter by the second. I loved that he teased me, but sometimes I wanted him so much that it hurt by the time he was inside me.

"Lie back."

I followed his directions and settled back on the bed while he kissed me, my core throbbing as he slid his finger inside me. His tongue swirled around my clit, and I moaned. My hands ran across his neck and slipped into his curls while he lifted my hips to his mouth.

"You taste so damn good," he murmured.

I gasped as he sucked on me, teasing me until I thought I'd come undone with anticipation. His slick fingers pumped me as he continued, his pace quickening. The comforter bunched up beneath my fingers as I cried out and climaxed.

He reached for the condom on his nightstand. After rolling it on, he lay down next to me on his back. "Come here," he said, his voice raspy.

I straddled him and slowly lowered myself down, allowing his large shaft to move deeper inside me.

My eyes grew wide as I took in every inch of him and then tentatively rocked my hips.

"You feel so damn good," he said. He lifted me up and gently brought me down on him again. Our movements became more urgent as we found our rhythm together.

"I love you," I said. "I love everything about you." I ran my fingernails down his abs and then reached behind me, cupping his balls and massaging them. He stopped moving for a moment, and a throaty growl escaped him. I rocked my hips and continued to slide up and down the length of him.

"I love every inch of you," I said, breathlessly.

"Shit, Hadlee." He gripped my waist. Sweat beaded his forehead, and I knew I'd found his sweet spot.

He groaned as I released his balls and leaned forward, resting my palms on his chest.

He flipped me over onto my back. "Turn around," he ordered, his voice gruff.

I positioned myself on all fours so he could enter me from behind. He moved inside me, one hand cupping my breast and the other tracing over my hip and between my legs.

"You're so wet," he whispered as I leaned against him, desire rippling through me, his hands and lips finding every sensitive place on my body. He moved slowly at first, his fingers massaging my clit, the other hand teasing my nipple. My senses threatened to go on overload.

"You're so amazing," he panted, his pace quickening. "How did I ever get so lucky to have you?" he whispered.

I grasped his thigh, my fingernails raking his skin.

"That's it. Let it go. Feel me inside you," he said, his breath brushing against my ear. "Right here," he said, thrusting inside me again and gently pulling my clit between his fingers. Black spots floated before my vision as I gasped for air.

"Oh. My. God. Don't stop, Kaisen." My breath hitched, and I moaned, teetering between pleasure and sheer ecstasy. I gripped his hand, holding it against my hip as he plunged into me and ripples of pure euphoria crashed through me. Kaisen's hold on me tightened, and my core clenched around him. He rocked against me, and my world stopped as he exploded inside me. Every nerve in my body came alive as he shuddered, and I climaxed with him.

Spent, we dropped to the mattress, tired and elated.

I smiled at him while we lay next to each other in the silence, his fingers stroking my hair.

"No," he said, smiling at me. "It's not illegal to be this happy."

I snuggled into him and drifted off to sleep to the steady beat of his heart.

My ears perked up at the sound of music from the TV. I bolted upright and glanced around. Shit, I'd fallen asleep on Kaisen. I searched his room, located a T-shirt on his dresser, and slipped it on. It reached my knees and hung off my shoulders, but it was the next best thing to his arms around me.

He'd piled my clothes on the dining room table. I gathered them up and joined him in the living room. "Sorry, I didn't mean to fall asleep on you," I said.

His smile widened as he saw me in his shirt. "You should keep it," he said, patting the seat next to him. I sank down into the cushions and rested my head against him.

"You hungry? The prime rib turned out perfectly."

My stomach growled in response.

"I'll take that as a yes," he laughed, kissing my nose before he stood.

While he went to the kitchen, I slipped my jeans back on. The fire was roaring in the woodstove, making the room toasty and warm, so I decided to leave my socks off.

"Here," he said, bringing me a plate and utensils. "Stay on the couch. Relax." In the next minute, he had produced a TV tray for me.

"Thanks," I said, smiling. "It smells so good."

Kaisen settled in next to me and began flipping through the TV channels. "How about *How the Grinch Stole Christmas*?"

"With Jim Carey or the cartoon?" I asked between bites.

"Jim."

I nodded, taking another bite, my eyes rolling with pleasure. "So damn good. I'm going to have to keep you around," I teased.

"You should definitely keep me." He laughed. "I'm glad you like it."

I ate while we watched the movie and then curled up next to him.

"Look," he said, pointing outside. "It's snowing."

"It's beautiful." I strolled to the large windows.

"So are you," he said, joining me. His arms wrapped around my waist, and I leaned back against his chest.

"Our first Christmas together," he said, placing a kiss on the top of my head.

My heart sang as I gazed at him in the reflection. There wasn't any place I'd have rather been. I turned and pushed off my tiptoes, my lips brushing against his. "I'm going to clean up my mess. Be right back."

My bare feet didn't make any noise while I padded into the kitchen with my empty plate. I busied myself by putting away the food on the counter, loading the dishwasher, and pouring myself a glass of water. My focus dropped to a cookbook on the counter and a white piece of paper hanging out of it. Thin, tight handwriting caught my attention.

I peeked over my shoulder to see where Kaisen was and noted that he was sitting on the couch again. I didn't want him to catch me snooping. My focus returned to the paper. I took a drink and pulled it out of the book, wondering if this were his mother's script. I scanned the writing, expecting to see a recipe. Confusion swirled through me when I saw my name. I set the glass down quietly on the counter and searched for Kaisen again, but he hadn't moved. I turned back to the letter.

Dear Kaisen,

I haven't heard from you in a while, so I'm writing again. How is Hadlee? Does she suspect anything? I'll never be able to thank you enough for keeping an eye on her. I just needed to know. I'm so sorry I pulled you into all of this, but please, you have to keep my secret. She can't ever know the truth.

Please write soon with any update you have on her.

Sincerely,

Jedd

My hands shook, and nausea rolled through my stomach. Who was Jedd? What the hell was going on? Kaisen was watching over me for someone? Was that what I was to him, a favor? Fear shot down my spine as I realized Kaisen wasn't who he said he was.

I yelped and whirled around at his touch.

"Don't!" I shrieked at him, jumping back. "Don't touch me! I don't know who you are," I accused, tears spilling down my face.

"Hadlee, what are you talking about? Why are you crying? Babe, it's okay . . ." His voice trailed off as I held up the letter.

"Who are you, and what do you want from me? Who the fuck is Jedd?" I demanded, the pitch of my voice climbing.

Kaisen stepped toward me again, and I stepped backward, my back in the corner, against the kitchen counter. I had nowhere to run.

"Get back," I said, grabbing a knife from his butcher block.

"Hadlee, it's not what you think. Please, let me explain. I'll back up. I'm not trying to hurt you. You know who I am; you know everything about me." Confusion clouded his face.

"No, I don't!" I shouted, shaking the paper at him as I darted to the left, out of the corner. I dropped the knife and letter and shot past him.

Kaisen shook his head. "Hadlee!" Desperation filled his voice. He stepped out of my way as I gathered my socks, boots, and purse. "You don't understand," he exclaimed, his eyes wide with fear.

I made a beeline out the front door, my bare feet not even registering the cold while I ran through the snow and to the car.

"Hadlee, please. Stop!" Kaisen said, alarm ringing in his voice as he hurried after me.

"Don't call me ever again," I said, opening the car door and climbing in. My breathing came in sharp gasps as I shut and locked the door behind me, then started the car. My heart pounded in my ears as I looked at Kaisen one last time and my world came crashing down. He waved frantically, attempting to stop me, but it was too late. He could report to whomever

Jedd was that I was gone for good.

I sped as fast as I dared down Fertile Valley Road, but it was dark and snowing, and I was struggling to see through my tears.

He'd lied to me. I'd just had sex with a stranger; I'd given him my heart. Had he run into me that day at the grocery store on purpose? Was it all just a show? And what did Jedd mean by "the truth"? That Kaisen didn't love me?

My salty tears burned my chapped lips, but there was no switch to flip my emotions off. It had been easier when I'd not let anyone in, but I'd been stupid enough to think that this was different—that he was different.

Fertile Valley Road ended, and I turned onto Highway 2 and headed toward home. Since it was Christmas Eve, I scanned the area for any cops. Not seeing any, I pushed on the accelerator, anxious to get home. I choked on my sobs as the speedometer reached ninety.

Thirty minutes later, I drove up my driveway and slammed on the brakes. The tires screeched as I shoved the gear shift into park. Tears continued to drench my face while I turned the car off and collected my things. My body trembled, and I realized I'd left my coat at Kaisen's house. I hopped out of the car and ran up the porch steps. The front door wasn't locked, thank goodness.

"Syd!" I hiccupped, attempting to calm down. "Syd," I called again, dropping everything on the living room floor. My feet padded through the house as I looked for her in the kitchen, but she wasn't there. Where was she? She'd said she wasn't going anywhere tonight. I rounded the hallway corner and ran toward our bedroom. I passed the bathroom, stopped short, and backed up, slowly opening the door wider.

And then I screamed.

"Syd! Syd!" I cried, stepping over the pool of blood. Her limp body lay sprawled on the floor, her jeans soaked.

"Syd, honey," I said, sitting down next to her and picking up her head gently. "Syd," I cried. "Talk to me." I held her against me and rocked her back and forth. My eyes caught the corner of her phone next to the toilet; I leaned over and seized it. My hands shook violently as I dialed 911.

"Help," I said into the phone. "She's bleeding everywhere, and I can't wake her."

"Ma'am, what's your address? We're on our way."

"It's 31521 Sycamore Lane. Please, hurry."

"Does she have a pulse?"

"I have to put you on speaker," I whispered, fumbling for the button. "Can you hear me?" I hiccupped, gently touching Syd's neck, searching for a heartbeat or any other sign that she was alive. "Come on Syd, don't you dare fucking leave me. Don't you dare. I found it! I found a pulse!" I yelled. I held her and rocked her against me as her blood seeped into my clothes. "The front door is unlocked. Just, please, hurry."

I refused to leave Syd's side until the ambulance pulled up and the EMTs entered the house. They placed an oxygen mask over her face and lifted her limp body onto the gurney. I tucked myself into the corner as everything unfolded in slow motion.

"I'm right behind you," I said, wiping my tears while they took her out of the bathroom. I gathered the few towels hanging on the rack and tossed them on top of the bloody mess. My heart racing, I located Marcus's name on Syd's phone and tapped the call button.

"Hey, babe," he said.

"Marcus, it's Hadlee."

"Why are you calling on Syd's phone?"

"She's on the way to the hospital," I hiccupped. "She was passed out in the bathroom, and there was so much blood," I said, sobbing so hard I could barely speak.

"The baby," he gasped. "Hadlee, she was pregnant."

"What?"

"I'm on my way to the hospital. Do I need to pick you up, or can you drive her car? Hadlee?"

I shook off my shock at his news. Damn it, I needed to pull myself together. I could lose my shit later. I wiped my mascara-smeared face with the back of my hand. "I'm okay. Syd will need her car when she gets discharged, so I'll meet you there in a few minutes. See you when I get there."

I disconnected the call, shoved the phone in my back pocket, and hurried to the kitchen. I'd have to leave the towels in the bathroom until I got back. Until I came home with Syd.

I grabbed some water and slammed it down. Then, I hurried into the living room, slipped on my boots. My stomach lurched as I realized I needed to call Camille and Jonathon. I rummaged through all the crap in my purse for my phone. How was I going to tell them we didn't know if their daughter was going to live past Christmas Eve? I swallowed hard and pushed down the tears that threatened to reappear.

In moments, I had locked the door and started the BMW.

I located Camille's number and tapped the speaker button. It rang while I backed out of the driveway and drove toward the hospital as fast as I could without ending up in an accident. One person in the hospital tonight was enough. Her voicemail picked up on the fourth ring. "Damn it," I said, searching for Jonathon's number at a red light. He didn't answer either. "Shit!" I said, banging on the steering wheel.

My phone buzzed, and Kaisen's name flashed across my screen. "Fuck you!" I screamed. He wasn't anywhere on my list of priorities right now.

Minutes later, I pulled into the far end of the hospital parking lot and sprinted into the emergency room and to the desk.

"I'm Hadlee. I'm Sydney Davidson's sister. She came by ambulance," I stuttered, trying to regain my breath.

"Fill this out for me, please," the nurse said. "We'll need her insurance information."

"I don't have it, but our parents, I'm trying to reach them. Can you still treat her?"

"We won't refuse any treatment. It'll be okay," she said, patting my hand. "I'll find you in the waiting room the moment we know something, Hadlee."

"Thank you." I walked away in a haze. Fear gripped my chest as I scanned the waiting room. A family in the corner cried together, and a little girl rested her head against the shoulder of a woman who was singing to her softly. A guy who seemed to be my age peered up at me, his face purple and swollen, his lip fat. He held his right leg, grimacing and rocking back and forth. Everywhere I turned, there was loss and brokenness.

Panic surged through me as I took it all in, and then everything crashed down on me. My knees buckled, and I slid down the wall and to the floor, sobs racking my body. The outside air rushed over me as the ER doors flew open, and seconds later, arms wrapped around me.

"Hadlee," Marcus said, kneeling down. "She'll be okay. She's strong.

You found her in time."

My fingers clutched at his coat and held on with everything I had while I sobbed until my emotions ran dry. Minutes later, we held hands in silence, my mind imagining the worst for Syd. How in the hell would I make it without her?

I stared mindlessly at the clock as the tick of the hand moved with each agonizing second.

Hours later, my butt was numb from sitting on the floor. The doctor entered the waiting room.

"Hadlee," he said, approaching us. Marcus and I stood.

"Yes, sir." My voice was thick with fear.

"She's going to be okay. She lost a lot of blood, but we stopped the hemorrhaging during surgery."

"Surgery?" Marcus asked, worry draining his face of color.

"Yes, we had to stop the bleeding, or we would've lost her," the doctor said.

I covered my face again as the tears returned. I leaned against Marcus's shoulder; he wrapped his arm around me, attempting to calm me down.

"But she's okay?" he asked, his voice barely above a whisper.

"She's going to be fine," the doctor said. "She's asking for you, Hadlee. She's pretty groggy, but she'd like to see you."

I looked at Marcus through my tears.

"Go," he said, shoving his hands in his coat pockets. "I'll call her parents again."

"Okay." I wiped my face and followed the doctor to her room. I knew my attempts to look calm and collected were futile, but I didn't want her to know how terrified we all were. She didn't need to concern herself with us, only her recovery.

I paused, took a deep breath, and stepped inside. Her skin was so pale against her jet-black hair.

"Hi," she said, attempting a smile. Her eyes were slightly glassy.

I hurried toward her. "I don't know whether to hug you or beat your ass for not telling me," I said.

"I'm sorry I didn't say anything." Her grip was weak, but she attempted to squeeze my hand.

"I want to ask you a million questions, but I know you're tired, and from the looks of it, they gave you some heavy-duty drugs."

"Mm-hmm. It's okay," she slurred, patting the space on the bed next to her. I took her cue and crawled in next to her. Her thin frame made it easy for us to both fit.

"I thought we'd lost you," I said, unable to hold back the tears. "There was so much blood, Syd."

"I tried to call 911, but then I guess I passed out." Her eyes closed briefly as she took a deep breath. "I was almost five months pregnant, Had."

My jaw clenched, and I struggled not to scream at the universe for all the wrong that had happened tonight. There was no way in hell Syd and Marcus deserved this. And I hadn't deserved to have Kaisen break my heart. I shoved him out of my head. This wasn't the time for him to be creeping around in my thoughts.

"I lost our baby," she hiccupped, tears spilling down her cheeks.

"I don't know how, but we'll get through this." I pulled her close to me as we clung to each other and cried.

"I feel like I hitchhiked my way to hell and haven't been able to find my way back," I said, sitting down next to Marcus.

"No shit," he said, leaning his head against the wall. We'd moved to the chairs, and although they were better than the floor, it was difficult to sit still or sleep in the hard, plastic seats. Maybe they didn't want to encourage people to get too comfortable.

Marcus and I had both spent a few minutes with Sydney, and we were waiting for her parents. Not that we wanted to leave her, but I needed to shower and wash her blood off me.

"Were you excited to be a father?" I asked gently, unwilling to look at him. I was barely managing my own feelings, and if I saw the expression on his face, I'd lose my shit again.

"Scared, mostly. Honestly, I know you're upset with her, but we'd only found out a few weeks ago, and she was already four months along. She's so tiny that she wasn't even beginning to show, so we were trying to figure out our next step and how to tell you and her parents."

I shifted in my chair, trying to find a better position, but nothing was working. "I thought she was dead when I saw her," I said, finally glancing up at him. "I thought I'd gone to Kaisen's and left her there to die alone." I chewed my lip and forced the tears back. "And then everything went to hell in a handbasket."

"There's no way you could've known, Had. Don't beat yourself up. I was going to go over there earlier tonight, but she told me she wanted to be alone for a while. I don't know if she wasn't feeling well or what, but she talked me out of stopping by."

I reached over and squeezed his arm.

"You're an okay guy, Marcus. Thanks for being there for both of us."

"Well, ya know," he said, blushing, "when I marry her, you and I will be in-laws."

My eyebrows shot up. "Are you going to ask her? She's going to kill me for telling you this, but she heard you talking to someone on the phone about proposing, and it freaked her out."

Marcus shook his head. "I want to, but I was going to wait. I thought a year after we graduate would be a good time. Of course, I wouldn't propose now even if I wanted to. I think she needs to heal . . . about the baby. We both do."

"Are you okay?" I asked.

Marcus's gaze drifted down to the floor and back to me. "I don't care about kids; I care about her. She's my entire world, Hadlee. If I ever lost her, I'd have nothing left."

"Same here," I replied softly. "But she's okay, and we all have each other."

He nodded.

The emergency room doors whooshed open, and Camille and Jonathon burst into the waiting room. We stood, hugged them, and gave them an update on their daughter.

The metallic stench of blood overwhelmed me as I entered the bathroom. Fighting back tears, I picked up the ruined towels that were caked with Syd's loss. Thank God the roomies were gone for the holiday vacation. Syd would have withered of embarrassment if Lionel or anyone else had witnessed the evidence of such personal devastation. Marcus hadn't even seen the bathroom in its current condition.

An hour later, the bathroom reeked of bleach. I flipped the switch, turning the fan on, and threw out the toothbrush I'd used to remove the stains from the floor crevices. The towels quickly followed. Her blood had stained my clothes, so I removed them and threw them away, too. Finally, it was time for a shower. I just needed to wait for the water to heat up.

My iPhone lay facedown on the counter; I'd refused to look at it until after I had cleaned the bathroom. I picked it up—twelve text messages. My pulse quickened, but I ignored it and placed the phone back down. Kaisen wasn't taking a hint. No meant no. The only positive thing about all the shit with Syd was that I hadn't had time to dwell on Kaisen. Until now.

Hot water steamed from the shower head, and I stepped in, pulling the curtain closed behind me. Blood had clung to my skin and now pooled at my feet. I inhaled deeply, trying to calm myself, and turned my face into the water. What had happened tonight? How had everything gone from perfect to fucked up in a matter of hours?

I clutched my stomach and realized I'd lost Kaisen and almost Syd. My knees buckled, and I sank down into the tub, the water pouring over my body. Finally, I allowed my heart to shatter into tiny pieces. I'd lost everything I loved. Again. How had I not seen it coming? Sobs shook my body as I fell apart.

Dreams *taunted me all night,* and then images of Syd's limp body woke me abruptly. I flung the covers off and sat up. My swollen eyes traveled to Syd's unmade bed. I crossed the room, pulled the blankets up, and straightened her comforter. I fluffed her pillows, too. It was the least I could do. But she should have been here—in this room, with me, giggling and wishing me a merry Christmas as we prepared for the festivities at her parents' house.

At least Syd had been discharged and was at her parents' house. I'd offered to give them family time together and come over at one in the afternoon instead of this morning. Even though I wanted to be there to see her, it was the right thing to do.

A heavy sigh escaped me, and tears threatened to return. I was sick of crying, but I couldn't seem to stop, so the next best thing was to not think about it. The scent of fresh coffee tickled my nose. I didn't remember setting the alarm on the pot last night, but I must have. At least my brain had its priorities straight while it was running on autopilot.

My Minion slippers scuffed the hardwood floor as I made my way to the kitchen and located a mug. I filled it, poured in some milk, and slumped into the chair at the bar. As often as I'd prayed for silence during my college years of constant roommates, it wasn't what I'd hoped it would be. It was overwhelming, threatening to crush me. Yet the clock over the sink ticked loudly with each second that passed. I set my cup down and hurried to get dressed. I couldn't take it; I had to get out of there.

Starbucks would be open. I'd grab a muffin, sit in a crowd of people, and pretend that I belonged somewhere.

Twenty minutes later, I pulled up to the crowded shop and stepped out of the car. Never in my wildest dreams had I imagined I'd be spending today alone. I sat near the window in the back corner, where I could see everyone. Kids jumped with excitement and pulled at their mom's sleeves as they waited in line. Exhausted dads carried holders full of everyone's favorite beverages, stifling yawns as they joined their families.

It was funny how someone could be surrounded by people and feel so alone.

The peppermint mocha burned my throat as my attention landed on a guy at the end of the line. My heart skipped a beat. Was it Kaisen? My throat tightened when I realized it wasn't. Was this what it would be like? Thinking I saw him everywhere I went? The memories of his scent tickling my nose, the warmth of his body next to mine, his mad skills in the kitchen?

I leaned back in my seat and rubbed my forehead, my breathing quickening. I needed to stay focused. Kaisen had lied to me. I'd slept with a hot guy and wrapped him up in a package with a bow on top, choosing to see the things I'd wanted to see instead of what was really in front of me—a stranger. Questions hammered my exhausted brain as I began to sift through the letter again.

My phone buzzed and interrupted my thoughts. Kaisen's name flashed across the top with *I'M SORRY*. I groaned, tapped the screen, and scrolled through his messages. He was sorry; he could explain; he loved me.

Not good enough, I screamed inside my head.

I resisted the urge to throw my phone against the wall and watch it shatter into a million pieces. Enough destruction had already taken place. Kaisen had shattered my heart. He'd pretended to love me when actually he'd just been doing someone a favor.

Fury bubbled up inside me when I envisioned the tiny, tight handwriting. Who the hell did Kaisen think he was, marching into my life like that? And who the fuck was Jedd?

I shoved my phone into my coat pocket, gathered my belongings, and tossed my empty cup in the trash. An elderly gentleman held the door open for me. "Merry Christmas," he said as I strolled past him.

"You, too," I muttered. I dug through my bag for my sunglasses and slipped them on. The sun was glaring at the world, its rays brighter than normal as they ricocheted off the snow.

I stared at the sidewalk, took a deep breath, and trudged forward. I had no idea where I was going, but I had to breathe. I needed the sun on my face, its warmth against my skin, melting away the memories of

Kaisen's arms around me. Of his strong arms lifting me out of the pickup when I'd gotten into the wrong one, his fingers on my cheek, and his mouth all over my body.

My chest tightened, but I kept walking, the memories bombarding me with every step. The salt crunched beneath my boots as my pace quickened, and I found myself hurrying across the crosswalk toward Francis Avenue. Nothing mattered except that I keep moving. I looked over my shoulder and saw the shopping centers growing smaller with each step.

An hour later, I stopped at a house up the street from Syd's. I checked my Fitbit clock and scolded myself. It was only twelve fifteen. What in the hell was I going to do for forty-five minutes? Glancing around, I noted the driveway was empty. Maybe I'd wait here for a bit. I sat down in the snow, leaned against the neighbor's mailbox, and waited. My head tilted toward the golden rays and soaked them up.

A cold, wet nose touched my cheek, and I jumped. I must have dozed off.

"Hadlee!" Rosa exclaimed. "Miss Hadlee, what are you doing here in the snow? Come here Chloe," she said, picking up Camille's terrier.

"Rosa, what time is it?" I asked.

"Twelve forty. Come with me. You can't be out here like this."

"I'm not supposed to be here until one. It's okay," I said, standing slowly. The snow had soaked the back of my pants, but I didn't care. My backside was now numb, just like the rest of me.

"Nonsense! They'd have a fit if they knew you were out here waiting all alone."

"Please don't tell them. Please," I pleaded. My eyes dropped to the ground, and my cheeks flushed with embarrassment. She knew I had nowhere else to go. No family. I didn't belong anywhere.

As if that weren't bad enough, I was also so tired that I had dozed off on their sidewalk!

"If you want me to keep my mouth shut, come with me so we can get you some dry clothes. I have some of Sydney's clothes in the laundry room. You can wear some of her pants?"

"Yeah, we share stuff all the time."

"Good. Come on now." She shook her head and waited for me to follow her. "Don't know if I should hug you or smack your behind for sitting out here alone in the cold. And Sydney will be so glad you're here, too. She's exhausted. Her parents have had a stern talking to her for most of the day. She'll be relieved to have a break," Rosa said as we meandered up the driveway. "She gave us all a good scare," she added, her voice dropping to a whisper.

"How's she doing this morning?"

"She ate some soft scrambled eggs, so that was a good sign."

The thought of eggs brought the image of Kaisen cooking. I guess that was the only thing not fake about him—he was good in the kitchen. He would have made me fat if we'd stayed together anyway, so I should be counting my blessings.

The sound of Rosa's boots against the back stairs of the house brought me back to reality. She held her finger to her lips while she cracked the door open and poked her head in.

"This way," she whispered. She ushered me into the laundry room and quickly found a pair of jeans, then motioned me toward the bathroom. I slipped inside and changed into dry clothes. Syd wouldn't think anything of me wearing them if she noticed, especially since we traded all the time.

Once I returned to the laundry room, I leaned down and hugged Rosa. "Merry Christmas," I whispered, raw emotions making my voice crack.

"You, too, Hadlee," she said, rubbing my back. "And don't you worry—I'll wash your pants and send them back with Sydney when she goes home. Now, go out the back and run around to the front so you can ring the doorbell. It's one o'clock, and I'll be serving the food soon."

I chuckled at her, snuck out the back, and hurried around the house. I wondered how many times she'd helped Syd sneak in after curfew. Rosa seemed to know exactly what she was doing.

My finger pressed the doorbell, and seconds later, Jonathon welcomed me in.

"Merry Christmas," he said, hugging me. "How's our girl?"

"Good, thanks. How's Syd?" I asked, unable to hide my concern.

"On the mend." He guided me into the living room. "What would you like to drink, Hadlee? We have white or red wine, or I can make you something stronger, if you'd like."

I frowned. Jonathon never offered the hard stuff. "No, thank you. I don't feel like having anything yet." Fear gripped the back of my neck. Was something else wrong with Syd?

"Sit," he said, motioning to the dark-brown wingback chair.

I sat.

He took the seat across from me. "I just wanted to talk to you for a minute." He hesitated as a torrent of anguish rippled across his face. "If you hadn't found Sydney last night, she wouldn't be with us today," he said, his voice thick with gratitude. "I can't imagine how difficult that had to have been for you, but you kept a clear enough head to call 911."

I nodded, unsure of what to say. "She's family. You're all my family," I said softly. I swallowed hard, shoving the ball of emotion down.

"She wants to go home already," he said, chuckling.

"Really? Is she able to? I mean, can she?"

"We're going to keep her here until New Year's Eve to make sure there aren't any complications or issues."

My jaw tightened with the news. I didn't know if I could make it without her for a week. In fact, I wasn't sure if any of my roomies would be there until school started again, which meant that the large house would be empty.

"Would you like to stay? There's an extra bedroom, or for that matter, there's another twin bed in Sydney's room. You're welcome to stay with us. I think she'd like you to as well."

"Oh. Wow. Thank you! How about I stay for a few days and then play it by ear? I have to go back to work and stuff."

Jonathon nodded. "You stay as long as you want," he said, standing. "Now that it's settled, let's go eat." He rubbed his stomach and grinned.

The lazy afternoon drifted by while we ate and laughed together. Even though I was trying to not think about Kaisen, my mind drifted toward him more often than I cared to admit. At least I had Syd and her family for now, and I didn't have to listen to the screaming silence at our house. And the thought of that house made me suddenly wonder how I would get there.

I scratched my head, searching for the words. "It's getting late . . . would it be too much trouble to ask for your driver to take me to Starbucks?" I asked Camille.

"You don't have to go to Starbucks, hon. We have coffee right here."

"No, I really do. I—I walked here. Syd's car is parked in front of the Starbucks at Wandermere."

Everyone's eyes grew wide. The sudden silence reminded me of my own house.

"That's ten miles," Camille exclaimed.

"Yeah. I found that out," I said, attempting a smile. "I needed some air."

Syd reached for my hand. She knew me well enough to know when I was stressed beyond words, I took off walking or running. She just didn't know the full extent of my stress.

"Of course. Yes. Let's get you taken care of." Camille excused herself from the table.

"Thank you for staying," Syd said.

"You're doing me a favor, too," I said, giving her a reassuring smile. "I much rather hang out here than sit in an empty house."

"He'll be here any minute," Camille said, smiling gently and returning to her seat.

"Thank you. I'm sorry I needed to ask."

"No, it's fine. You just get whatever you need from the house and then come on home."

My face fell with her words. Home. I nodded, glancing at Sydney, her expression growing intense while she searched my face. Had she realized something else was going on with me? I turned away, not wanting her to know yet.

"I'm back," I said, knocking on Syd's bedroom door and entering the purple-and-pink oasis. "I see nothing has changed." I dropped my overnight bag on the floor and flopped onto the twin bed across from hers. "The setup is almost like our place, huh?"

"Yeah, except Barney didn't vomit all over the walls," she laughed.

"Did you know Demi Lovato was on *Barney* when she was young?"

"No," she said, sitting up in bed. She grimaced as she attempted to get comfortable.

"You okay?" I asked, jumping up to help.

"I'm still in a lot of pain, but I'm going to be fine."

I sat gently on the side of her bed.

"What happened?" I asked barely above a whisper. "Why didn't you tell me?"

Syd leaned against her headboard and rubbed her face. "I was going to tell you after Christmas. I'd only known for a few weeks. Marcus and I were still trying to wrap our heads around everything. We obviously weren't planning to have a kid, and—I guess it doesn't matter anymore," she said, her shoulders sagging with grief.

"I don't know how, but it's going to be okay. I'll help you in any way I can."

"They aren't really sure what happened. They say I can try again, but of course, I don't want to. I'm too young to have kids. This broke me into pieces, and I—I don't think I could live through it again."

"I can't live through almost losing you again, so if you and Marcus decide down the road that this is what you want, maybe you should talk to a doctor first. And when you get pregnant again, you need to speak up so everyone can bug the shit out of you," I said, laughing. "You won't even be able to go pee by yourself."

Syd covered her face with her hands and groaned. "You're so right! Can you imagine what a mess Marcus would be?"

"He was a disaster last night. He really loves you," I said.

She nodded. "I know. I'm lucky to have him."

"Yes, you are. And now that I'm here and putting all the pieces together . . . all that talk over the last few weeks, about how Kaisen looked at me? How Marcus wasn't looking at you the same? How you were jealous of me? All of that was about the baby, wasn't it?"

"I'm sorry," she said. "My hormones and emotions were all over the place."

I patted her leg. "At least it makes sense now. The important thing is that you're okay and we're here together." My gaze fell to the floor as I realized I was missing Kaisen. He'd let me down when I'd needed him the most.

"Ten miles, huh? Is that a record?"

My nose scrunched up at her. "Probably, but I had a lot on my mind."

"All for me?" she asked, her eyebrows raised in anticipation.

I answered her question with silence.

"Shit. Kaisen? Wait, you weren't even supposed to be home last night. But you found me, right?" Syd scooted up in her bed and leaned forward.

"What did he do? What happened? Things were going so well." She held up her hand, palm out. "Wait, did he hurt you?"

"It's nothing," I muttered.

"Ten miles isn't nothing. What happened?"

Over the next few minutes, I filled Syd in on the mysterious letter. She sat still, mouth slightly open, until I ran out of words.

"Well, fuck me runnin' sideways." Shock flickered across her face as she processed the news.

"I don't think we could figure that one out together, Syd," I said, attempting to inject some humor into the conversation.

She eyed me and rested her hand on her chin. "You haven't talked to him yet, have you? You have no idea what this is all about?"

I shook my head.

"Hadlee! You have to find out. You need to talk to him!" She urged.

"Why? So he can lie to me some more?" I asked, hopping off her bed. "That's all it was. He was watching me for someone, and, like, what the hell do I even do with that? I slept with him, Syd. I mean, multiple times. And—I fell in love with him," I said, my voice gaining an octave.

"Oh Hadlee, that guy loves you. The way he watches you, how protective he is, there's something to this. You need to find out what's going on so you can make an informed decision. Right now, you're terrified, but being terrified of the truth won't help you. Find out who Jedd is and what this is all about. Then figure out how you feel about Kaisen. Text him that you'll meet him at the bar and grill. Sit in Kara's section, where you're in public and safe. I'd go with you, but I have to rest for a few days, and you really shouldn't wait that long."

I stared at her in disbelief. "You do understand I have no idea who he really is, right?"

"Yes, you do. He's even tried to text you and explain that it's not what you think. In no way do I believe he's someone awful. But you'll never find out for yourself if you don't sit down and talk to him."

"Isn't it your bedtime or something?" I asked, giving her the best evil glare I could manage.

"You're funny. Don't ignore me. You know I'm right."

I sank down on the bed opposite her. "What if it's something horrible?"

"What if it's not?" she challenged.

I flopped backward, realizing there was no way I'd win this battle with her.

"I need some time first." I pressed the palms of my hands against my forehead, trying to clear my head.

"I wouldn't wait too long; your phone is going to blow up," she said, nodding at it.

I fumbled around for it on the nightstand and frowned. "More texts from Kaisen."

"What do they say?" Syd asked.

"Same stuff. He loves me, and he wants me to please talk to him."

"If you need some time, fine, but at least tell him that."

"I miss him," I admitted, my emotions in a continual tug-of-war.

"I know, and we'll figure this out like we do everything else. Text him back." Syd sank back into her pillow, her eyes narrowing. "Now's a great time," she said.

My forehead creased in frustration as I struggled with what I wanted to say.

I need some time.

Hadlee? Are you okay?

I need some time, Kaisen. I'll text you when I'm ready.

I held down the power button and turned off my phone.

"What did you say?" Syd asked.

"That I needed some time. Which I do. I told him I'd text him when I was ready."

Syd nodded. "Good. Just make it soon. I need to know what the hell is going on," she said, an exhausted smile easing across her face.

I couldn't help but laugh at her. Little did I know it would be awhile before I laughed again.

The New Year was rung in quietly by Syd, Marcus, Kara, Michael, and me at our place. We stuck with board games and some drinks. Life had returned to normal as much as it could with a constant nagging hole inside me. I'd tried to build up the courage to text Kaisen, but I couldn't. He'd respected my space; I hadn't heard from him in the last week.

The next morning, Syd and I hopped in her car and returned to Whitworth. I only had two classes without Kara and Syd this semester. I guess part of me figured that if I kept them around most of the time, I wouldn't break down and message Kaisen.

I was on my way to class when my phone vibrated. I pulled it out of my backpack, leaned against the side of the science building, and tapped my screen.

Sometimes our perception isn't the truth. I'll tell you everything. Please say you'll meet me somewhere so we can talk. I can't take it anymore. I miss you, and I love you more than I thought was humanly possible.

My chest ached. Syd's words rang in my ears, and Kaisen's words swam before my eyes. Was my perception of what had happened incorrect? Was I being unfair by pushing him away and refusing to let him explain? Kara and Hank were both working tonight, and even Syd could go with me now. I'd have all the support I could hope for.

Fine. In public, at the grill. Seven tonight.

Thank you! And no matter what, never question how much I love you.

That was debatable, depending on what came out of his mouth. I tucked my phone away and proceeded to class.

Sometimes your brain can fuck with you more than the truth can, but that wasn't the case in this situation. Nothing I'd imagined since Christmas Eve could have even come close.

My stomach rolled, and my hand trembled as I pulled open the door to the grill and Syd and I stepped inside the crowded restaurant. I slipped off my coat and nodded at Kara. While we waited for her to approach, I blew on the palms of my sweaty hands. How could they possibly be sweating when it was twelve degrees outside?

"Hey, you ready?" Kara asked. Without waiting for a reply, she added, "You're doing the right thing."

"Is he here?" My nerves jittered, and my voice cracked.

"Yeah. I put you two in the corner but with your back against the wall so you will be able to see Syd, Hank, and me at all times. If it helps any, he looked scared shitless when he came in here."

"Really?"

"Yeah," she said gently.

"Okay," I said, taking a deep breath. Anxiety hummed beneath my skin as I glanced toward the corner. I couldn't see him yet due to the crowd.

"You've got this," Syd said, rubbing my back.

I attempted a smile that turned out more like a grimace and moved toward him, leaving the girls behind me.

My feet felt as though I were trudging through mud. I had walked this aisle a million times over the last few years, yet I felt like I'd never seen it before. Five more steps to go, and then I'd face him for the first time since I'd run from his house. Butterflies fluttered in my belly as I swallowed hard and approached his booth. Tired eyes searched mine as I paused for a moment. If I was guessing correctly, he'd lost some weight, too. Strings of anxiety tugged at my heart.

"Hadlee," he whispered, his expression a mix of relief and sadness.

"I'm not here to get back together, so just tell me what the hell is going on and who you really are." I slid into the seat across from him and scanned the room for my friends. Kara was waiting on a couple not far from us, and Syd and Hank were watching from the bar.

Kaisen's hand reached for mine, his touch sending a shock of electricity through me. My eyes narrowed, and I jerked it away, placing my hands in my lap.

"You said you'd tell me everything. I'm listening," I snapped, glaring at him.

"Okay," he nodded, wiping his hands on his jeans. Was he scared? "First, I need you to listen to everything. Some of it won't make sense, so I have to back up a little in order to explain it." He ran his hand through his hair. My heart skipped a beat as I remembered how soft his curls were.

I crossed my arms over my chest and waited. He probably thought I was pissed, which was good. I couldn't allow him to see how badly I was shaking.

"Everything between us is real, Hadlee. You know who I am, but what you don't know . . . what you don't know is . . ." His voice faltered, and he cleared his throat. "Our fathers . . . I . . . fuck."

"Spit it out, for God's sake, or I'm leaving," I hissed, leaning toward him.

Kaisen rubbed his face with his hands and swore under his breath. "We know each other."

"Of course we do. In fact, if my memory serves me correctly, I was in your bed, naked, with you inside of me on Christmas Eve," I reminded him, my tone scathing.

"That's not what I meant."

My eyebrows arched as frustration nipped at me. "Who are you? And what do you want from me?" I asked, almost choking on my anger.

"I'm a friend, Hadlee. Our fathers were best friends growing up."

My mouth dropped open. "Wait, what? Your dad knew mine?" My spine went rigid as my brain attempted to digest this new information. "Kaisen, if they knew each other, did you know my dad, too?" A flood of hope and fear simultaneously swirled inside me.

"I met him a few times," he replied.

My head dropped forward, my eyes stared vacantly at the table, and thankfully, my hair draped down, shielding my face. Thoughts raced through my mind as I fought the tears and implemented an anxiety technique I'd learned from a psych professor. "Feet on the floor, feet on the floor," I muttered.

My head snapped up when pieces of the puzzle began to float loosely into place. "If you knew him before he died, did you know about me? Did you know who I was that day at the grocery store? Were you following me?" I asked, panic gnawing at me as my mind returned to the letter.

"I knew who you were because I'd seen you in here a few times when I came in with the guys. I had no idea you were going to be at the store that day, though. But there's more."

I searched his face in an attempt to discover any clue that might help to prepare me for what he was about to say next. My head tilted as I waited for him to continue.

"Hadlee, the letter you found at my house . . . it was from your father. He's alive. Your father's alive."

Shock splintered through me as I struggled to understand what Kaisen had just said. I was stunned into silence.

"I didn't know this for a while, but a guy named Jedd, a friend of my dad's, contacted him several months ago and asked if he could help find you. He agreed, made some calls to an attorney and a detective, and a search began for women your age who could be a potential fit. You came up with a ninety-two percent possibility."

"What?" I sputtered. "What the fuck? You're sitting here telling me my dad's alive and, in the same sentence, he *thinks* I'm his kid? Because the last time I checked, ninety-two percent doesn't equal one hundred percent. Do you know how many people mistake someone as their parent? And wouldn't he remember my name? I mean, it was on the birth certificate he signed." I paused. "You're not making sense, Kaisen. My father was in a car accident!"

Kaisen paused. "Hadlee, I know you found the death notice, but your mom could have written anything she wanted to on it. And he thinks your mom changed your name to protect your identity while you were growing up, so you wouldn't be tormented by other kids and their parents."

"That's absurd! What in the world would I need to be protected from?" I leaned forward, my eyes narrowing. "I'm going to keep firing at your theory until I blow it apart, Kaisen. For instance, what about Jedd's name? My father's name was Christopher."

"As far as I know, it's a nickname; my dad has always referred to him as Jedd. Look, I know you have a lot of questions, but I need to tell you everything first. A few months ago, I received a letter from Jedd at the construction company. He explained some of his situation and asked if I would get to know you. I refused, but the letters kept coming, pleading for my help. Finally, I showed them to my dad. He'd had no idea Jedd had been writing me. That was when I learned about the search for you. After talking to him, I realized that Jedd wasn't asking me to be a creeper; he just wanted to see how you were doing."

My head was spinning. "Is this some kind of really sick joke, Kaisen? Of all people, you should know what losing a parent feels like. Or was that a lie, too?" I asked, tilting my head.

"No," Kaisen said, sincerity written across his face. "I never lied to you about who I was or how I felt about you. The only thing I kept from you was Jedd."

A slightly hysterical laugh escaped me. "Kaisen, if that's all it was, you can relax because this is all one big, big misunderstanding," I said. "My father has been dead since I was eight. You have the wrong girl. I'm the ninety-two, not the one hundred-percent girl." I leaned back and rubbed my forehead. This was just one awful mistake that we could have talked about on Christmas Eve if I hadn't panicked and run out of his house. But then I would've never found Syd. Sadness drifted over me, and I remembered how quickly someone could disappear from my life. First Dad and then almost Syd. Was I about to lose Kaisen, too, or could we work things out? I wanted to, but there was still a problem hanging over us. He thought I was someone I wasn't.

Kaisen took my hand. "Hadlee, I'm pretty sure we're not mistaken."

"No. Listen to me—you're wrong. Like, really wrong. In fact, I can prove to you that I'm not the person you think I am. Tell me—where is this guy, this *Jedd*, right now? I'll meet him, and then we can move past this nonsense and put it behind us."

Kaisen's grip tightened on my hand.

"Idaho Maximum Security Institution," he said, hesitating. "On death row," he whispered.

Blindsided, my mouth dropped open. "What? No. That's your proof right there. My dad would never. No," I stammered, shaking my head.

"After I visited Jedd with Dad and talked to him, heard his story, I finally agreed to meet you and let him know how you were doing. It was a harmless agreement. I never in a million years expected to fall in love with you. And when I realized I had, I stopped writing to him. I wasn't willing to tell him anything else."

"Hmm. So, you agreed to spy on me for a monster on death row? Do you have any idea how insane this sounds?" My eyes widened. Oh, shit—the letter. I paused for a moment, thinking back. "You really did stop writing to him, didn't you? You're telling me the truth. He said he hadn't heard from you in a while."

"Yes, I'm telling you the truth. I knew who you were from the detective, and then I'd seen you in here a few times when you were working. The thought of approaching you was off the table since I didn't want to scare you, so I wrote to him that you seemed happy and healthy. That's it. I've never lied to you. I swear on my mom's grave."

As I filtered through the information, I realized Kaisen was being honest with me, and the tension eased from my shoulders. My head pounded while I considered how I could convince him that I wasn't Jedd's daughter.

"Let's clear this up really quick. Show me a picture," I suggested, my fingers tapping on the table.

Kaisen rubbed his jaw, and frustration clouded his features. "We looked. Dad doesn't have any pictures of Jedd after their college graduation. He got married, traveled all the time for work, and Dad didn't see him often."

"Shit. Really?" I chewed my lip as I realized people didn't take pictures back then like they do now. That only left me with one other option—one that I didn't want to do, but I would for Kaisen. "Fine. Take me to visit him, and then you'll see for yourself I don't know him and we in no way are related."

"It's not going to be tonight or tomorrow, Hadlee. Dad said he would contact Jedd's lawyer to see how fast we could get your application processed, but it could be a few weeks. You have to complete paperwork, and they run a full background check on you before you can visit someone on death row even if you're family. But I do have one with me, so we can fill it out and, hopefully, get it pushed through quickly."

"Fine. Where is it?" I asked, fumbling in my purse for a pen. "There is no way in hell Jedd is my father. My dad would have never murdered someone or done whatever other awful things you have to do to be put on death row."

Kaisen reached into his front pocket and pulled out the form. "I printed it off for you. I'll get it to my dad tonight, and he'll deliver it to Jedd's attorney in the morning."

I uncapped my pen and scanned the form. This was the most ludicrous thing I'd ever heard, but if it allowed me to straighten things out with Kaisen, then I'd do it. My heart sank as I realized nothing would get cleared up until I came face-to-face with a monster and Kaisen had proof that there was no relation. I completed the form and slid it across the table to him.

"I can't see you again," I muttered. His face fell, and my heart dropped into my stomach.

"What? Hadlee, don't say that."

"Kaisen, I'm not saying we can't work this out, but I can't be with you until you've realized that I'm not this guy's daughter. Every time we're together, you'll think you're spending time with someone who isn't me."

He frowned. "That makes no fucking sense."

"And neither does this." I gestured to the paper, attempting to get a grip on my emotions. "You think I'm someone I'm not. I'm not saying you don't love me, but until you realize that I'm not Jedd's daughter, you're going to be thinking I am. I can't have you looking at me like that, like I'm the offspring of a murderer."

He reached up and rubbed his stubbled chin. After a minute of silence, he nodded. "Okay, I'll give you that. But what about the letter and stuff? Can we move past that? Is there hope that we can get back together?"

"I understand why you wanted to help your dad, and I believe you weren't following me. But I'm mad at you for hiding this, and I need some time to think it through."

"I didn't know how to tell you," he said, pausing. "And then I fell in love with you and tried to put the letters behind me. I just wanted you—to be with you, to build a life with you."

My pulse raced as I held his gaze. "Build a life with me?" I asked softly.

"Yeah. All of a sudden, I found myself rethinking my plans after graduation. In my mind, you were next to me. I wasn't concerned about finances or the business; I was only concerned about what you wanted. Did you want to stay in Spokane? Would you be able to find a job in your field? If not, would you want to start your own clinic? What did your future look like, and how did I fit into it?"

Dazed, I rested my head on the back of the booth and stared at the ceiling, his words a painful reminder of how much I missed him. Whatever the hell was going on with us, I knew one thing—I loved him.

I looked at him and reached for his hand.

"I love you, and I've missed you so bad, but we need to clear this up first."

"Then I better hurry up and get this to the attorney," he said, standing.

I stood with him. He leaned down and kissed the top of my head. "I love you, Hadlee Jameson," he whispered in my ear. And with that, he strolled away.

"That is some crazy shit," Kara said, crunching on a carrot stick in our kitchen.

I'd invited her over so I could talk to Syd and her at the same time. I wasn't sure I could repeat this story twice.

"Right?" Syd chimed in as she leaned against the sink, sipping a soda.

"Why would my mom pretend to bury someone who wasn't dead? I think Kaisen's heart is in the right place . . ." I was hoping for confirmation I hadn't fallen off my rocker and hit my head so hard I was no longer capable of seeing the truth for myself.

"Well, it really would have saved everyone a lot of hassle if he'd told you up front," Syd said.

"Mm-hmm, I can hear that conversation now," Kara said, almost laughing. "'Hi, we don't know each other, but there's this guy on death row who thinks you're his daughter, so I'd like to get to know you and tell him how you're doing.' Nope, not happenin.'"

We giggled at Kara's impersonation of Kaisen.

"That would have been beyond awkward," Syd agreed, smiling.

"Here's the real question," Kara said, leaning her elbows on the kitchen counter. "When are you two working things out?"

"I don't know. I'm waiting for him to call me. There's this application process to visit someone on death row, and it includes a background check. I guess they're trying to get me through as fast as they can, but it could take up to several weeks. Until then, I can't see Kaisen. It sends chills down my back to even imagine he would think I'm related to some monster on death row! So, we have to settle this first." My lips quirked. "Then, I'm taking off his clothes and screwing him senseless."

"Oh my God! Did you hear her, Kara? Our Hadlee is all grown up," Syd said, laughing so hard that tears formed in her eyes. "I've never heard you say anything like that."

"Hey, it's true." Kara shrugged. "Once you start, it's hard to stop. But are you sure you can't just have a quickie before everything gets settled?"

"Are you implying that I should use him for sex?"

"Hell yeah, I am."

I snickered and then sobered with the realization that I wasn't sure when I'd see him next.

"I just hope all this shit is put behind us soon," I said quietly.

The girls stopped laughing.

"Keep us posted," Kara said. "Whatever happens, it'll work out."

A full week had passed, and I'd heard nothing from Kaisen. Unfortunately, instead of lessening, I ached for him more with each new day. And as much as I tried, I couldn't stop thinking about the insane situation concerning Jedd. I knew Kaisen and this guy were wrong, but my entire life seemed stalled until I could get past it.

I checked my hair and makeup in front of my vanity mirror. Richard anticipated a busy night at the grill, and I wanted to be ready. Hopefully, it would help me think about something other than this shit with Kaisen. But I doubted anything was going to make me feel better right now.

Thirty minutes later, I pushed through the restaurant door. Today, my shift started at five, and the restaurant was already busy.

"Hey, hey," I said to Hank, putting my backpack behind the bar. "How was your New Year's?"

"Good! How about you?"

"Quiet, but that's okay, right?" I said, smiling. I drew his attention to a large-busommed girl leaning across the bar, attempting to gain his attention. He winked at me as I tied my apron on and grabbed my tray.

After scanning my section, I wandered over to Kara at the computer station.

"Anything yet?" she asked as soon as she saw me.

"Nope, I haven't heard a word from Kaisen." I sighed loudly. Sometimes, it sucks when people do what you ask them to do."

"You should text him. It'll put you both out of your misery."

I perked up at that. "He's miserable?"

"Michael said he's driving him nuts and all he does is talk about you. He goes on and on about how much he loves you and how he blew it."

"Kara, I've had some time to think things through, and yes, he made a mistake, but I can't imagine how hard it must have been to try to help a friend who is important to your dad. Kaisen has basically taken care of his father since his mom died."

"That's what Michael was saying, too."

"I'm not mad at him anymore. I just wish he'd been honest about it upfront so we could have moved past it already."

"So, you've forgiven him?"

"Yeah," I muttered. "I probably would have done the same thing if I'd been in his shoes."

"Then call him, Hadlee. If you want to be with him, what's the problem?" She rolled her eyes. "You two can be so frustrating."

My nose wrinkled at her. "Although I hear you, think about this for a minute: imagine that Michael thought your father was a guy on death row—*death row*, Kara. How would you feel? What if he looked at you differently? I mean, do you know the shit you have to do to even be put there? Like, what the hell?"

Kara nodded. "I know. It would rattle me. I'd wonder if there were something wrong with me, too. Like, could I hurt someone? And, would Michael wonder the same thing?"

"Exactly." I jabbed the air with my finger. "That's my point right there."

"I get it, Had, I really do. I just know you two belong together."

The evening dragged by. I tried to engage with everyone at work, but I was growing antsy with each passing hour.

When my break time arrived, I ordered something to eat and dug my phone out of my backpack. I had a missed call. I hurried to the breakroom to listen to the message from Kaisen.

"Call me. You're approved."

My pulse raced as I listened. The sound of his voice alone stirred up everything inside me. No one had any idea how much I dreaded going to a prison, especially that one. I had no clue what to expect, but I was about to find out.

"Feet on the ground." I inhaled and then tapped the callback option. My legs turned to jelly while I waited for him to pick up.

"Hadlee," he said.

"Hi."

"How are you?"

"Good. I'm at work but on a break. I heard your messages."

"Okay. The drive is about six and a half hours."

"Oh, jeez," I said, rubbing my forehead. "That means I'll have to take off work and school?"

"Probably. Visiting time isn't very long either, so we'll grab a bite to eat and come right back. That way you'll only miss a day of classes. It'll be better if we take off really early in the morning, around three."

"Three in the morning?" I squeaked.

"I'm sorry. It's the only way we will make it there for visiting time. It's the same time each day."

Silence hung in the air as I considered my school and work schedule.

"What day are you thinking?" I asked, my nerves tingling. This shit was getting real. I willed myself to focus on the positive. After this, we'd finish working things out, and I'd be in his arms again.

"Tonight, if we can. If not, we will have to wait another day."

"No, I can borrow notes for history and psych. I'm ready to get this over with so we can move on."

"You are?" he asked. Did I detect a hopeful note in his voice?

"Yeah. And Kaisen, after this is over, I don't want to talk about it anymore. But, if you ever hold out on me again, we're done."

"I promise," he said, releasing a sigh.

"I close tonight, so I'll go home and shower. Just text me when you get to my place so we don't wake anyone. Lionel and the other invisible roomies are back now that the holiday break is over."

"Okay. Hadlee?"

"Yeah?"

"Can I kiss you when I see you?"

A smile pulled at the corner of my mouth. "One thing at a time. We need to stay focused, and if you kiss me, I'm going to pull you into the house and take advantage of you."

"Please do," he said, chuckling. "Seriously, though, as long as I know you're coming back to me, I'll wait."

My heart skipped a beat with his words. "All right. I'll see you in a few hours."

"I love you," he said and then disconnected the call.

I frowned, shoving the phone into the back pocket of my jeans. Why had he hung up so fast? Was he afraid I wouldn't tell him that I loved him back?

His text came through as I drank the last bit of coffee. Since I was pulling an all-nighter, I figured it was in order, but it hadn't helped my anxiety any.

"Hey," I said as I opened the front door, my eyes drifting over his face and down his chest, stomach, and those jeans . . . my body shivered, remembering exactly what was underneath his clothes.

"You okay?" he asked, moving toward me and grabbing my backpack.

"Yeah. Ready to get this over with," I said.

He nodded, and I pulled the door closed behind me and locked up. A few minutes later, we were on the way.

"I've never been to a prison before."

"It's not fun. I wish I could prepare you, but there's nothing I can really say. It's bleak. But I'm here with you. And the sooner you see him and confirm everything, the sooner we'll be able to put it behind us, right?" he asked.

Something was off. He seemed unsettled. Was he worried? About what exactly?

"Where is this hellhole?"

"Kuna, Idaho," Kaisen said. "If you want to get some sleep, go ahead. I brought snacks if you get hungry, too."

"Thanks," I muttered, stifling a yawn. "Maybe I should try to get some rest."

Kaisen reached over and squeezed my hand. I situated myself in the seat, and within minutes, I drifted off to sleep, my fingers linked with his.

Apparently, having Kaisen next to me again helped me to sleep. I hadn't realized how exhausted I'd become since the horrors of Christmas Eve.

The sunshine woke me, and I peeled my eyes open. I winced as I turned my head toward Kaisen, my neck screaming in protest.

"Morning," he said.

"Where are we?" I stretched my cramped body the best I could.

"We're about half an hour away. We have time to stop and get some food."

"I don't know if I can eat, but I gotta pee. And I definitely need a cup of strong coffee." I pulled the visor down and peered in the mirror. "Jeez. Remind me never to sleep in your pickup again."

"You're beautiful in the morning," he told me gently.

"This wasn't how I pictured spending our first night alone back together," I said, attempting a smile.

"Me neither."

Silence settled between us as my mind woke up. Ten minutes later, Kaisen pulled up to a small diner and parked.

I pushed the door open and breathed in the fresh air.

He came around and offered me his hand. Our gazes locked while I took it and hopped out.

As soon as my feet touched the pavement, he dropped my hand and turned to walk away.

"Kaisen!" I tugged on his shoulder. Once he turned around, I grabbed him by the biceps and pulled him back with me as I leaned against his truck.

"This is torture," I said, running my hands through his curls. "Kiss me."

In his eyes, I saw a mix of hope, longing, and caution. "You sure?"

"Yeah."

He smoothed my hair back and brushed his lips against mine. My body vibrated as I slid my hands down his back and around his waist.

"I've missed you so much," he murmured between kisses.

Our mouths parted, and his tongue swept over mine. I moaned against him and then gently pulled away.

"I don't think having sex in a diner's parking lot is the right thing to do. We should probably go inside." I sighed.

"I guess you're right, but what is it with you and parking lots?" he asked, his laughter filling the air. His fingers slipped through mine, and we headed for the front door.

I hadn't meant to kiss him until after the visit to the prison, but being in the truck with him had brought back so many good memories. And, if I allowed myself to think about it, I was scared shitless about this visit to the penitentiary. I needed something solid, something normal. I willed my thoughts to shift toward what was waiting for me after this crazy visit. I'd be grateful when things were settled between Kaisen and me. It seemed like an eternity since we'd been together.

The small restaurant was buzzing with people chatting. The aroma of breakfast and sound of clanking dishes made me miss the grill. I realized it was silly, but the grill was my safe place.

I focused on the little girl who was squealing and giggling while her father laughed and attempted to feed her. My chest tightened as he made *choo choo* noises to get her to open her mouth. My dad had done the same with me.

Kaisen and I located a seat next to the window, and I stared mindlessly out of it, watching the cars pass on the interstate while he ate and I drank my coffee. Plenty of those cars were pulling up to the diner. For such a small place, I was surprised at how busy it was.

"How ya doing?" he asked, wiping his mouth with a napkin.

"It's almost over," I said, unsure whether I was reassuring him or myself.

"Just know that I'll be waiting for you when you're done. And when you visit, you'll be on the opposite side of the glass, talking to him on the phone."

"Like in the movies?" I said, trying to lighten the mood with a grin.

"Pretty much like that, except it's grim, Hadlee. Those guys in there . . . I'm not sure some of them have a soul. It's eerie, and you can almost smell the death."

"You're scaring me," I whispered. "But this is why I have to go there. I can't have you looking at me like I might be the same way."

"What?" He reared back in the booth, his eyes flaring. "No!" In the next instant, he was leaning across the table and grabbing my hand, squeezing it as if he'd never let go.

My anxiety calmed with his touch, but I knew I needed to be responsible for me. He wouldn't be with me when I walked into the visiting area.

"We're almost through this."

I nodded, unable to speak. My stomach lurched, my liquid breakfast threatening to come back up. I was only minutes away from stepping into a place that would most likely haunt me for the rest of my days.

Nothing in my life could have prepared me for this.

Kaisen slowed as we approached the sign that announced the maximum security prison. When he turned the corner into the parking lot, I gasped.

"So many cars . . . do all of these people work here? How many people does it take to keep them in here?" I asked.

He just glanced at me, his eyebrows raised.

"Shit," I muttered, the reality seeping in. I was about to enter one of the most highly guarded places.

My breath came in short gasps as Kaisen pulled up to the gate. The guard stepped out of his small station booth and approached the driver's side window.

"What's the purpose of your visit today?" the guard asked, offering a friendly smile.

How in the world could anyone smile while working here? Maybe it was because he wasn't on the inside?

Kaisen explained the reason for our arrival, and the guard asked us to step out of the truck and open all of the doors. I shivered against the cold and stared at Kaisen. He'd done this before.

After the guard finished searching the vehicle, we were allowed through, and Kaisen pulled into the parking lot.

The bleak, gray buildings were surrounded by tall fences topped with razor wire. The ground was covered in snow. Only the bright blue of the sky showed any sign of something positive.

"You'll need to leave your phone and purse with me," Kaisen told me. "They won't let you take anything with you, other than your picture ID, and they'll need it to issue a visitor's badge. You can take change for the vending machines, too."

"I'm not hungry. I'm just trying to keep my coffee down," I muttered.

"It's not only for you. You can buy inmates food."

"Oh." I fumbled with my phone and handed it to him, my hands shaking. "I don't know if I can do this," I said, rubbing my arms as the gravity of the situation closed in on me.

He tipped my chin up. "You don't have to, Hadlee. We can turn around right now."

I hesitated. He made it sound so easy. "No. That's not fair to you. You've been up all night driving." I took a step back to steady myself. "Besides, I can't walk away. I have to put an end to all of this."

"Okay." He moved closer and kissed my cheek. "We need to go then."

My heart pounded in my ears as we waited to go through security. I squeezed my eyes closed while a stranger's hands patted every curve of my body. This wasn't anything like the airport security. I grimaced when the guard reached the inside of my thighs.

"Your clothes are appropriate for the visit," the security guard said.

"Um. Thank you." My head throbbed from the anxiety. The thought of my clothing hadn't even crossed my mind. I never dressed inappropriately, but even showing a small amount of cleavage might have been dangerous here.

The buzzer sounded, and I jumped. It was time to leave Kaisen behind. I looked his way one more time.

"I love you," he mouthed before I was escorted down the hall.

The guard led me toward the visitation building. I signed my name on a sheet. Door one. Door two. Door three. Door four. Finally, we reached the visitation room.

My feet were stubbornly rooted in place. I willed them forward, one heavy step at a time. I rubbed my clammy hands on my jeans and took in my new surroundings. The dingy cinderblock walls, vending machines, and scattered small tables all reminded me of the middle school cafeteria. And then I saw the dreaded visitation booths.

The minutes ticked by as I paced the room, waiting for Jedd—waiting to look into the eyes of a man who had done something so horrid a jury had sentenced him to death. Kaisen's words rang in my head: *no soul.*

The metallic taste of blood filled my mouth, and I realized I'd chewed my lip raw.

My gaze traveled to the booths, small cubicles, really. A thick sheet of safety glass separated the prisoners' side from where I stood—on the side that offered freedom.

The clanging of chains and handcuffs broke the eerie silence of the room.

"Hadlee Jameson, you have one hour."

My feet froze, and my heart pounded so hard that black dots floated across my vision. I stared at the floor, refusing to look up. The security guard patted the back of the chair for me. It was bolted to the floor.

"Ms. Jameson?"

I stood there, stupid and frozen, each second ticking by. Sucking in a deep breath, I shoved the fear away and nodded, still refusing to look at the inmate on the other side of the glass. My feet scuffed across the floor, and I kept my head down, staring at the speckled gray-and-black floor. I lowered myself onto the edge of the chair and counted to ten.

A black corded phone hung on the wall to my right. I slowly picked it up, pausing while I held it a few inches from my ear. This was it, the moment where I proved everyone wrong. All I had to do was look this man in the eye, and then I could leave and run back to Kaisen as fast as my legs would carry me. He was waiting for me. And the minute we finished here, we could go eat lunch and kiss in his pickup until we were breathless. We'd laugh about this entire situation. His apologies would roll off his tongue, and I'd forgive him and snuggle up to him on the drive home.

Just. Look. Up.

I took a deep breath and brought the phone to my ear.

"Hello," a deep baritone voice sounded through the phone.

Fear rolled inside me, but the only response I offered was silence as I stared blankly at my lap.

"Can you look at me? Please? I just need to know," he said.

He needed to know? I needed to know so I could get my life back, get Kaisen back. My heart rate spiked. All I had to do was glance up. Simple. I'd be face-to-face with a monster I'd never seen in my life, and then I'd leave.

Five, four, three, two, one.

My head snapped up, and I met his gaze. Time stopped as we stared at each other, neither of us speaking. And then a blood-curdling scream ripped through the air. The phone clattered against the wall. My legs propelled me out of the chair and scurried backward. My eyes never left his while I stumbled, my screams never-ending as the guard grabbed me.

"Ma'am, you need to stop screaming."

Violent tremors jolted through my body as Jedd's features clouded.

Few words could have described what I saw. It was . . .

Me.

I was looking at the spitting image of myself in an older, male body. We had the same color hair, eyes . . . even the shape of my nose was his. In sixty seconds, I'd gone from a 92-percent to a full-blown 100-percent match.

His forehead creased. Was he worried? How could someone like that even care?

"I'm done," I stuttered to the guard. "Please, get me out of here."

The door buzzed, and I numbly followed the guard back the way we had come.

Tears streamed down my cheeks with each step. Who was I? Was I like him? What had happened? Why was he here? Why had my mother lied to me for all these years? The questions swirled through my mind so fast I didn't even realize I was back in the main building.

"Hadlee." Kaisen was suddenly there, in front of me.

"Kaisen," I whispered, collapsing against him. "Get me out of here."

He wrapped his arm around me, and I hid my face against his body, allowing him to guide me the rest of the way out of the prison. The cold, fresh air signaled my escape as we stepped outside—we were free. My knees buckled, and I collapsed to the ground.

"Hadlee, my Hadlee," Kaisen murmured in my ear as my entire world crashed down on me. "I'm here. I've got you."

Sobs shook my body as Jedd's eyes haunted me. My eyes. My father was alive and on death row. How could this be possible?

"You're in shock. But it's going to be okay, Hadlee."

As he scooped me up and carried me to the truck, I buried my face against his neck and tried to catch my breath.

Life had just knocked the wind out of me.

Stress has a funny way of manifesting. Apparently, it made me tired. Limp, drunk tired.

And my sleep-addled mind took me to the safest place I knew— Kaisen's bed. Memories of the soft sheets, plush mattress, and musky, woodsy scent filled me with longing for the safety it offered. He was all I wanted. My body tingled with anticipation, and I stretched my arm out for him, but he wasn't there.

A cry stuck in my throat as I forced my eyes open and bolted upright, attempting to adjust to the darkness. Panic surged through me. Where was he? Where was I?

"Hey, it's okay," Kaisen said, turning on the lamp and approaching me. Worry flickered across his face as he lowered himself next to me. I really was in his bed.

My groggy mind also noted that I was fully clothed.

"How did I get here?" I asked softly.

"You slept the entire way home, so I just brought you here. I wanted to watch out for you. You know, to make sure you were okay."

"What? What time is it? It's dark out! I have to call Syd. She'll be worried. I promised I'd text her." I struggled with the sheets, scrambling to free myself.

"Had, it's okay." He gripped my arms lightly. "It's a little after seven at night, and I already talked to her. She knows you're here, and so does Kara."

"They know? Did you . . . did you tell them?" I asked, afraid to hear the answer. No one could know yet. I couldn't even face the truth.

"No. I just told Syd that we were fine and you fell asleep so I brought you here. She's worried. I didn't tell her anything, but she asked if I'd stay with you. Then she mentioned the past few weeks have been shit—for more than one reason. I'm sorry about Syd and Marcus's baby," he said, moving his hand down my arm and taking my hand in his. "I'm grateful you found her, but I can't imagine how awful it must have been. And I'm so sorry I wasn't there for you."

I chewed my lip and shut my eyes against everything in the world that threatened to take me down. How had everything changed so fast?

"Do you think you can eat?" he asked.

"I'll try. I need some coffee," I said softly. I slid from the warm cocoon of his bed, my bare feet touching the oyster-colored carpet of his bedroom.

"I'm sorry."

"Why?"

"I'm not the 92 percent." The words came slowly, thick in my throat. "Did you know? Did you know that Jedd . . .?" My voice trailed off, the words nothing but a thought.

"I can tell you more if you'd like, but I need you to try to eat something first."

I nodded, took his hand again, and allowed him to guide me into the kitchen. He pulled a chair out for me, and I sat down, numb and dizzy with a million thoughts rushing through my exhausted mind.

Within a few minutes, a plate of eggs and hash browns appeared in front of me.

"Just breakfast. It's the fastest thing I could make. I think you might still be in shock over everything, so I just want to keep you warm. Keep you close," he said, laying a blanket over my shoulders before sitting in the chair across from me.

"I'll never look at this table the same again," I said, attempting a smile.

"You and me both." A grin drifted across his face and then faded. "You scared me."

My brows knitted together. "I'm sorry," I said taking a small bite of my food. "I just. I just freaked out." I laid my fork down and looked away. Tears threatened again as my stomach clenched. His eyes. Jedd's eyes haunted me everywhere I looked.

"Tell me everything you know."

"Hadlee, this can wait. I don't want to stress you out any more than you already are."

"Please," I pleaded. "I need to know."

"Okay, but you have to eat at least half of your food first."

I frowned and then quickly beamed at him. "Does that mean I get dessert?" I asked, wiggling my eyebrows in an attempt to break through the gloom.

His chuckle filled the space between us as I took another bite.

"I'm trying," I whispered, fighting back tears. "I'm trying not to be that girl who loses her shit."

"No need to worry. I'm here. And so are your friends."

He made a sandwich for himself while I focused on my food. As soon as he placed a cup in front of me, though, I pushed the plate away and picked up the mug filled with steaming liquid.

"What's this?" I asked, sniffing it. I'd expected coffee.

"A hot toddy," he said, unable to hide a smile as he sat down. "It's courtesy of Syd."

I rolled my eyes, half laughing and crying at the same time.

"Take a few sips while I talk? You might need them." He rubbed his face with his hands and then leaned back in his chair.

The breath whooshed out of me. No more laughter. All of the humor had suddenly been sucked out of the room.

"Remember I said I knew your dad?"

I nodded and took a sip, not really tasting anything.

"You and I actually met years ago, too."

I set my cup down. "When?"

"The day you buried him, I was the kid who gave you the rose for his headstone."

A gasp escaped me. I slapped my hands over my mouth and stared at him. Silence hung in the air as I tried to digest what he was saying. Kaisen? He was the boy in the Mariner's hat?

I leaned closer, staring him straight in his eyes, searching. His eyes. Those big, deep brown eyes, the ones that had touched my heart all those years ago, were staring back at me. I'd just never made the connection. My hands dropped into my lap, and I dug my nails into my palms as every minute and every detail of the most horrible day ripped me apart all over again.

"My mind wants to tell me you're kidding," I said after several tense moments. "There's no way you were there, Kaisen. This is crazy."

He nodded as if expecting my response. "I can show you. I have proof." He pulled his wallet from the back pocket of his jeans. My gaze was intent while he opened it, producing a small, worn photo.

"My dad took this," he said and handed the picture to me.

I hesitated for a second and then snatched it out of his hand. My focus dropped to the small image. In the next instant, my eyes slammed shut. But there was no escaping it—the snow, the damn tombstone, my mom . . . and the boy with the rose, his hand extended toward me.

All the facts were unarguably before me.

"Dad and I were at the cemetery, and he sent me over to you. He stayed out of sight so you and your mom could grieve in private. From what he's told me, she always had a strong distaste for him."

"That's no surprise; that woman doesn't like anyone." I sniffled and finally opened my eyes. They were drawn to the photo. "Why didn't you show me the picture the night at the restaurant?"

"I wasn't sure what to do, Hadlee. You were so adamant I was wrong. And

I was afraid to push too hard; I was afraid I'd lose you forever." Silence hung between us. "I was with you even then, Hadlee. I'll never forget your face. You were so sad, broken, and I wanted to reach inside you and fix everything. I knew—I knew how empty and horrifying it was to lose a parent."

My head hung, tears slipping down my cheeks.

"Did you talk to him?" Kaisen asked so softly that I almost didn't hear him.

"No, I couldn't. I saw his eyes, Kaisen. I saw my own face looking back at me. I look just like him." My palms pushed against my forehead as if pushing away the memory. "This can't be real. It just can't be!" My brain scrambled through memories, so many years old, and then flashed back to earlier today. It all seemed like a dream, one awful nightmare. "And the same nose and hair . . . you'd think my mother had nothing to do with making me. He basically created a spitting image of himself in a girl's body. You knew when you saw me at the grocery store, didn't you?"

He shrugged. "There's always room for error, but yeah. I was pretty sure."

"Shit!" I smacked my hand against the table. "Shit! My goddamn mother!" Boiling rage blasted inside me. "She knew! She knew and buried an empty casket! What the fuck?" I jumped to my feet, sending my mug flying into the other room. My mouth hung open as my eyes darted from Kaisen to the mess on the floor. "I'm sorry. I didn't mean to," I said, scurrying to pick it up.

"Babe, stop. It's okay. I've got it."

"I'll help," I said, reaching across the kitchen counter and grabbing the paper towels. I scooped the shards off the floor.

Kaisen crouched down next to me, mopping up the drink with a napkin. "It's fine. It won't even leave a spot on the carpet," he assured me.

My gaze drifted to his face. "I need to see her. Please take me there?"

His face fell, and then he checked his watch. "Okay."

I leaned in, kissed him, and walked out of the room.

My brain shifted to a steely calm, and my rage turned to ice while I considered what I was going to say to my lying mother.

15

The truck idled as we sat in my mother's driveway. The living room lamp glowed softly against the darkness, and I glimpsed movement inside.

"Big house," Kaisen muttered.

"It's empty inside. She might live there, but I can count the good memories on one hand."

"Is this the same house you lived in when you lost your dad?"

"No." I looked at the window and clenched my jaw.

"I'll stay here and keep the heat running, but take your time."

"Kaisen, go grab a bite to eat or something. It's probably going to be a while."

"But what if it's not? I want to be here if you need me."

There was no arguing with him. And he had a point. Honestly, I wasn't sure if I'd talk to her for two minutes or two hours.

The crisp night air chilled me as I got out and shut the door behind me.

My shoes scuffed against the stone stairs. I approached the front door and struggled to control my breathing. The knocker split the evening's silence; I pounded it hard and fast against her door. Never in my wildest dreams would I have considered that, after having kicked her out of my house weeks ago, I would find myself on her front porch.

The door opened, and my gaze traveled up to the cold, shrewd face of the woman I called Mother.

"What are you doing here?" she asked, her tone sharp.

I pushed my way inside.

She closed the door, wearing an expression of disgust. "If this is more of your drama, Hadlee, then I'm not interested."

"Jedd." I said, my chin jutting in defiance.

The day we'd buried my dad, my mother changed; any warmth or motherly inclination had disappeared that day right along with him. Over the years, she had mastered her poker face. But now, as I glared at her, I saw her face falter for a split second, and I knew she'd been lying to me all these years.

Her heels clicked against the marble floor as she waltzed past me into the living room. "I don't know anyone named Jedd."

"Stop lying," I said, following her, my anger starting to stir.

"Hadlee, you're acting ridiculous, just creating chaos, like usual. I think you should leave." She sat in the armchair, crossed her legs, and gestured to the door.

"All these years," I said quietly. "All these years, Mother, I tried so damn hard to make you love me, to earn a smile from you. Imagine my shock when I found out Dad is alive. Well, at least for a while, I guess. I was so stunned when I was face-to-face with him, only a thick glass separating us, that I never got around to asking him why he was there. Or why my mother turned into a heartless shrew the day she pretended to bury him."

"Don't be a bitch, Hadlee." She smirked. "You have no idea what you're talking about."

"Then tell me. Stop lying for once in your life and tell me what in the hell happened!" I yelled, my manners forgotten.

She stood and sauntered toward the fireplace, the crackling flames and wood the only sound in the room.

"I can't talk about this," she said. "You need to leave this alone." She turned to face me and warned, "Do not dig up the past."

My jaw tensed. "Your past is my *present,* and I need to understand."

She whirled away from me, her back rigid, shutting me out. Her silence snapped the last shred of decency I felt toward her.

"Do you know what's really so fucked up? The simple fact that I love you as much as I hate you. When you buried him that day, you took away my choice," I said, my voice growing cold as I continued. "You and Dad took it away and built this world of secrets that ripped us apart. But now? Now I'm grown. And I'm taking it back. I'm taking my choice back, and I choose to see him!" I shouted.

"You think you know everything?" She turned and strode toward me. "You see a man who looks like you, and you think you've got all the answers?" she asked.

"No!" I cried. "But you're not talking to me. You're not leaving me any other option except to see him again, to figure out what you've been keeping from me."

Sadness flickered across her face. "Do you know why he's there? You do realize what death row means?" she asked, her tone so typically condescending.

"Of course I know what it means. Something went horribly wrong."

"You were too young to understand, and the only way I could protect us was to bury him along with the awful truth. No one would have talked to us, Hadlee. You could have forgotten sleepovers, friends, and invitations to dinner. Everything you had growing up would have been gone." She sighed heavily, her shoulders sagging under the weight of her secret. "I'll tell you, but don't you ever speak his name in front of me again."

I nodded, waiting, my pulse quickening with each second.

"He raped and murdered an eleven-year-old girl," she said. She paused, waiting for the horror to register on my face, and when it did, a sneer slowly crept over hers.

It took everything inside me not to slap her.

"I lied to protect us, you ungrateful girl."

"If you wanted to protect me, then why did you treat me the way you did? Why did you ignore me for years? You never even hugged me again after . . ."—I took a breath, willed steel into my voice—"after he was gone."

She tilted her head to the side, studying me as if I were a mere curiosity. "Of course I didn't! You look just like him. Every day was a constant reminder of his betrayal. And how could I know whether you were just like him? Was there evil within you? Would you become a murderer, too?"

She folded her arms across her chest. "If you'd turned out like me, I would have considered it a blessing."

Her words punched me swift and hard in the gut. My own mother thought I was bad? That I was just like him? That I was capable of harming another human being? Agony ripped through me, shredding me to ribbons with each second that passed.

"I'm not like you," I spat, my fingernails digging into the palms of my hands. "I don't treat people like shit, walk on them for personal gain, or build a company based on lies. I hope you rot in hell along with my father," I hissed, spinning on my heels and marching out the door.

Nothing in life was really what it'd seemed. I'd lived a lie for years, my choices taken from me, the truth hidden, and my heart shattered by the two people who were supposed to have protected it. Their decisions had left me empty and alone, and I couldn't seem to regain my footing.

I'd studied enough psychology to understand how the brain protected us when life's events were too difficult to deal with. My brain needed alcohol in order to shut the fuck down.

Kaisen reached his hand out to me when I hopped in the truck, but at the expression on my face, he placed both hands on the steering wheel. He understood. I wasn't interested in talking. He didn't press. A thick silence hung between us while he drove toward my place. A part of me wanted to stay with him, make love to him, and shudder from the feel of his hot mouth against my skin. I wanted to allow everything else to slip away as we danced our way into ecstasy. But I couldn't give him my heart tonight; that wouldn't have been fair to him.

He pulled up in front of my house, and I stared at the structure, hardly recognizing my life anymore. It seemed like days had passed since he'd picked me up and taken me to Idaho, but it'd been less than twenty-four hours.

Kaisen shifted into park.

"Are you going to be okay?" he asked quietly.

My attention turned toward him as I searched his face, finding nothing but love and compassion. "I don't know," I said. "But thank you for everything you've done. I just need time to process. Some time alone."

His face fell, but he nodded and didn't push me. I now wondered if he'd known, in some small way, that once I looked Jedd in the face, the old Hadlee would be gone forever. Nothing would be the same again.

Maybe I just needed some sleep. Maybe things would look better in the morning.

Maybe.

"I love you," he said, his voice trembling.

A sad smile pulled at the corner of my mouth. "I'll call you soon." My heart sank to hear my own words. Tonight, I couldn't give him what he needed. I couldn't tell him I loved him. I didn't even know what love meant anymore.

Kaisen ran his hand through his hair, worry lining his forehead. I couldn't concern myself with his worry, though—I had nothing left. I scooped my backpack from the floor, hopped out of his truck, and walked into the house.

Listening to the rumble of his engine easing down the street, I leaned against the door, gasping for air. How in the world could someone suffocate when the room was full of oxygen?

"Hadlee?" Syd's voice floated around the corner. "Is that you?"

"Hey," I said, slipping off my boots and leaving them next to the door.

"What happened? Are you okay? I was super worried when Kaisen called and said you were at his place asleep. I wasn't concerned that you were sleeping, of course. But his tone said so much more."

I followed her into the kitchen and went straight for the Jim Beam. Syd's brow rose when I mixed it with soda, but she didn't say anything.

"If Kara has the night off, maybe she should be here, too," I said after downing half the glass. "That way I can tell you both at once."

Syd grabbed her phone. Within seconds, it vibrated with a response. "She's on her way."

I sank onto the barstool and laid my head against the cold laminate countertop while I waited for her to arrive. A few minutes later, the door flew open.

"I'm here," Kara said, tossing her purse on the table. "Hugs," she said to Syd and then me. "Okay, someone tell me what the hell is going on."

I sipped my drink and stumbled around in my head for the right words, but there were none.

"My dad's alive."

Tension filled the room as they waited for me to continue.

"On death row."

"Well, fuck me runnin' sideways," Syd expelled on a breath.

I glanced at them. "My mom knew the coffin that was lowered into the ground and covered with dirt was empty. All this time, he's been alive."

My head throbbed with the weight of the words.

"Why is he on death row?" Kara asked, reaching for the Jim Beam. She had the right idea; this entire ball of shit needed to be dealt with through alcohol.

I paused while she poured herself a shot and tilted the glass until it was empty.

Then I topped off my own glass, took a giant swig. "He raped and murdered an eleven-year-old girl," I said, choking on the foul words. It was the first time I'd spoken those words aloud, and my stomach was churning, fighting against the truth. "My father is a monster, and he deserves to die," I stammered, gazing down into my glass.

"Oh, Hadlee. I'm sorry," Syd said as she lowered herself into the seat next to me. "I won't even pretend I know what you're going through right now."

"Hell, I don't even know what I'm going through right now. I don't know how to begin digesting this information. And when I was there, when I sat on the other side of the glass, I couldn't look at him. It was like a part of me knew it was him. I don't know how long I sat there before I put the phone against my ear. He finally asked me to look at him so he could know. Then, I did. I . . . I couldn't believe it—I look just like him. I look just like a murderer," I whispered.

Kara pursed her lips together. "Just because you look like him doesn't mean you *are* him," she observed matter-of-factly.

My head snapped up, and I really looked at her for the first time since she'd arrived.

"I'm serious, Hadlee. Don't think there's something wrong with you. You're. Not. Him."

"How do you know?" I asked, finally considering the question I'd been trying to avoid.

Syd barked out a laugh. "Are you serious? Do I need to list the million and one ways you're nothing like a murderer? It's going to be a long night, then."

"I am, though. I am serious."

"And so are we," Syd said, holding my gaze. "You do not have the makings of a rapist and murderer. If you did, you would have left me on the floor to die on Christmas Eve."

I winced at the memory. "No way could I have done that. To anyone."

"And that's the point," Kara said, gesturing with her empty glass for emphasis. "You don't lead some mysterious life, Hadlee. You're in classes, working, or with one of us the majority of the time. You just can't go down that road."

Syd poured us more alcohol as I struggled to sift through their argument.

I took a swallow and grimaced. "Here's the kicker," I said. "I never told either of you this, but the day we buried my dad, a boy brought me a rose to put on the grave. He was a few years older than I was and wore a baseball hat. It—I can't believe I'm saying this—it was Kaisen."

"What?" Kara asked, sloshing her drink across the countertop. "Shit." She hopped off her chair and grabbed the paper towels.

"No worries, we have plenty more," Syd sang, holding up the bottle to show that it was still two-thirds full.

Kara finished cleaning up the countertop, poured another shot, and settled back in.

I continued. "He was there because our dads knew each other."

"Holy hell. Do they still?" Syd asked.

"Yeah, they must." I rubbed my aching forehead, and the girls stared at me, waiting for details. "When Kaisen first told me about Jedd, he mentioned our dads were best friends growing up." I hesitated as I thought back to our conversation. "As for now, I know his dad visits mine, and he said something about an attorney and a detective. And that's all I know about it."

"Had, did you ever meet Kaisen's dad? I mean, Kaisen is a great guy, and they are close, from what Michael has said. I just can't imagine his dad being good friends with a man who did those awful things. We still might not have the full story, but someone does, and that person is within your reach," Kara said.

"Why would I even want to know? The facts are right in front of me. My father is alive and in a maximum security prison for a horrific crime."

"Well, your mom certainly won't be of any help. She's lied to you for this long, and her perception will certainly be different from someone else's. Had, can you imagine being married to the love of your life, being happy, and then, all of a sudden, having him sent to prison? Do you know how horrible that would be?" Syd asked.

"Are you taking up for my mother?" I asked, rearing back in disapproval.

"No, I'm just realizing it wasn't easy for her either. She had to make hard choices to protect you, and those choices included lying to her own daughter."

"She said she treated me that way because I was a constant reminder of him. She wondered if I'd turn out evil just like him." She threw up her hands in surrender. "I can't help who I look like!"

"Of course not," Kara chimed in.

"Holy hell," I said, sitting up straight. "My name."

"What about it?" Syd asked, her face clouding in confusion.

"When Kaisen was talking to me, he mentioned that Jedd thought Mom had changed my name to protect me. That was why he needed help finding me. Fuck. I don't even know what my real name is," I said, gasping.

We all stared at each other as we processed this new piece of information.

"Hadlee, call Kaisen and see if you can talk to his dad. I think your chances of gaining honest answers are better with him than with anyone else." Kara nodded toward my phone.

It was after midnight, but I texted Kaisen anyway.

Hey.

My phone buzzed within seconds.

Hey. I was just thinking about you.

I'm sorry I'm such a mess right now.

You have nothing to apologize for. I just want to help.

You can, actually. I glanced up at the girls before I continued typing. *Do you think I can meet your dad and ask him some questions?*

My phone remained silent for a few minutes.

"What did he say?" Kara asked.

"Still waiting for a response," I replied, frowning.

How about dinner with him tomorrow at six?

I mentally flipped through my schedule to see if I was working or not.

I'm off tomorrow night again, so that works.

Great. I'll pick you up at five thirty.

Thank you.

Love you. Get some sleep, and I'll see you tomorrow.

You too. Night.

For the second time, I felt like an ass for not telling Kaisen I loved him, too. A part of me realized he was hanging on the edge, waiting for me to show up again in our relationship. My intention wasn't to hurt him, but I was a mess right now; I needed to stay focused on finding the truth. And my moods and feelings were ricocheting in every direction possible. I was spinning from an emotional storm right now; I couldn't add anything else to it.

"Tomorrow," I told Syd and Kara.

"Good! Maybe someone will finally give you some answers," Syd said.

I cringed as I realized my head had been so far up my ass I hadn't asked Syd how she was feeling. I did so right away.

"I'm okay, which is surprising," Syd told me. "I'm certainly in no hurry to get pregnant again, but the thought lingers in the back of my mind. I wonder, if it had been a boy or a girl, who it might have looked like. Would the baby have had Marcus's red hair or my blue eyes? But, we're young, and once we graduate and have stable careers, we want to try again."

"Wow! That's a shitload of planning," Kara remarked.

She shrugged. "Even though I only knew about the baby for a few weeks, something changed inside me. I actually started really considering Marcus long-term, past college, and thinking about what kind of parent he would be. I feel like me but not. It's hard to explain. It's like, somewhere inside me, I know I'm missing something—someone."

"I'm just glad you're okay," I said. "I'm not sure how I'd sleep without you snoring every night."

"You do realize we won't share a room forever, though, right?" Syd asked, giggling.

"It is going to be so weird after we graduate," Kara said, tilting her head. "I have no idea what will happen between Michael and me."

"What do you mean?" I asked.

"It's a little while away. I mean, look at all of us and how much our lives have changed in just the last month."

"Hell, mine turned upside down in twenty-four hours," I said, shaking my head.

"Yeah, so how do you plan for a future?"

"Make the plans, prepare for the worst, and hope for the best." Syd tilted her chin up and placed her hands on her hips.

I grinned at her. "No shit."

16

The morning didn't greet me with open arms. I smacked my alarm clock, which was rudely blaring and announcing the arrival of 7:15 a.m. Kara groaned while she rubbed the sleep from her eyes and peered at me.

"Thanks for letting me crash," she said, "but this really sucks." She patted her hair down.

"Yeah. Not sure who had the bright idea of drinking when we had to get up so early. But, on the other hand, I haven't been sleeping much, so maybe it was a good thing? Except for the monstrous taste in my mouth. Yuck," I said, sticking my tongue out, hopping out of bed, and running toward the bathroom to brush my teeth.

Once I returned to the bedroom, my mouth now fresh and clean, I saw that Syd had already provided us with cups of coffee.

"Grab up, ladies," she said. "I have an announcement." She patiently waited for us to raise our mugs, then stated, "I think we should find our own place together."

"Really?" Kara asked.

"Sure, why not?" she said. "We all work. Well, my daddy works, but he would much rather I live with a few other girls than with three guys he doesn't really know. I mean, Lionel is fine, but we should really consider it. There's a super-cute three-bedroom apartment that's going to be available next month. Daddy already said he would cover the deposits for us."

"I think it's a great idea," I responded. "Kara?"

"Hell yeah, but more importantly, will he adopt me?" Kara asked.

"Right?" I sipped my steaming cup of java, then started pulling out clothes for the day. "Syd, can I catch a ride with you this morning?"

"Yup."

"And don't forget I have dinner scheduled with Kaisen and his dad tonight." I paused, two potential sweaters in my hands, as they stared at me.

"You're meeting the boyfriend's father. You do realize that, right?" Kara asked.

My heart suddenly burst into overdrive. "Shit, no. I didn't think of it like that. I was just . . . shit." I threw both sweaters on the floor.

"Kara," Syd, said with a hint of warning in her voice. "You're going to scare the baby deer off."

My eyes narrowed, and I tossed a dirty sock at her. "You're lucky it's not dirty underwear," I threatened, smirking.

"That's some nasty shit right there," Kara said, giggling. "But, ya know, Syd's right. Forget I said anything. Go find out about Jedd. Stay focused and just remember Kaisen's father was Jedd's friend before he was your boyfriend's dad."

"Damn. That's a lot to wrap my addled brain around this early in the morning," I said, frowning.

"Well, either way, I had a blast, and I'm off to class. Keep me posted," Kara said, hugging us goodbye.

Oddly enough, my day whizzed by as I buried myself in my classes again. It was a welcome change from the past month.

The doorbell rang at five thirty sharp, and a smile pulled at the corner of my mouth. I loved it when a guy was prompt.

I hurried down the hall, gathered my coat, and slipped out the front door. He was waiting on the porch with his back to me. My gaze dropped to his ass, and I chewed my lip.

"Hey," he said, turning toward me and placing a kiss on the top of my head.

"Hi." My gaze flickered up to his face and then rested on his mouth. I pushed up on my tiptoes and kissed him. "I miss you," I said quietly.

"Thank you. I know you're going through a lot, but I wasn't quite sure where I stood at the moment."

"Next to me." I took his hand.

My brain and heart had warred all night long, and even though I'd told myself I should keep my walls up with him, he had already gotten behind them. I was just lying to myself. Syd and Kara had reminded me of that as well. Their faces lit up when they talked about the guys even though they'd had their challenges. It's what I wanted, too. With Kaisen.

"Ready?" he asked, pulling me close, his fingers stroking my cheek.

I nodded.

"Dad's really excited about meeting you."

In a matter of minutes, Martha was roaring to life, and we were on our way. My nerves hummed. I'd had my share of surprises, and I wasn't sure I was up for any more, but maybe this would be different.

Fifteen minutes later, Kaisen pulled off Highway 395 and then turned onto Calamity Lane.

"His place is small, but it's good for him; it's just big enough for company."

He pulled into the driveway and turned off the truck lights before I had a chance to see the house and property.

"He has a few acres, not as many as I do, but he doesn't want to have to maintain the land, so it works out."

I didn't respond, too anxious to even try to form an answer.

The walkway had been cleared, and salt crystals crunched beneath my boots. Kaisen held my hand, knocked on the door, opened it up, and ushered me in ahead of him.

"Hey, we're here," he hollered.

"Come in!" A man strolled out of the kitchen and wiped his hands off with a dish towel.

"Hi, son," he said, hugging Kaisen and patting him on the back.

"Dad, this is Hadlee. Hadlee, my dad."

"Hi, Mr. Sinclair," I said, extending my hand.

"Please, call me Cameron."

A warm smile crossed his face as he took my hand in his and covered it with his other one. He stood a few inches taller than Kaisen but had a similar build. Strokes of gray ran through his light-brown hair, and his smile reached his eyes. I didn't see a great resemblance; maybe Kaisen took after his mother instead.

"Welcome. It's so nice to meet you. Kaisen was right—you look just like Jedd. Wow. You gave him quite a start when you visited the other day."

"Um, maybe give her a minute before we dive right in?" Kaisen asked, nudging his father.

"Oh, sure. Sorry. Don't mind me. I can't tell you how excited I am to meet his kid all grown up, though."

"Dad," Kaisen warned again. "You do want her to stay, don't you?"

"Yes, yes, of course. Are you hungry?" he asked, meandering back into the kitchen. "I bought a brisket from Gary's farm. Hadlee, it's the best grass-fed beef you'll ever taste. It melts in your mouth."

"It sounds wonderful. Thank you."

Kaisen led me into the kitchen, and we sat down at the dining table while Cameron continued to cook. He made the salad, checked the meat, and moved around the kitchen as though he had been born there.

"I see where you get it," I said, smiling at Kaisen.

He leaned on his elbows. "Get what?"

My eyes cut back to his father, and then I leaned over and kissed him quickly. "Your kitchen moves."

Kaisen chuckled. "He taught me everything I know."

"Oh, so we're dining with the master?" I asked, trying to keep the mood light.

"Here we go," Cameron said, placing the food down in front of us. "Kaisen, can you grab the silverware? I'll get the plates."

Kaisen hopped up and assisted him. They were poetry in motion, perfect complements. Their years of experience working together were taking center stage. Some struggles split families apart, but the loss of Kaisen's mom had molded their relationship into something strong, unbreakable.

Something suddenly pulled at me, something I'd never experienced before—a feeling of belonging. Cameron was the link to my missing past, and his son owned my heart.

Minutes later, we began to eat.

Cameron chatted about the construction business that would belong to Kaisen soon and how he would continue to work with him, leading the crews.

We finished dinner, and Cameron surprised us with strawberry cheesecake.

"I'm pretty sure I just gained a few pounds," I said, smiling and rubbing my belly.

Kaisen smiled. This was nice; it felt right. But my mood shifted after Cameron finished the dishes and returned to us, carrying a photo album.

"I'm really sorry you had to meet Jedd like that, Hadlee. I can't imagine what a horrible shock this has all been."

I nodded, unsure how I should respond.

"I met your dad in junior high," he proceeded. "We've been friends ever since. In fact, I saw you at the hospital after you were born. You were so tiny. He was excited to have a daughter. He chose your name, but I guess your mother changed it after everything happened."

"You know my real name?" I asked, leaning forward in anticipation.

"Jayden Amanda Mackenzie."

My mouth hung open slightly, and then I peeked at Kaisen.

"Your dad had a sense of humor back then; he wanted your initials to spell a word," Cameron explained. "Your mom, on the other hand, wasn't impressed. That's the name you were born with, though."

"Jayden? I don't think *Jayden* fits. Do you, Kaisen?" I asked, frowning.

"I think you're probably always going to be Hadlee to me."

I nodded as he winked at me.

Cameron flipped open the photo album and pulled out a picture.

"This is us before you were born. He'd wanted this car for a long time and loved it, especially that shade of blue." Cameron chuckled. "Jedd ended up with quite a few speeding tickets, though." He grinned and handed me the photo.

"A 280ZX?"

"Yup."

My skin hummed as an eeriness crept over me. I stared at my dad's picture, a piece of him from before I entered his life—him and Cameron, grinning like idiots next to the sports car. My stomach dropped. It should have been him sharing these memories with me, not Cameron.

"Here's another one. This was his college graduation photo. You look just like him."

I glanced up at Cameron as I took the picture.

"What was he like? I don't have a lot of memories of him other than watching cartoons, having tickle fests, and being carried to bed when he was home."

"Smart, almost too smart for his own good. He challenged every teacher he ever had," Cameron said, laughing. "It got him sent to the high school principal's office on a regular basis, too. But that's where he met your mom. She helped out in the office. She made copies, filed, stuff like that. They fell in love, fast and hard. There was no separating them. After college, they got married and bought the house you probably remember. Your dad's job had him traveling, and even though your mom liked the money, she got lonely. It wore on her. She said she felt like a single parent most of the time. They agreed he'd keep the job until you started kindergarten, and then he'd find something else, but it never happened. She liked to shop too much. As you got older, spending and some other things started putting a strain on the marriage."

He leaned back, tension around his eyes. "You were eight when things went haywire."

My hands slid into my lap, my fingers wringing together while I stared at the floor. This is where it wasn't going to be pretty. Was I ready? Was I finally about to hear the truth?

"One evening, he was home for the week, and he had tucked you into bed. He left the house afterward, and we went out to shoot pool and have some beers across the state line in Idaho. We'd been to this same bar a hundred times before. It was harmless fun, two married men taking a break from family life. No big deal." Cameron paused, his brows pinching together. "Eleven o' clock rolled around, and we called it a night. I'd driven, and as we walked around to the back alley where I'd parked, we heard a loud commotion. We took off around the corner to see what had happened, but we were too late." He shook his head as his gaze fell to the floor. He cleared his throat and then looked back up at me. "I've regretted this next part my entire life, but we scrambled backward and ran as fast as we could to the car. Those images of that little girl . . . her dress was bunched up over her waist, and blood from the back of her head was all over the ground. A little brown teddy bear lay next to her." His voice caught in his throat. "By the time we got in and took off, we realized we needed to go to the police station. We reported it, but she didn't make it. If I'd been thinking straight, we would have gone back in the bar and called 911 from there."

"Cameron, you can't blame yourself. I don't know anyone who wouldn't have panicked."

"Maybe, but she might have lived if I'd kept my thoughts straight."

"Maybe she wouldn't have, though. And maybe it would have been worse if she had, with those memories haunting her for the rest of her life. She would have relived the trauma over and over," I said, tears brimming in my eyes. "I wouldn't have wanted that," I said softly.

Kaisen reached over and took my hand.

A soft, sad smile spread across Cameron's face. "I guess it's a possibility I've never considered before.

"Unfortunately, we were in the wrong place at the wrong time. When the police investigated the crime, an eyewitness came forward and described your dad. And I don't mean a rough sketch; they provided an in-depth description. What he was wearing, the color of his shirt, his hair color and style . . ." he said, his voice trailing off. "He didn't have a chance. When I tried to explain to the police why we had been there, they weren't interested. They just wanted to make an arrest, and because of the witness, it held up, and your father was sentenced to death. Hadlee, he's innocent. He never hurt anyone. I was there with him all night. Some cop just had a burr up his ass and refused to listen."

I leaned toward him, afraid to hope. "So, you're telling me he was with you all night and never hurt anyone? He never raped or murdered an eleven-year-old girl?"

My chest tightened as I held his gaze, searching for any sign that he was covering for Jedd or trying to spare me the agony.

"That's precisely what I'm telling you. We've been fighting it for years, but we ran out of funds. We just got an attorney to take his case on pro bono. He said he was going to call for DNA tests."

"Oh my God. DNA testing wasn't around when all this happened?"

"It was, but it wasn't as inclusive as it is today. But, Hadlee, he was sentenced without any DNA tests. This attorney wants them done. And, if it comes out that the results do not match your dad's DNA, it will prove he's not guilty."

My head pounded while I tried to wrap my brain around this shocking new information.

"You're sure he never left your side?" I asked, fear lacing cold fingers around my spine.

Cameron's face fell. "He did, Hadlee. I'm not going to lie to you. He went to the bathroom and then to my car to search for his cell phone. It was dark and difficult to see between the seats and underneath them, so it took him a bit. He was gone long enough to raise suspicion."

"So, there's still a chance that he did it?" I asked, my voice lowering an octave. I turned my head away, unable to look at him, my hopes plummeting. Cameron had offered a lifeline, and seconds later, a tidal wave of contradiction had torn it away—crushing me beneath it.

"Listen to me. We grew up together. I knew him then, and I know him now. No way in hell was he capable of such a heinous crime. I'd bet my life on it."

His eyes never wavered from mine. "Take some time to think about it, okay? It's a lot to process. I've got a meeting with the attorney tomorrow, so if you have any questions or want an update on the case, I'd be happy to get information for you."

"Okay. Thank you for sharing all of this with me. I have to admit my head is spinning faster than I can sort anything out."

"I understand." He sighed, leaning back in his seat.

I hesitated for a second. "Why do they call him Jedd?" I asked quietly. "His name is Christopher."

"Jedidiah is his middle name."

My chest ached as I grabbed onto another piece of my past I hadn't known before. Was what Cameron told me true? Was my dad innocent in all this? My head swam while I tried to sort things out.

A beat of silence filled the room.

"Can I tell Jedd I talked with you?" he asked gently.

"Cameron, thank you for your time and the amazing food. But, for now, I think I'm going to ask you not tell anyone about our conversation. I just need some time to process everything."

"Of course. I completely understand. And, Hadlee, you're welcome here anytime, as Jedd's daughter and my son's girlfriend. I know this has been a strange situation for you."

"I appreciate it," I said, smiling.

Minutes later, we took our leave and got into the pickup. I shivered as my butt hit the cold leather seat.

"How are you doing?" Kaisen asked.

I turned toward him.

"Can I stay with you tonight? I have classes in the morning, and I know it's a lot to ask you to take me back early—"

"Hadlee, stop. I'll drive you anywhere you need to be and get up at four in the morning if I have to. Yes, please, stay with me tonight."

"Thanks," I said. My cheeks warmed as I realized I'd just invited myself over, but he didn't seem to mind, and I needed to be somewhere where I didn't have to answer a million questions.

I texted Syd where I'd be while he headed toward his house.

My feet never hit the floor. Kaisen lifted me out of the truck and carried me into his house and straight to his bedroom before placing me on his bed. We removed our coats and lay on the plush comforter, facing each other.

"I love you," he said, kissing the back of my hand.

"Are you sure? Something has been bothering me, but I couldn't put my finger on it." I hesitated. "Are you sure you're not in the middle of some fantasy about saving the daughter whose father is on death row?"

"Had, I've never looked at you that way. Yeah, I knew about your past. I saw a picture of you when you were younger, and I had the photo from the day in the cemetery, but you'll never be 'that girl.' You don't need to be saved. And I've said it before, but I'll say it again now—I did *not* write to your dad after I fell in love with you. I couldn't do it without your permission. It felt dishonest, and I was already regretting my decision to say yes to begin with."

"Where's the first place that you saw me? I mean, other than at his fake grave?"

"The grill. The guys and I went in there one night to grab some beers, and there you were. I knew it was you because Dad had mentioned you looked just like Jedd. I didn't need anyone to tell me you were his daughter."

"I wonder how much like him I really am." My wistful thoughts suddenly darkened. "Kaisen, what if he did do it? He left for a few minutes. What if the little girl was lost or—"

"She belonged to one of the chefs who worked in the kitchen. She would go outside to play whenever he was busy."

My eyes widened with this new information. "So, he really could have done it?" I bolted upright. "Kaisen, all I have is your dad's perception of what happened. I mean, look at Ted Bundy. The ladies loved him, and he functioned normally in society for years. The BTK killer worked at a security company and murdered people for twenty years!" My tone grew more and more pinched with each syllable.

"I understand why you're scared, but after hearing everything and talking to him, I believe him."

"You do?"

He nodded. "My father is a good man, and it devastated him when your dad was taken away. Then he lost my mom. He's suffered a lot of loss, but somehow, he found a way to keep his chin up. And when he couldn't,

I helped him through it. There are several things he's taught me, and one is that the truth is in front of you—as long as you choose to see it."

"And he taught you the three things about women," I reminded him, a small smile pulling at the corner of my mouth.

"Yeah. He's a smart man. If he thinks Jedd is innocent, then I'm going to take his opinion into consideration. But, after meeting him myself, looking him in the face, I believe him, too. I don't think he belongs there."

I nodded. "Okay. I just need some time to think through everything. But in the meantime," I said, pushing him on his back and straddling him, "I've missed you." I whispered in his ear, "It seems like nothing is for keeps in this world. So, can I keep you here with me—just for tonight?"

A growl erupted from his chest as he pulled my mouth down to his. His desire was evident as our mouths parted and he slid his hands underneath my shirt, grazing my bare skin.

I sat up, and he slid my shirt off. The cold air stirred goose bumps across my skin as he unhooked my pink bra and slid the straps down slowly. His eyes never left me as my breasts were exposed, my nipples hardening in anticipation of his touch.

My breath caught while he cupped my breasts; I leaned into his strong hands, rocking against him.

Kaisen opened the button on my jeans, unzipped them, and slid his middle finger inside. I leaned back, allowing him access, and he gently stroked me through the sheer material of my panties. A soft moan escaped me while he teased my sensitive skin.

"You missed me?" he asked, his voice low and husky.

"More than you could ever know," I moaned.

"Stand up."

He helped me to stand on the mattress. In one swift movement, he had my jeans and panties around my ankles and his mouth on my core.

His tongue massaged and caressed me, making my knees threaten to buckle. I gasped, grabbing his hair for balance. His fingers dug into my ass cheeks; in response, my pulse fluttered, and heat curled down my spine.

"Kaisen," I whimpered. "I can't stand any longer."

His chuckle vibrated through me, and then he pulled me down onto his lap and rolled me over on the bed. When he slipped off his shirt, my eyes devoured his pecs and abs.

"Why are you still wearing these?" I asked, slipping my fingers beneath the waistband of his jeans. "They're in my way." I flipped open the button and wrestled him free from them. My hand wrapped around him and gently stroked him. He balanced above me, the muscles in his arms and chest tightening.

"I've missed you," he said, trailing kisses down my neck as he settled down on top of me.

As soon as I released him, I felt his hardness against my leg, throbbing and at full attention. "Now," I said, kissing him.

He grabbed a condom from the drawer of his nightstand and rolled it on. The absence of his body heat sent a chill down me. My hips tilted up and off the bed as he lowered himself again. I guided him inside me and lay very still.

Uncertainty clouded his gaze. "You okay?"

"Yeah," I said. "I just wanted to feel you inside me." My fingernails raked down his back, and I thrust upward. A growl escaped him while he lifted my legs and placed them on his shoulders. He pulled out agonizingly slowly and then buried himself inside me, over and over, until I was pleading for him to move faster. I arched off his bed as he consumed every part of me—my body, mind, and heart.

Our breaths came in short bursts, our mouths and hands devouring each other, our bodies melting together. He released my legs, adjusted me, and moved his hips in a circular motion.

"Holy hell," I squeaked, his pace quickening.

"I want to watch you," he said, his voice husky. "Come for me."

The more his hips moved, the more he reached parts of me I never knew existed. And the sweet, familiar, warm sensation began to build inside me.

"Nothing feels as good as when you're soaking wet and wrapped tight around me," he murmured.

He thrust inside me one final time, and I exploded. My core tightened around him while he released with me.

He collapsed on me, our bodies sweaty and limp.

"Baby," he said. "Don't ever leave me again. Please."

Our gazes locked. I stared into those eyes, the same eyes I had seen at the cemetery. He'd left his mark on me then; maybe it was destiny that we'd made our way back to each other, maybe not. Regardless, I had fallen for him harder than I thought possible.

"I won't," I vowed, kissing him.

We lay there, still connected, as our heartbeats kept rhythm and my thoughts finally relaxed.

"I could stay like this with you forever," I said.

"You don't have to go. You can stay every night."

A sad smile eased across my face. "I do have to go, but leave the door open for me, and I promise I'll be back."

17

nyone who didn't like shower sex first thing in the morning needed their head examined. I waltzed out of Kaisen's house and to the truck with a massive smile on my face. Maybe the rest of my life was screwed up, but at least my relationship with him wasn't. He was the one thing I was sure about, and when he kissed me, nothing else seemed to matter.

My classes passed without incident that day. To be honest, I was in a bit of a daze, considering the thoughts that were spinning in my mind. I needed to get my act together and focus. I vowed to do better tomorrow. No matter what my dad had done and no matter how amazing Kaisen was, I needed to get my degree as soon as possible.

Five o'clock rolled around, and I waved at Kara as I stepped out of the freezing late-January weather and into the grill.

I stepped into the break room, Kara was already waiting for me. I smiled, closing the door behind me. Kara tapped the seat next to her impatiently.

"That's a good sign," she said as I took a seat. "Your smile, I mean."

"We'll see. I am super curious to get your and Syd's thoughts on all this. I've tried to think it through, but how do you even begin to find the end of the string to pull in order to unravel this big ball of mess?"

"I'm listening," she said, checking the clock. "But we have, like, four minutes, so talk fast."

"Kaisen's father is really nice. He cooked—"

"Yup, that's all great, but we have to get straight to the stuff about Jedd; you can fill me in on the niceties later. The clock's a tickin'." She tapped her wrist for emphasis.

"Okay. He thinks my dad's innocent."

"That's great news! But why?" Kara asked, leaning toward me. "Um, no offense."

I waved off that last remark. "He was with my dad the night the girl was raped and murdered," I said, my voice hovering above a whisper.

Kara's face flashed with sadness.

"He and Jedd were having a guys' night out, and then everything turned to shit."

Kara never took her eyes off me as I updated her about the events that had happened in the alley and my own concern since Jedd had left Cameron's side for a bit during the evening.

"I'll bet the time unaccounted for was what clinched the jury's decision—he used the bathroom, and the door to the alley was right there."

"I know. That's what has me hung up, too. Kaisen said he believes him, but—"

"'But' is right," Kara said, pausing. "What are you going to do? Are you considering seeing him again? Acting like it never happened? Having copious amounts of sex?"

There was nothing better than a moment of comedy relief to break the tension of a shitty situation.

"Yes to the sex," I said, grinning mischievously. "But I'm not sure about Jedd. I want to believe he was and is incapable of doing something so horrible, but . . . Kara, what if he's not? What if he really belongs there?"

"If I were in your shoes, which I'm not, because they're too small, I'd want to see him and find out what I thought for myself."

"You would?"

"Hell yeah. I mean, he's literally back from the dead, and you have an opportunity to talk to him and say anything you want to. Cuss him out, tell him you hate him, you love him, you think he's a bastard, or that you want to know more about him. No matter what, he's your father. Take this time with him and find out who he is for yourself. Kaisen, his dad, your mom—they can say whatever they want to, but you're the only one who can decide for you."

Her words sank into my heart. She was right. And no matter how fucked up it would be to visit the prison again, I realized I'd never forgive myself if I didn't try.

"I'll text Kaisen and see if he'll take me back." My throat tightened as the words left my mouth.

"Good. I've gotta get to my customers." She stood up and stretched. "But, Had, don't keep me waiting so long again. That was torture," she said. "I was worried."

"Sorry. It's been so much to take in. At times, I'm so numb I think I'm living in someone else's nightmare." I sighed, standing up and hugging her.

We exited the break room, and I began my shift. Although I tried to avoid it, my mind continually returned to my conversation with Cameron. The question wasn't whether I could trust his sincerity—of course I could; he was Kaisen's dad. But could I trust his judgment concerning Jedd? Maybe Kara was right, though. I'd never gain any peace unless I found out for myself.

The evening progressed slowly, and my customers were happy, so I slipped behind the bar to grab my phone and text Kaisen during a lull. His name flashed across my screen with earlier messages. Unable to hide my smile, I hurried out of sight and scrolled through them.

I wanted you to read this message when you took your break tonight. I love you, and I miss you. I'm watching the seconds tick by until you're in my arms again.

Damn it. How could I not love this guy?

I love you, too, I texted. *And I have a small favor to ask.*

My back leaned against the wall as I stared at my phone and waited for the dots to flicker across the bottom of our messages.

I peeked around the corner to check on my tables and then returned to my screen.

Yeah? You want to take my clothes off and ravage my body tonight?

LOL. Yes, that, too. My chest tightened. Was I doing the right thing? Would he even support my choice after my meltdown the last time?

But . . . can you take me to see Jedd again? I'd ask the girls, but I don't want them anywhere near the prison.

Silence. Had he changed his mind? Did he no longer want to help me? It'd taken everything I had to even ask for his help. Where had he gone? I peered around the corner again, and a customer raised her hand to gain my attention. Kaisen would have to wait. I placed my phone behind the bar and returned to my job.

Maybe the snow had thawed and people had decided to get out of their houses, because all of a sudden, we were busy. Although it was good for my checking account, I really wanted to look at my phone again. Anxiety prickled my skin as I imagined another visit to the prison. I wasn't sure I could do it without Kaisen.

I welcomed my new customers and hustled for the next few hours. People were in good moods, which also helped my tips. If Kaisen would take me back to Idaho, I wanted to help pay for gas and food. I inwardly groaned and outwardly smiled while I took more orders, served more alcohol, and welcomed more guests. My mind drifted toward my phone again as I loaded up the dirty dishes and half-full beer glasses.

"I just gave you another two-top!" I heard right behind me.

Startled, I jerked my tray up, and beer spilled down the front of my cream-colored shirt and black pants. The cold liquid soaked through to my skin, instantly chilling me.

"Oh, Hadlee, I'm so sorry!" Jamie squealed. Every person in the grill turned toward us. My cheeks flamed as my nipples hardened, showing through my bra and top.

"I'll move them," she said, the expression on her face apologetic.

"I need to clean up," I muttered. I held my tray in front of me while I passed the customers on the way to the bathroom.

Thank goodness the restroom was empty. It was bad enough I'd had to walk through a busy restaurant to get there.

I groaned. Instead of removing the large brown beer stain from my chest, the paper towels only managed to leave little brown tufts on my top. I growled in frustration. Maybe Richard had a spare top I could borrow.

The bathroom door squeaked as I opened it and stepped out, turning left down the hall.

"Your tits look hot, all wet like that," someone said behind me.

My nostrils flared as I turned, my hand raised, ready to smack the shit out of someone.

"Kaisen? What are you doing here?" I playfully wrapped my hands around his neck while he lifted me up off the ground and hugged me.

"I just needed a quick hug and kiss," he said, setting me down and brushing his lips against mine.

"That just made everything better," I mumbled against his mouth. "Oh shit, I'm getting you all wet."

"Not the first time you've gotten me wet." He chuckled.

I bounced my eyebrows in response.

"Plus, I wanted to talk to you about Idaho."

My face fell. "Is something wrong? You don't want to take me?"

"No, no. I do want to be there with you. This is a huge step."

"Then, what is it?"

"Well, visitation is only for a few hours, so I wondered what you thought about taking a few days off and staying in a hotel so you can spend more time with Jedd. If we do that, you'll be able to ask the questions you need to. The upside is you and I will get to have those days to ourselves other than the time you're with Jedd. But, the downside is you'll be missing work and school."

"Oh," I said. He'd summarized that perfectly. The thought of having him all to myself warred with the lost wages and missed classes.

"You don't have to say anything tonight," he said, tucking a stray hair behind my ear.

"No, I think you're right. I think it would be the best use of our time. Making three to four trips over time doesn't make sense. Can you set it up? Then I'll talk to Richard and my instructors. Maybe Kara can pick up a shift or two for me."

"Are you sure? I don't want to push you. I just thought it would give you more time with him."

"Nuh-uh, you just want me in your bed every night," I said, running my hand over his chest.

"That, too," he said, leaning down and kissing the top of my head. "I'm going to grab a seat. I'm starving."

I glanced down at myself. "And I need to see if Richard has another shirt, so I'll see you in a bit."

My heart fluttered while he strolled back into the main part of the bar and grill. Jamie smiled at him and sat Kaisen in my section.

"Just hanging out with nothing to do?" Richard asked, approaching me from his office.

"Ha, ha. Do you have an extra top in your office? As you can see, I had a tussle with a customer's beer. It won," I said, pursing my lips together.

Kaisen didn't skimp on the hotel in Idaho. My mouth dropped as I realized he'd reserved the honeymoon suite for us. Fresh rose petals were sprinkled across the floor all the way to the bed, and champagne was already chilling. A box of chocolates sat next to it, just waiting to be savored, and a two-person jetted tub was sitting empty, waiting to be filled.

"Why?" I asked, stunned into stupidity.

"Don't you like it? We can change rooms," he stammered.

"No, I didn't mean it like that! I'm just surprised." Guilt flooded me. "It's perfect, Kaisen." I laid a hand on his arm. "I just don't understand why you went to all this trouble. I guess I'm so used to budgeting every penny I make and spend, and it's not our honeymoon, and . . ."

Kaisen placed our bags on the dresser, and then his fingers gently brushed across my cheek. He cupped my chin and tilted it upward.

"Hadlee, I know this isn't a vacation or a romantic getaway, but for the next few days, you're going to need something to help you through. I want you to know that you're safe and loved. You're going to walk into the death row visitor's room and see terrible human beings; you're going to pick up the phone and talk to a man who might be guilty. You're going to be confused, probably cry a lot, and overthink things. But when we're here, I need you to know my entire world revolves around you and what you need."

Tears welled in my eyes. "Thank you."

His lips brushed against my cheek, wiping my tears away.

"Before all of that happens, I need one thing," I said, emotion swelling in my chest.

"Anything," he said gently.

"You. I just need you."

I had flat-out lied to myself. For some ridiculous reason, I'd thought since I'd visited the prison already, it wouldn't bother me. But with every step, every buzz of the security doors, every evil eye that lurked at me, I had to force myself not to run in the opposite direction.

One thing was different, though. When I sat down and picked up that phone, I looked at him. I looked Christopher Jedidiah Mackenzie square in the eyes.

"Jayden," he said.

The deepness of his tone rumbled everything inside me. My breath hitched with the sudden memory of him reading *The Cat in the Hat* to me.

"My name is Hadlee," I replied, my chin jutting up.

"Okay, I understand. 'Hadlee' has a nice ring to it."

Silence filled the telephone line while we stared at each other.

"I guess it'd be dumb to tell you that you look just like your aunt Jessica."

"Who?"

"You probably don't remember my sister. You were two the last time you saw her. After everything—after I ended up here—your mom cut all ties with my side of the family. And they cut all ties with me, too."

"Can you blame them?" I blurted.

Sadness pulled at his handsome features, and guilt snaked through me.

"Everyone says I look like you. But it doesn't matter." I paused. My throat tightened from the stress of the situation, then a surge of anger rushed through me. "You left me. You left me there with her," I hissed into the phone. "Do you have any idea what it's been like?" I laughed. "Of course you don't because you've been in this disgusting hellhole my entire life."

"I'm so sorry, Hadlee." He shook his head. "You were my little girl, and everything I did was for you."

"Murdering someone was for me?" I asked, the pitch of my voice climbing.

Too much. It was all too much. My head hung down, and my pointer finger thrust upward, demanding a minute so I could collect myself.

Once my gaze returned to him, his eyes filled with tears.

"When you were just a baby and you weren't talking yet, I—I got a seat for you on my bicycle. Your mom bought a few little bonnets to protect your fair skin, and we started going out together. I loved taking you out with me. And you loved the fresh air!" He smiled at the memory, and I felt my heart constrict. "One day, I pedaled down the driveway, hit a rock, and lost my balance. The bike fell with you strapped in the seat, and your scream split the air. I scrambled to you as fast as I could, picked you up, and checked you for cuts, bruises, bumps . . . you name it. My heart split wide open at the mere thought I might have hurt you. I held you and just teared up. And then, out of the blue, you started jabbering. You weren't speaking yet, so it was all gibberish. And then you smiled at me. It was as though you were trying to tell me that everything was okay. I'll never forget it."

"Dad," I whispered, covering my mouth with my hand, the tears brimming over.

"You will never know how much I regret going out that night." His voice trembled with the admission. "It cost me everything I loved, but mostly, it cost me you."

I choked on my pain while I struggled to control my flood of tears. I pulled in a deep breath, wiped my cheeks, and accepted the burning ache that his confession delivered.

"She never told me. Mom never said a word. We buried you. I stood there and sobbed while she lied and never shed a tear. And, Cameron—he and his son were there, too."

Jedd nodded. "I asked him to go." He paused. "After I arrived here, your mother wrote me a letter. She told me her plans to bury me, change your name, and tell you I was dead. I hated her for it, but I also understood why. You would have grown up a murderer's daughter, and you deserved so much more."

"Why don't I remember her changing my name? After the funeral, no matter how hard I tried to keep going, things just went dark. I've never told anyone before. It's one of the reasons I wanted to study psychology."

"Psychology? Wow. That's amazing." He paused for a minute. "Your mom said you got really sick after my death. She said your migraines were so extreme you'd vomit if she turned your bedroom lamp on. The doctor said it wasn't uncommon for people to get sick after a stressful period. They called it something like the—"

"The let-down effect," I supplied. "I don't remember any of that. I guess my brain was trying to protect me, but the hole inside me never allowed me to stay still for long. I didn't make a lot of friends, have slumber parties, or anything most girls growing up did. I was a loner for the most part. Mom changed, too."

He nodded. "I know." Silence filled the line. "What about now? Do you have a lot of friends? A boyfriend?"

"You haven't earned the right to know me yet. You're sitting on death row, and there's no way I'm telling you about anything personal other than school," I snapped. Just because we'd had a moment didn't mean he had the right to ask personal questions. I swallowed against the bile in my throat as reality reminded me where I was.

"Did you do it?"

His hazel eyes locked on mine, and for a split second, I swore I could see his soul.

"I. Am. Not. Guilty."

Chills rippled through me. He was so convincing. Was he lying or telling me the truth? Could I even trust myself to believe the right thing? How would I even know?

"What's next?" I asked.

Jedd leaned back in his chair, his gaze dropping to the table.

"I'm out of appeals, Hadlee."

"What does that mean?" I asked, unsure I wanted to know.

"My execution could be scheduled at any time."

I gasped. "But, Cameron—he said an attorney . . . I just fucking found you," I sputtered.

He offered a wan smile. "My attorney is still working on the case, but we're running out of time. That's why I wanted to find you."

My vision flicked upward toward the ceiling as I struggled to control the tears that threatened.

"What do we do?" I asked, refusing to look at him again.

"Hope the attorney is able to get the DNA tests and they prove my innocence."

"And if not?"

"It's only a matter of time. Once the execution papers are signed, they have about sixty days to see it through. I suspect the papers will come through any day now."

"That's not long," I said, my heart splintering. As much as I distrusted him, I couldn't bear the thought of anything happening to him. He was Jedd. But he was also my dad. I leaned forward earnestly. "What can I do? I don't know if you're guilty or not, but I don't want you to die."

Jedd gave a nod of thanks. "There is nothing to be done. But will you come back tomorrow?"

"Yes. I'll be here."

He nodded. I hung up the phone, and the guard stepped up to take him back to his cell. My stomach churned as he shuffled out the door in chains.

"**W**hat's he saying?" I asked Kaisen, pacing our hotel room.

"No update yet," he said and leaned against the dresser.

"Well, what in the hell is this attorney doing, for God's sake? We're on a deadline." I rubbed my face with my hands and released a frustrated groan.

"Hang on. Yeah, Dad. Okay. Thanks." Kaisen tapped his phone screen and ended the call. "Had, unfortunately, this attorney is pro bono, so we can't yell and scream since we're not paying him."

"Damn it. I don't know what to do, Kaisen."

He gently grabbed my arms, effectively stopping my unproductive pacing.

"The only thing I can suggest right now is to use this time the best you can. We're playing Russian roulette, and no one has any clue what's going to happen. But you should expect the worst."

My knees turned to jelly; I sank onto the bed.

"I—I . . ." My voice refused to cooperate as I attempted to articulate my thoughts. "I can't bury him twice." My voice was hardly more than a breath. "I can't do it."

Kaisen crossed the room and sat next to me. He pulled me against him, and I laid my head against his chest. His heartbeat reminded me he was here with me. But another heartbeat might not be around much longer.

Although the bed was comfortable, I tossed and turned all night, trying to find some loophole that could stop the execution. Was this life's cruel joke? Had I done something so wrong that I was being punished by having to bury my dad twice?

Kaisen's soft snore distracted me from my dark thoughts. My eyes wandered over his peaceful face. A heavy sigh escaped me as my thoughts returned to the craziness called my life. If my dad was executed, would there be enough of me left to give to Kaisen? Or would I become an empty shell? That wouldn't be fair to him. I'd rather be alone than hurt him.

"Can't sleep?" he asked, his voice thick and groggy.

"Sorry, did I wake you?"

"No, you're fine. I figured some late-night conversations would happen. Part of the gig, I think."

"At least we don't have to get up too early," I said.

He reached out and smoothed my hair. "Do I need to rock you to sleep?" he asked.

I scooted across the bed and straddled him. "I think that's a great idea," I replied, leaning down to kiss him.

My thoughts focused on him as he made love to me, slowly, gently. Somehow, he had the ability to reach inside me and massage my heart when I thought it would no longer beat on its own. And every time he did, he brought me back to him and gave me something to live for, something to hold on to when everything else around me turned dark.

In reality, there's no black or white; the world is filled with shades of gray. The constant political argument concerning execution had now become a truth for me. Maybe Jedd had done it, maybe he hadn't, but did he deserve to die instead of living out his life in prison? I wasn't capable of making that decision. My judgment was clouded with the simple fact that he was my father.

I was staring out the window of my hotel room, lost in thought, when my phone vibrated. I tapped my screen and saw that Syd was checking in since this was my last day before Kaisen and I headed back to Spokane.

How are you holding up?

I don't know. A part of me wants to run and never come back here, and the other part never wants to leave. How am I supposed to deal with this?

The three dots flitted across the bottom of the message as I waited for her response.

There's no right or wrong here. You're not supposed to solve anything—you can't. This trip was for you to see if you wanted to connect with him, maybe find out who he is, who you are. That's happening. No matter what else goes on, you've gotten some answers.

I glanced toward the bathroom and listened to Kaisen's shower running. *I need to know if he did it. That's why I'm here. But I still don't know.*

Hadlee, no one knows the truth except him. You might never get the answer!

I heaved a sigh of frustration. Deep inside, I knew she was right, but logic had nothing to do with it.

When do you see him again?

I spotted the clock on my phone. In an hour.

We'll leave here in thirty. Sometimes they let me in on time, and sometimes I have to wait for what feels like days. The visitation room is dark and dingy, and I hate sitting there.

Can you message me?

No, no phones allowed. I responded.

Okay. Then let me know when you guys are on your way home. Be safe.

I will.

I pushed the button on my phone, the screen fading to black. My head leaned against the back of the chair. I inhaled deeply, the scent of Kaisen's soap tickling my nose.

He stepped out of the bathroom, a white towel hung low on his hips. Beads of water traveled down his abs and vanished beneath the thick, cotton fabric. My breath caught, and for a split second, I forgot why we were there. A sad smile spread across his face. "I'm ready to go back to Spokane, but I'm not ready for the bed to be empty next to me."

"Me, too," I said. An ache had already formed inside my chest just thinking about being away from him again. "I'm a little worried about my classes, too. My concentration has slipped over these last few weeks."

"Can you talk to your professors? Maybe you can ask for an extension and just tell them you've had a family emergency."

I nodded. I didn't want to. I didn't want anyone to know about my dad. Guilt speared me as I admitted it to myself, but having that dark cloud follow me in public was more than I could handle right now.

"I'll figure it out," I said, standing. "Thank you for helping with everything—driving, paying for the room, keeping me sane. I'm not sure how I could have managed everything without you."

"I wanted to, Had. You mean everything to me, and I love you."

I crossed the room, pushed up on my tiptoes, and kissed him.

"As much as I'd love to continue, I need to get dressed so we're not late." He turned and sauntered away, dropping the towel on the floor right before he closed the bathroom door behind him.

"Not fair!" I called through the door.

He responded with a deep chuckle.

The corded phone felt heavy in my hand as I picked it up and held it to my ear.

"Hey," I said.

"Hey, good to see you again. You've been the highlight of my days this week."

A small smile pulled at the corner of my mouth.

"I'm going home after I leave here."

Jedd nodded, the corners of his eyes creasing while he stared at me. "Do you think you'll come back?"

"I don't know. I wish I had an answer for you, but this is a lot to process. I'm just not sure of anything right now."

"Can I write?"

I bit my lip. If I agreed, he'd have my address. And not only mine, but Syd's and the address of everyone else who lived there.

"I'll have to get back to you on that. I'm not the only one who lives there."

"I understand. Having a father on death row probably won't go over well, huh?"

I shook my head. "I came here to see if I could find out if you were guilty or not. Everyone else has shared their opinion, but I needed to decide for myself." I rolled my eyes, more at myself than anyone else. "I thought I could figure it all out in three days, three visits."

Jedd waited for me to continue.

I inhaled sharply, remembering Kara's words. She was right—this was my time to say whatever I needed to, no matter how ugly. "I don't know if you did it or not, Jedd. I wasn't there that night. You should have been home instead. You should have never left me, no matter what, and you should have fought for me. But you didn't. You allowed Mom to have your funeral and change my name. Maybe I was too young to understand, but you could have refused. You both made a decision for me and literally took my choices away. I needed to be able to decide if I wanted to walk in here and see you. And every day, your death has haunted me. You were my entire world. I loved you, but it just wasn't enough."

"I didn't know what to do, Hadlee. I didn't know how to take care of you or protect you from it all. Life turned on me, and I found myself behind bars and filing appeals. I couldn't bring you into this world. You're probably right; you should have had the option to decide, but sometimes we don't make the best decisions in those life-crushing moments. I'm so sorry. Please . . ." His plea hung in the air. "Forgive me."

While I sat there in the cold chair that was bolted to the floor, I wondered if I'd ever find out the truth about that night. Probably not, but maybe I had another choice in front of me. Maybe I needed to let the past go and face the present. Maybe Jedd didn't deserve a chance in the outside world, but maybe he deserved another chance with me. Or maybe I owed it to myself.

"I can't just flip a switch and forgive you, but I'm willing to try," I whispered.

"That's all I can ask."

He raised his arm tentatively and flattened his large palm against the glass.

"I love you," he said softly through the phone.

I stared at his hand and then slowly raised mine, pressing it against the glass on the other side.

Time was called, they escorted Jedd back through the door, and I stood. My heart sank as I realized it might be the last time I saw him.

You don't walk out of a maximum security prison as the same person who entered it. I'd glimpsed a world so vastly different than my own, yet a part of me lived there. My dreams were haunted by the prison, the guards, and Jedd. I couldn't shake the heaviness that followed me everywhere I went.

It seemed as though time had moved forward without me, and the end of March had arrived. The few months since Kaisen and I had returned from Idaho were filled with playing catch-up with my classes and work. My time with Kaisen and the girls plummeted while I scrambled to pull my life back together.

Kaisen offered to let Jedd write to me at his address; all I had to do was reach out first. I'd mulled over what to include in the letter a thousand times. My attempts overflowed the wastebasket. What could I possibly say? *How's your day going?* didn't fit. Nothing seemed right, so I finally wrote down the only word I could think of: *Hi.* And then I mailed it. And waited for his reply.

Tonight, our house was fairly quiet, so I was taking advantage of it. My biology book rested on my lap, the words an empty blur no matter how many times I read them. As stupid as it was, I wondered what Jedd was doing. From what I understood, the inmates spent approximately twenty-three hours a day in their cells. Did he study? Read? If so, what did he read? Did he stare at the walls? Nothing I imagined probably came close to the truth of what that life was like.

I leaned my head against the wall and struggled to stay focused.

"You're so cute when you drool."

My eyes fluttered open.

Kaisen was standing beside me, kissing my forehead.

"What?" I asked, peering around my bedroom. "Shit, I must have dozed off while I was studying." My neck popped as I straightened it; I winced at the tightness.

Kaisen lowered himself next to me and took my hand. "I'm glad you got a bit of sleep. I know things have been tough lately."

I looked at him, searching his face, and wondered how in the hell I'd gotten so lucky. "I love you."

He leaned in for a kiss. "Love you, too."

"What time is it?"

"A little after five. I was on my way to Dad's house for dinner and thought I'd swing by."

"How'd you get in?"

"Lionel was on his way out, so he let me in."

I chewed my lip as I remembered when he'd let my mom in on Thanksgiving. The same day I'd kicked her out of my house. A glorious moment. Such irony to think I was relieved to be rid of the woman who had raised me and concerned about the man on death row.

"He seems to let just anyone in. I'm going to have to talk to him about that," I said, gently jabbing Kaisen in the ribs with my elbow.

He offered me a fleeting grin and then turned serious. "I want to give you something."

"Yeah? What's that?" I asked, turning to face him fully.

He reached into his jacket pocket and pulled out a small package, a petite white bow resting on the top of a maroon velvet box. I frowned as he handed it to me.

"A gift?" I asked, puzzled. Valentine's Day was over, it wasn't my birthday, and no major holidays were even close.

He nodded.

My heart skipped a beat as I lifted the lid. The light glinted off the silver of a single key.

"To my house," he said, softly.

I frowned. "Kaisen, are you sure?"

"Yes. You don't even have to ask; just show up and go in anytime, whether I'm there or not."

I lifted my gaze from the key to his face.

"Really?"

"Yeah. If you'd just shoot me a text or let me know you're there so I don't think someone's broken in, that would be helpful, though."

"Ya think?" I said, giggling. "Thank you."

His mouth rested against mine, his lips tender. "I have to go, but if you need to study and want to stay the night, have Syd or Kara drop you off."

"Are you hinting?" I asked as he stood.

"I'm strongly suggesting," he said, standing. "But it's up to you. I don't know what your schedule is like."

"I have to be at class at eight," I said, my eyes rolling. "A stupid test. Which I need to study for if I hope to pass."

His face clouded with disappointment. "Okay, maybe tomorrow?"

"I think that might work," I said, smiling at him. "Tell your dad I said hello?"

"You bet," he said, leaning down for another kiss.

After he left, I turned the key over in my hand, my heart thumping against my chest. He'd just offered to share his living space with me. I frowned as I heard the front door slam shut and footsteps pound into the kitchen. If I were at Kaisen's, I could crawl into his bed and be surrounded by quiet. If I had a car, I could drive to his place even for a few hours to study. The idea of not having my own transportation had never bothered me before, but now, with Kaisen living outside Spokane, I needed to figure something out. I couldn't depend on someone to drive me up there all the time.

Kitchen cabinets slammed closed, and what I suspected was a plate came into contact with the counter. The slide of the drawer and sound of clinking silverware was enough to make me cringe. I'd never realized how noisy everything was until this moment, when I was, quite literally, holding in my hand the key to peace and quiet.

I opened my biology book, which must have folded shut during my nap, and rustled through the pages in an attempt to find my chapter again. Determined to pass this test, I popped my earbuds in, located the Spotify app on my phone, and cranked the music. The sounds of my roommate faded into the background while classical notes filled my ears.

Thirty minutes later, Syd peeked through the crack in our bedroom door. I smiled and waved her in as I pulled out my earbuds.

"Noisy, huh?" she asked, dropping her purse and backpack on her bed.

"Very. I guess I've gotten spoiled with Kaisen."

"How are you doing? Anything from Jedd?"

"No. Kaisen would have mentioned it if he'd heard anything. Maybe my father doesn't want to write to me."

"Um, Hadlee, what else would he do?"

"Syd!" I scolded her.

She gave me an innocent shrug as she slipped off her shoes and sat down. One day, we would no longer share this room, and our in-depth, intellectual conversations would be over the phone instead of stretched out on our beds, face-to-face.

"Well, it hasn't been that long since you wrote to him. Maybe he's struggling with what to say just like you did," she offered.

"Maybe. It would make sense." I paused. "I do have other news, though. Kaisen gave me a key to his house," I said, smiling shyly.

"Well, fuck me runnin' sideways," Syd said, grinning and clapping her hands together.

"He stopped by earlier and gave it to me. He also suggested I stay there with him tonight, but I said I had to be at school at eight so I needed to stay here."

"Girl, you need a car."

I groaned. "I was thinking the same thing. It would be so nice to go up there and study."

"Study? Really?"

"Yes! Do you realize how noisy this house is with a million people in and out?"

"That's what noise-canceling headphones are for," Syd said. "But I get it—just having a place to go would be so awesome."

"Speaking of which, I completely forgot about that possible apartment for you, Kara, and me. I was so caught up at the time, going to the prison . . . what happened?"

"We all got busy. That's what happened. And I had been pretty serious about it, actually."

"Well, have you talked to Kara again? She's in the same position we are—a house full of college students. It would be nice if we could manage it financially."

"Do you want me to keep looking?"

"Yeah! Let's see what shows up over the next few months."

19

The persistent ringing of the doorbell shot me out of bed a little after midnight.

"Are you fucking kidding me?" I muttered under my breath as I rubbed the sleep from my eyes and stumbled down the hall. I flipped the deadbolt and pulled the door open a few inches.

"What is it? What's wrong?" I asked Kaisen, ushering him inside. "What are you doing here? Is Cameron okay?"

"You need to get dressed and grab your stuff. Dad's in the truck waiting for us."

I froze. "Kaisen, what's going on? You're scaring me."

After glancing into the living room and seeing one of the jocks passed out on the couch, he took my hand and gently guided me back to my bedroom, where Syd remained asleep.

"They just moved your dad. Hadlee, his execution will take place at ten tomorrow morning. We need to hurry if we want to get there in time."

"I don't understand." I changed out of my pajamas and into jeans and a sweatshirt, my mind a complete blank. "How can that be possible?" I asked.

"Hey, what's going on?" Syd sat up in bed.

"They're going to execute Jedd tomorrow," I said numbly. "I have to go." How strange, I didn't recognize my own voice. Those words couldn't really be coming out of my mouth.

"Oh my God," Syd gasped as I grabbed my purse. "Text me. Please, take care of her, Kaisen."

He nodded and picked up my coat from the floor.

"Go to the bathroom, and I'll dig around in the fridge and find something for you to eat on the way there."

I nodded and finished getting myself together for the trip. Before we left, I walked up to Syd and squeezed her hands. "I'm not going to be okay," I stated matter-of-factly.

"Yes, you will." She shook our joined hands for emphasis. "We will all figure it out together. I promise." She wrapped her arms around me and held me tight. I wished she would never let go, that I could stay frozen in this moment and never face tomorrow.

"I'll text you as soon as I can," I said, failing in my attempt at a smile.

Within minutes, Kaisen and I were situated in the front of his dad's truck. Even though the heat was on, I shivered.

"Hadlee. I'm sorry to see you under these circumstances," Cameron said as he pulled out of the driveway. "I got the call a few hours ago, and I've been on the phone with Jedd's attorney, or I would have been here sooner." He paused, cleared his throat. "I don't know if you'll get to talk to him before—before . . ." His voice trailed off.

I looked at Kaisen. Fear bubbled up inside me. What if I never had another opportunity to say anything to Jedd? I'd foolishly wasted my time with him, yelling at him and feeling sorry for myself.

"I don't understand how this all happened. What about the attorney? What about the DNA tests? Cameron, how can this be happening?" I heard the shrill desperation in my voice, but I couldn't control it; I needed to grasp even the smallest shred of hope.

"I don't have all the information yet, hon. I'm so sorry."

I sank into the seat and stared out the front window. I didn't even realize Kaisen had taken my hand in his as questions whipped around inside my head.

Silence filled the air, and the moon shone brightly, breaking through all the darkness that surrounded us. I wondered where I'd be this time tomorrow night.

Thoughts of all the articles I'd read about executions by lethal injection came rolling back. Nausea hit the back of my throat as reality began to sink in. We'd be in a room, glass between us, Dad lying on the cot. They'd strap him down before they introduced the lethal drug into the IV.

I choked on the images. My hands covered my face as the tears drenched me. Kaisen pulled me to him, and I brought my legs up, curling into myself the best I could. How could life be so cruel? I'd buried him when I was eight and would be watching his execution at the age of twenty-one. Wasn't one time enough? How in the hell would I ever live through it again?

"Stop the truck," I gasped. "I'm going to be sick."

Cameron slowed and turned off the interstate. I released my seat belt, scrambled over Kaisen's lap and out of the pickup, and then deposited the contents of my stomach into the snow on the side of the road. Why was I even doing this? Why? And at what point would I get to choose what happened in my life?

Kaisen knelt down with tissues and a bottle of water.

"Thanks," I said, wiping my mouth and taking a sip.

I leaned on Kaisen as I stood, and he led me into the back of the extended cab. He settled in and fastened his seat belt.

"Don't worry about buckling in; just come here," he said.

I stretched out my legs on the seat and leaned into his chest, his arms wrapping around me like a safe cocoon. My ears filled with the steady beat of his heart as the tears flowed down my cheeks.

"I'm here," he said, rubbing my back and planting a kiss on the top of my head. "I'm so sorry, Hadlee. I'm so sorry," he whispered into my hair.

I'm not sure how much time passed as I cried, but eventually, the tears stopped, and I drifted off to sleep.

"Babe, wake up. We're here," Kaisen said.

My swollen eyes slowly peeled open as I took in my surroundings. And then it all came back to me: Cameron, Idaho—the execution.

I sat up and placed my feet on the floor. Kaisen opened the door and hopped out. The burst of unseasonably cold air sent an instant shiver through my body. I slid out behind him, but my knees buckled when my feet made contact with the ground.

"I've got you," he said, catching me. "Your legs are probably asleep. Just stand here for a second and get your bearings."

I nodded as I realized that, once again, there was snow on the ground. And, once again, Kaisen would be with me on the day I said goodbye to my father.

"We need to go, kids." Cameron looked at his watch and then motioned toward the bleak prison.

I inhaled sharply and grasped Kaisen's hand. He was the only thing that would keep me from shattering into tiny pieces when we left here. But, even then, I wasn't sure he'd be enough.

I proceeded through the security checks and pat down in a heavy daze. Nothing seemed real as we were escorted to the waiting area.

"Cameron?" I looked at him, hope making a brief appearance inside me. "Did we get here in time? For me to say goodbye?" My voice broke over the last word.

"No. I'm so sorry."

I chewed my lip and nodded, tears threatening. Maybe it was better this way.

Maybe I needed to believe that he'd raped and murdered an eleven-year-old little girl and left her for dead in the back alleyway of a bar. Steel shot through my spine. Did I really believe he would be here if they didn't have enough proof? Had I just been hoping so deeply for something different that I'd almost convinced myself he wasn't a monster?

I stiffened as my brain latched onto the facts. An eleven-year-old girl—dead. My father—a murderer.

My chin tilted up as the guard opened the door, and we were escorted into a tiny room. A curtain hung from the ceiling on the other side of the glass partition, blocking our view. It moved slightly, and I realized there were people in the . . . in the execution room.

I couldn't sit down. I had to remember why we were here. This wasn't about me; this was about justice, and I had to hold on to that.

Footsteps sounded in the hall and broke through my thoughts. An older couple stepped into the room. Tears stained the women's plump face. Her black hair was streaked with shades of gray. She leaned against the taller man, his arm holding her protectively. His eyes flashed with a mixture of anger and grief.

"We've waited a long time for this," he said to her as he led her to a seat.

My eyebrows rose, and I realized they were the victim's parents. These were the people who had lost their little girl. She'd only been three years older than me at the time. She'd have been twenty-four today if she'd lived.

My heart sank as I sat down as far from them as possible. How could I even look at them? Shame washed over me, and I dared a glance toward them. This was the day they'd waited for. It'd been years since they'd lost their daughter. Nothing would ever bring her back. A flicker of compassion for them shot through me. But their long-awaited day was about to become my worst nightmare.

The air was thick and stifling inside the little room. The large clock ticked loudly while we waited.

The curtain finally moved. I rose to my feet. My emotions flip-flopped as I took a deep breath and tried to steady myself. Somehow, I managed to choke down a rush of vomit. I felt Kaisen's arm wrap around my waist. I glanced past him and saw Cameron standing stoically beside him.

A small cry escaped me as the curtain opened to reveal the horrific scene in front of us—the gurney, the straps, the IVs, the warden, guards, and medical professional. And then—Jedd—Dad, strapped down to a gurney in jeans and a short-sleeve shirt. My eyes traveled along the IV tubes that ran from his arms to a screen. From what I understood, three anonymous people waited to push the buttons that would end his life.

I turned into Kaisen, hiding my face. All of a sudden, my myriad pep talks about guilt or innocence seemed weak and small compared to what was unfolding in front of me.

Jedd turned his head and scanned the room. Our gazes locked. His face twisted with grief, his eyes filling with tears.

"I love you," he mouthed to me.

Everything closed in on me. My pulse raced. This shouldn't be happening. I couldn't lose him again. I'd just found him. A desperate, strangled scream ripped from my throat.

"Daddy! No! No!"

"Ma'am, you have to calm down, or I'll escort you out," the guard said sternly.

My vision blurred as tears cascaded over my cheeks and down my face. I gasped for breath.

What had I done? How could I have wasted the few precious visits I'd had with him? Why had I allowed my anger to take over instead of just letting him be my father one last time? Why couldn't I have just been thankful he was alive and I'd learned the truth? My heart splintered as I realized I'd screwed up. I should have come back again. All I'd had to do was ask Kaisen, but I'd been so wrapped up in school and work I'd lost the one thing that had genuinely mattered to me, the one thing I couldn't get back—time with my dad.

I was unable to control the violent tremors that seized my body as I leaned into Kaisen, both of his arms wrapping tightly around me. I felt his own tears land softly in my hair. I stared at my father as the medical professional checked the IV in each arm and the heart rate monitor.

The maximum-security warden stood at the foot of the injection table and read the death warrant, his voice crackling through the speaker. "Do you have any last words?" he asked.

A heavy pause hung in the air, and then Jedd's voice, thick with emotion filled the room. "Jayden, I'm so sorry. Please know I'm innocent and I love you."

In that split second, I no longer had control of my impulses. I ripped away from Kaisen's embrace and ran to the glass. The palm of my hand pounded on it again and again.

"No! Daddy! No!" My screams ripped through the room, overpowering everyone's muffled cries.

"Hadlee. Babe." Kaisen grabbed my waist and tried to pull me away.

My hand fisted as I pounded against the glass again before I was lifted off my feet. My body rebelled, screams ripping from my throat, my legs kicking whomever had secured me.

"I've got her," I heard the guard say.

I dug my heels into the floor as I realized I was going to be removed from the room. Then I was simply lifted off the floor.

"Daddy! Daddy! No, put me down!" My arms and legs flailed in the air, my fists and feet making contact. Then the guard abruptly stopped moving. My cries fell flat as the medical professional inside the execution room stepped away. What was going on? Another man hurried away from Dad and stepped out of view. I strained my neck, no longer able to see him.

My focus darted to Kaisen and Cameron, but they stood glued in place, their eyes bouncing from me to the gurney. The guard's grip slipped away, and my feet touched the floor again.

Finally mobile, I walked closer. The medical professional was removing the IVs from my father's arms.

"What's happening?" I rasped, my voice hoarse from screaming. No one responded. "What's happening?" I asked, a little louder this time.

My mouth dropped open as they unfastened the straps holding Dad in place and helped him to stand. He searched the room for me, a look of disbelief on his face.

"I can take her," Kaisen said to the guard. Silent now, I collapsed against Kaisen, clutching his shirt for support. But my focus remained trained on my dad as he stepped through the door and out of view, leaving the execution room behind him. At least for today.

"I don't know what's going on," Kaisen said. "Dad?"

"I don't know, son, but today wasn't Jedd's day to die," he mumbled, shock written all over his face.

"Does this mean they won't move forward with the execution?" I asked, hope filling my voice.

"Don't know. I need my phone so I can get some answers. Let's go."

Hope swelled in my chest while the guard escorted us out of the room and down the bleak path that had led us there. My body shook as I followed Cameron. Kaisen refused to let me go, and I leaned into him for support. Thoughts bombarded my brain, and my emotions spiked as I imagined the worst and best outcomes.

"Let Dad find out what's going on. Hang on, Had. I'm here." Kaisen placed a kiss on the top of my head.

I peered up into his face, his brows pinching together. He tried to reassure me. But I wasn't stupid, he was just as confused and scared as I was.

We stepped outside into the fresh, crisp air, and I inhaled it as though it were my first breath of life. The tiny room had reeked of death, and the images of Dad on the cot had threatened to choke me. But I wasn't the only one. Cameron's chest heaved while we continued to the truck in the parking lot, each of us tilting our heads toward the sun. I'd never been so grateful to be outside.

"Hang on, kids," Cameron said, taking out his cell phone. "I'm calling the lawyer now."

Kaisen squeezed me as I snuggled into him, my body calmer, but still shaking. But until we had answers, I realized I might have to walk back into that room and watch my father die. And if I walked in there again, it would be for the last time.

"It's ringing," Cameron said, pacing in front of his truck.

"This is Cameron Sinclair. I need to speak to Mr. Adams immediately, please."

Silence hung in the air between us while we waited for Cameron to speak again. My eyes were trained on his facial expressions and body language—any clue to what was going on.

"What the hell just happened?" Cameron asked.

I clutched Kaisen's shirt, his arm tightening around me. My breathing hitched as I listened and watched.

Cameron's hand covered his mouth, his eyes squeezing closed. He slowly bent over and rested his free hand on his knee.

Was that bad? What was the attorney saying?

"Dad, what's going on?" Kaisen asked, releasing me and approaching him.

Cameron straightened and took a deep breath.

"Okay, I'll wait for the update. Thank you."

"Cameron?" I asked breathlessly. "What?" My eyes grew wide in anticipation of the answer that could potentially be a game changer. My stomach churned with uneasiness at thoughts of returning to watch Dad be put to death.

"A stay of execution was signed. He finally got the judge to listen concerning the DNA testing. And, he's pushing to remove the death penalty. Not only do we have some hope, but we have some more time. And so does Jedd."

"He might not die?" I whispered, choking back my tears.

"That's what it's looking like, but I can't say for sure yet. We'll know soon. He said he's pushing as hard and fast as he can. That's why they stopped today. The phone call came in with the update. And I'll take it because right now your dad is alive."

My knees buckled, and I hit the ground, sobs racking my body with the news.

"That's good, babe. Just try to hold onto that until we know more."

Kaisen said, my emotions erupting. He scooped me into his arms, and we got into the back cab of the truck. He didn't bother with seatbelts.

"How long? How long before we know if he won't be executed?" I whispered.

I realized Cameron couldn't hear me over the rumble of the truck. Kaisen leaned forward a bit and repeated the question.

"He thinks we will know in a few weeks, but I'll be calling every day. I'll keep you updated, Hadlee," Cameron responded.

I sunk against Kaisen with exhaustion, but every time my eyelids fluttered closed, images of Dad strapped to the cot shot them back open. I wondered if I'd ever have a good night's sleep again.

Earlier that day, I'd known my life would never be the same when I left that prison, but I couldn't have imagined just how true that would be.

Spring was all about new beginnings. A time to blossom, grow, and recognize the beauty around us. Spokane was breathtaking at this time of year. The last patches of snow had melted, and life was blooming with color again. New life.

I rolled onto my back and yawned as I stared at the ceiling and listened to the peace and quiet around me.

"Hey, sleepyhead," Kaisen said, holding a cup of coffee out to me.

I scooted up into a sitting position and leaned against the headboard. "Thank you," I said, taking the offering and sniffing the freshly brewed liquid. I moved my leg over to make room for him on the side of the bed.

"How did you sleep?"

"Good. Better than I have in a long time, thanks to you."

"Glad to hear it." He placed a kiss on my forehead.

The sun filtered through the parted blackout curtains, and the chirping of birds filled the air.

"It's going to reach seventy today. A perfect moving day."

Placing my mug on the nightstand next to me, I laughed and scooted next to him, my feet dangling off the edge and grazing the soft carpet.

"You ready? You're all packed?" he asked.

My gaze flickered up to his beautiful brown eyes.

"Yeah, I'm ready," I said, smiling before I tilted my face up and kissed him. "Do you think Syd and Kara would get mad if we didn't show up?"

"We'd be in deep shit." He chuckled.

"Yeah, I suspect we would be," I replied, scrunching my nose.

"It all worked out well, though, didn't it? I know you'd originally planned on moving in with the girls, but I'm glad you're here with me instead."

"Me, too." I beamed at him. "Besides, Michael and Kara are ready to take that next step as well."

I stood and stretched, pulling down the bottom of my tank top. "I'm going to shower. I probably stink."

Kaisen's face wrinkled, and he waved a hand in front of his nose.

"Hey," I said, smacking him on the arm. "I don't smell *that* bad!"

"Oh yes, you do!" Kaisen yelled as he grabbed me and tossed me into the middle of his bed.

I giggled while he tickled my ribs.

"Stop!" I gasped, laughing harder.

His fingers slowed, and he lowered himself down next to me and smiled.

"I love you. I love your smile, your laugh, everything about you. I've never been this happy before. I didn't even know it was possible," he said, his face softening.

"I love you, too." I reached up and touched his cheek, his skin warm to the touch. "Tonight," I whispered, kissing him.

"Promise?"

"Yes," I said against his mouth. "We'd better get ready before we're late and have to deal with the wrath of Syd," I said, winking. My tongue darted across my lips, tasting the sweetness Kaisen had left behind.

"Where is it?" I asked, reading the street numbers. "There," I said, pointing.

Kaisen pulled into the driveway of the tan two-story house.

"We beat them?" I asked. "Seriously?"

"It's almost ten. I'm sure they'll be here in a few minutes."

I leaned back in the seat and studied the neighborhood. I waved at the mom pushing a baby stroller and watched an older gentleman as he began to prune his shrubs.

"I don't think these neighbors will want any wild parties," I said, smiling.

"Probably not. Definitely a different neighborhood but a good, safe one, from what I have gathered."

The *beep-beep* of a car horn sounded behind us.

"There they are!" I squealed and jumped out.

Syd parked her BMW next to the pickup in the driveway, and then she and Marcus got out. We laughed while we all hugged, and the guys smacked each other on the back.

"Hey, quit making so much noise," Michael yelled out of the car window as Kara pulled up to the curb.

I ran to her and hugged her before she could even get all the way out of the car. "Well, let's see it!" I squealed, jumping up and down like a little kid.

Syd hurried to the front door and slipped the key into the lock. She swung it open, and we all filed in behind her.

"Wow," I said, grinning. "It's awesome. You have a fireplace!"

"It's gas, too, which is perfect. If I wanted to stack cords of wood, I'd move out into the country, huh, Kaisen?" Kara said with a teasing smile.

"Come on," Syd said, motioning us into the sunny kitchen. "Great for parties—not like Lionel's parties, but our quieter parties."

Kaisen took my hand, and we explored the kitchen, dining room, and garage with everyone else. A pang of sadness filled me briefly.

"I have a surprise for you later," he said, squeezing my hand.

I chewed my lip while I studied him and tried to figure out what it was.

"The three bedrooms are upstairs," Syd said, running ahead of us.

Her happiness was infectious; soon, everyone in the house was laughing and chatting as we followed her.

"Michael's and my room," Kara said, pushing open the door. Michael bent down, kissed her, and took her hand; then, they stepped into the room together.

"Aww!" I blinked away my tears of joy. "I'm so excited for you two," I babbled while we inspected their new space.

A huge grin on her face, Kara leaned against Michael as he wrapped his arm around her.

"Ours is next," Syd trilled, practically skipping to the other end of the hall.

"What's the room in the middle?" Kaisen asked.

"Officially, it's the shared office, but really, it will give us all a bit of privacy between the bedrooms." Syd barked out a laugh.

"No more bathroom sex for you two, huh?" I asked, shooting a look at her and Marcus.

"Puh-lease. Sex was made to have anywhere." She continued the tour with a mischievous look in her eyes.

Kaisen chuckled.

"Oh! You guys have your own bathroom!" I burst into laughter. "Kara, you have no idea how lucky you are that it doesn't include a shared wall with your room." I winked at her.

We finished exploring the house and then all gathered in the kitchen. I wasn't sure why, but no matter whose house we were in, we always hung out there.

Syd had excused herself for a minute, and now she breezed in behind us. "Pizza's on the way, and of course, I have . . ."—she reached into the large brown paper bag she was holding—"booze!"

I shook my head as she pulled out multiple bottles, soda, and red Solo cups. After glancing at my phone, I decided that ten thirty wasn't too early to crack open a bottle.

Syd made everyone drinks, and then she raised her glass. The rest of us did the same.

"To new beginnings . . . and to family," she said, her face filling with emotion.

"Cheers," we all said together. I grimaced as the alcohol burned its way down my throat. A cough escaped me while I reached for the soda. "Damn, Syd, I forgot how strong your drinks are." I shot a wide-eyed look of desperation at Kaisen, and everyone broke into laughter.

Fifteen minutes later, the doorbell rang.

"I got it," Syd said, grabbing her wallet.

Marcus stood in the doorway of the kitchen, watching her every move. He glared at the delivery person until she closed the door behind her. Then he hurried toward her and muttered something in her ear.

She smiled, handed the pizzas to him, and placed a kiss on his cheek. I squeezed Kaisen's hand before I let it go and wandered to the other side of the kitchen, where I peeked into Syd's cup and then stole a sip. A smile played at the corners of my lips as I gathered the paper towels near the sink and joined everyone at the kitchen table.

While munching on the pizza, Syd turned on Spotify. Noah Cyrus's "I'm Stuck" blared through the speaker. She began to dance around the room, waving her slice in the air.

My foot tapped the kitchen linoleum, and Kara began to sing along to the lyrics.

I clapped, keeping the beat, and winked at Kaisen as he grabbed another slice for himself.

"You're stuck with me, Marcus," Syd said over the music. She smacked him on the butt and continued to dance around the room.

She twirled toward me. "Love you," she said, placing her head against my forehead.

I took her pizza and set it on the counter. "Let's go, girl!" I yelled.

Syd twirled underneath my arm as we all broke into laughter. "Kara, your turn!" We danced around each other, the guys laughing at us while we shared Noah's lyrics and the sentiment of being stuck with someone you loved. But this time was different. I wasn't stuck with anyone. I'd chosen this family, and if anyone was stuck, it was them with me.

The song ended, and I needed some air. I opened the slider and stepped outside.

"Isn't the yard great?" Syd asked as she joined me. She slid the door closed and glanced around at the green grass and the large clay flower pots someone had left behind.

"It really is," I said, reaching for her hand. Her poker face slipped for a minute as she realized what I was referring to. "How are you doing?"

"Happy," she said, brushing a stray dark hair out of her face.

"He loves you," I said, smiling. "And you two are going to have a beautiful baby. I'm so excited for you."

"What gave it away?"

I shot her a look and giggled. "Marcus did. He hasn't taken his eyes off you the entire time we've been here. And when the pizza arrived, you should have seen the way he was glaring. If the poor guy had raised his hand wrong, Marcus would have taken him down."

Syd laughed. "I'm pretty sure I'm going to get tired of having my every move observed but not yet." A shadow crossed her face, and her voice was a mere breath. "We have a long way to go before we're past the five-month point."

I forced back the tears that threatened when I thought of the last time she was nearly five months along. "I have no doubt that I'll be holding a healthy niece or nephew soon."

Syd's eyes teared up.

"You know, I'm so excited that you and Kara found this place, but when you said that one day everything would change and we'd no longer be roomies . . . I just didn't think it would happen so fast," I said softly.

"Well, I have a small confession."

My eyebrow rose while I waited for her to continue.

"I sort of saved the room in the middle for you in case you ever needed it," she said.

"You did?" I asked, tears welling in my eyes. I threw my arms around her and held on tight.

"Girl, just because things are changing doesn't mean you're not my family. It just means our family is growing."

I nodded, words eluding me. The sliding glass door opened, and we stepped apart.

"Hadlee, we need to go, babe."

"Okay, give me just a minute," I said, brushing my tears away.

"By the way, we haven't told anyone, so you'll keep our secret?" Syd asked, her voice low and her expression pleading.

"Only if you promise I get daily updates. And if you need me, I'll bring a sleeping bag and bunk in the office."

"Promise." She nodded and then tilted her head in puzzlement. "Why are you guys leaving anyway?"

"No clue! He said he has a surprise waiting for me."

"Oh! I love surprises," Syd said, grinning. "I gotta say, Had, never in a million years would I have thought a bag of coffee would have brought you and Kaisen together."

We quickly said our goodbyes and then stepped outside, closing the front door behind us. My heart sank a little. "A part of me feels like I should be here with them," I muttered.

Kaisen paused and turned me to face him.

"You can change your mind, Hadlee. I just want you to be happy."

"I am, and I'm ready." I nodded to emphasize my decision. "It's just all this change has been hard even though it's been good."

He scrutinized me for a moment. "Are you sure?"

"Positive," I said, pushing up onto my toes and kissing him.

"Good," he said softly. "Let's go."

We hurried to the truck, and I waved at Syd and Kara's new house as the pickup rumbled down the street.

"You're not going to give me any kind of hint at all?"

"Nope, not a clue."

My nose scrunched up at him, and I huffed.

"You're pretty damn cute when you pout," Kaisen said, smiling.

"I'm glad I could provide you with entertainment," I retorted, sticking my lower lip out. I glanced at him to see if it might be working, but I wasn't getting anywhere.

"Music?" he offered, turning his stereo on. "Just relax and enjoy."

I groaned and slid lower into the seat, staring out the window.

Twenty minutes later, we pulled into Cameron's driveway.

"You're surprising me with your dad?"

He took my hand and led me to the front door, but we didn't have time to knock. The door flew open, and so did my mouth.

"What? Are you kidding?" I squealed and ran right into my dad's arms.

"Hey, baby girl," he said as we clung to each other. I couldn't stop the tears from falling. All the emotion I'd struggled to contain over the last months spilled over.

"Oh my God, I haven't hugged you since I was eight," I said, refusing to let him go. "How can this be?" I asked, pulling back just a little to wipe my face.

"I'm so sorry. I'm here now. It's over, and you're not getting rid of me this time."

I finally stepped away and laughed, rubbing my face again in an attempt to regain some semblance of composure.

"Thank you," I said to Cameron, hugging him. "I'll never be able to repay you."

"Having Jedd cleared and home is all I need," he said.

"That's it? You're really done, Dad?" I covered my face as the tears slid down my cheeks again. I was afraid I was about to full-on ugly cry. "I need to sit down," I said, grabbing Kaisen's hand. He led me to the couch, and Cameron brought me some tissues. I dabbed my eyes and nodded to reassure them I was fine, but every time I looked at my dad, I started to cry again.

"What happened? I mean, we were there when the phone call came in, but I've been a little in the dark since then. All I knew was they weren't going to . . . to—" My voice broke off. I couldn't even say the word.

"The tests came through. The DNA came back, and there was no match. With the help of my attorney, I'm clear. They dropped all charges against me. It took a little over a week to get all the paperwork done and to get me out of there. I asked Cameron to keep quiet about it until I walked out of there a free man. I was terrified something might go sideways, but it didn't." He took a deep breath. "The nightmare is finally over." Dad swiped at a tear that had slid down his cheek. "I'll be staying here for a while, until I can get on my feet."

"Really? That's great! So, I can come over and bug you every day if I want to?" I asked, my eyes widening at the idea that I could see and touch him whenever I chose.

"That's exactly what it means, and I'll be working for these two."

I sighed with relief, so glad that he would be able to get settled back into a world without bars.

"Uh, you told him?" Kaisen asked Cameron.

Cameron shook his head. "All up to you."

I frowned, and then my mouth gaped as I shot a look at Kaisen. "Shit," I muttered.

Dad cleared his throat and frowned at me.

"Sorry," I said. My father had just scolded me for swearing. I didn't know whether to be embarrassed or thrilled.

"Should we get closer to the door so we can run?" I asked Kaisen softly.

Once he nodded, we stood together, hand in hand.

"Uh, well, Dad. This is awkward."

Cameron chuckled.

"Spit it out," he twirled his fingers. "I'm pretty sure I've seen, heard, and said it all."

"Kaisen and I moved in together yesterday. I mean, I still have to get the rest of my boxes but—" I said in a rush.

His face fell as my words registered. Then his eyes narrowed, settling on Kaisen.

I squeezed his hand for support, noticing it had turned clammy. He swallowed audibly and then squared his shoulders. I'd never seen him this nervous. If I'd had to face an ex-inmate and tell him I was sleeping with his daughter, I would have peed my pants already.

Silence hung in the air while we waited for his reaction.

"You going to marry her?" Dad finally asked Kaisen.

"Dad!"

"You wait a minute. This is man to man," he said, standing. His large frame towered over us, and his stern presence filled the room. He'd gotten the intimidation thing down frighteningly well over the years.

I looked at Cameron, but he'd grown serious, too. Was he worried? I sure was.

"Yes," Kaisen croaked. "Yes, I intend to marry her."

"You do?" I asked, my eyes widening as I looked at him.

"Well, yeah. I wouldn't have asked you to move in with me if I wasn't going to ask."

"Oh," I mumbled.

"When?" Dad asked Kaisen.

My mouth opened to protest again, but Dad held his finger up. I clamped my mouth shut before I said anything that might get me in trouble.

"Well, I graduate in a month, so I was planning on asking her afterward. I already have her ring," Kaisen said.

"What?" My eyebrows shot up into my hairline.

Dad turned his attention to Cameron. "What do you think of this?" he asked.

"I'm aware," Cameron said. "And, Jedd, honestly, I think they're perfect for each other. I'm absolutely thrilled about it."

Dad nodded and then returned his attention to us.

"Well, I would have preferred it the other way, marriage first and then living together, but I haven't been around. So, okay." He rubbed his chin and sat down.

"Okay?" I squeaked. "That's it?"

"Let me know when you two set a date."

"I need some air," I said, darting for the front door and closing it firmly behind me.

My head was spinning as I stepped into the sunlight and allowed it to warm my skin. Everything had moved so fast today. I hadn't even had time to process that my dad was alive and, in my life, again, much less that Kaisen was planning to propose.

I heard the door open and close but didn't turn around. "So much for coming up with a really good proposal, huh?" Kaisen said from behind me. "I'm sorry you had to find out this way."

"It's okay." I turned to face him, smiling slowly. "He's a little scary. I would have sung like a fat little canary."

He chuckled, but it was an uncomfortable sound.

"I'm just overwhelmed," I mumbled.

Kaisen's focus dropped to the ground as his tennis shoe kicked a rock on the driveway. "Do you think you'll say yes?" he whispered, a hint of fear threading through his words.

I searched his face and realized he was genuinely concerned. I closed the gap between us and placed my hand on his chest. His heart was racing beneath my touch. My gaze traveled to his face, and butterflies danced in my stomach.

"Kaisen, you've stood by me every step of the way, and I love you with every fiber of my being. I never even hoped to find someone like you. You're the best part of me, and I'd love to be your wife."

"Really?" His expression was brighter than the sun itself.

"Really," I said, laughing as he picked me up off the ground and twirled me around.

"She must have said yes," Cameron said from the front steps.

I peeked around Kaisen to see if Dad was with him. A grin eased across my face as I saw the smile that lit up his.

"Well, while we're at it," Dad said, motioning for Cameron to follow him.

I frowned when Kaisen set me down. "What's going on?"

"It's the second reason I brought you here today. Your father was the big surprise, of course, but this is an added bonus."

The brown garage door slowly lifted, and I caught a hint of blue.

"What is it?" I asked, tugging at Kaisen's hand like a little kid.

"Oh, wow," I said, stepping toward the blue 280ZX. "She's beautiful."

"Cameron kept it for me, kept her running good while I was gone," Dad said, looking at it fondly.

"Will you take me for a ride?" I asked, running my finger over the smooth edges.

"I think I've outgrown the car, Hadlee."

"What? No, you can't outgrow a sports car," I declared, looking in the driver's side window and noting the stick shift. At my mother's insistence, I had learned on a stick shift. I'd never appreciated it until now.

Keys jingled behind me, and I turned toward him.

"Let's go. Just you and me!" I said, clapping with excitement.

"She's all yours," he said.

My eyes narrowed. "I don't understand."

"I wasn't around to help you get a car, and I'd like something a little more practical for myself, so she's yours. All we have to do is sign the title over," he said, closing the space between us and reaching for my hand. He gently placed the keys in my palm and closed my fingers around them.

"Are you shitting me?"

He scowled at my language and then chuckled. "No, I'm not *shitting* you. Why don't you take your fiancé out for a spin?" My mouth hung open as I stood glued to the concrete floor of the garage, speechless. Fiancé? Car? Dad? How in the world could I have gained so much in one afternoon?

I turned toward the car and back to him.

"Are you sure?" I asked, excitement filling my voice.

"Absolutely, but please take good care of her. She's a fun car. And,"— he pointed a finger at me—"you're responsible for paying your own speeding tickets."

I laughed and threw my arms around him.

"Thank you," I said. Afraid I was going to cry again, I pulled away. I opened the door and slid in. My mouth formed a round O as I realized how close to the ground I was sitting. "This is way different from Kaisen's truck."

Dad smiled at me, and I slid the key into the ignition, turned it, and listened while the car purred to life. I shifted into reverse and backed out slowly, testing the clutch, accelerator, and brakes. I stopped at the end of the driveway, waiting for Kaisen to catch up, and lowered the passenger-side window.

"Wanna go for a ride, little boy?" I asked quietly and wiggled my eyebrows.

He laughed and got in. "Here," he said, handing me my sunglasses.

"I didn't even see you grab them. Thank you."

"You were getting into your car."

"Oh. My. God. I have a car!" I squealed. "Cameron really took care of her, too." I ran my fingers along the dashboard and gray interior. After turning the radio knob, I grinned while Halsey belted through the speakers.

I waved at Dad and Cameron as I backed out onto the gravel road.

"Shit. This is low," I muttered as rocks pinged off the bottom.

"Slow and steady," he advised.

We reached Highway 395, and I turned away from town.

"I just want to open her up for a minute. Help me look for cops?" I asked, grinning.

Kaisen pulled on his seatbelt, making sure it was secure. "Ready."

I pulled out, and within seconds, the speedometer shot upward. I whizzed past a car on the interstate and pushed the accelerator.

"We're at a hundred," I announced. "I'm going to push it a little more."

Kaisen responded with a wide grin.

"One ten, one fifteen, one twenty." I removed my foot from the pedal.

"You could probably push her a little more but only if you are comfortable."

I laughed. "I'm okay. I don't want anyone calling the cops on us. Dad would take the car back if he knew I got a ticket the first hour after he'd given it to me."

"It's so good to see you smiling," he said.

"Hell yeah! That was fun!"

"Summer is coming up, so you'll have plenty of time to get her out on the road."

"I can't believe I have a car! You don't have to drive me around anymore."

"I think I'm going to miss that, though."

"Really? You're going to miss playing chaperone?"

"I am not a picky guy," he said, patting his broad chest. "I will take any chance to be with you."

I shook my head at him and relaxed against the seat.

"Are you okay if we go back to Cameron's? I love the car, but—I just want to see my Dad," I said softly.

"Of course," Kaisen said, stroking the back of my hand with his thumb.

"I want to sit down, talk, and hug him every time I get the urge to." I glanced at Kaisen, his eyes gentle.

"I can't blame you. I'd want the same thing. Let's swing by the store on the way, pick up some drinks and dinner. I'll cook tonight so you can relax with him."

"Yeah?" I asked, grinning. I couldn't think of anything else that I wanted other than to spend the evening with my family.

Half an hour later, I darted through Cameron's front door like a little kid and hugged my dad again. He chuckled as he embraced me.

"Can't tell you how many years I've wanted to do that," he said, misty-eyed.

"Well, hope you don't get tired of it, because I'm a hugger," I said and giggled.

"Never will I take something like that for granted again." A beat of silence hung in the air.

"Me neither," I whispered. "Me neither."

Laughter filled the house, and the evening stretched into the early morning hours. But no one cared. Bellies were full, the liquor flowed, and our conversation never ran dry.

The lazy afternoon sunshine filled Kaisen's living room as we snuggled on the couch. Our couch. A smile pulled at my lips at the thought.

"Hey. Is your afternoon open today?" I asked, glancing at Kaisen.

"I'm all yours. But, I might be hungry."

I laughed. "I'll feed you while we're out."

A few minutes later, we pulled out of our driveway.

"You look really hot driving your car," he said, taking my hand. "I might have to take you home with me tonight."

"I might have to let you," I teased.

My mood sobered as I turned off Fertile Valley Road and headed toward Spokane.

In half an hour, I pulled into the large circular drive and shifted into park.

"You okay here for a few minutes?" I asked as I released the seatbelt and leaned in for a quick kiss.

"I'll just spend my time pushing the buttons and turning the knobs," he joked.

"Wish me luck," I said, stepping out of my car.

The day had turned out beautifully in every way, but my stomach sank as I looked at the mansion that was void of any real life. There had been no laughter in this house, no fun memories, no tickle games or hide-and-go-seek. It had been lonely and cold.

I proceeded toward the door, my heart pounding with each step. I rang the doorbell and waited, my lower lip trembling. No response. I banged the knocker against the hardwood, the heavy sound reverberating in my ears. As I admitted defeat and turned toward the walkway, the door opened. My back stiffened, and then I turned around and faced my mother.

"Mom?" Shock shot through me. For the first time in my life, I witnessed her without makeup. Her hair was a mess, and a housecoat was hanging loosely on her frame. Dark circles underneath her eyes overshadowed her face. "Are you sick?" I asked, unable to process her appearance.

"Come in," she said, patting her hair and stepping back, allowing me inside.

My nose wrinkled at the rank odor in the house.

"Is that your garbage I smell?" I asked, my forehead creasing in confusion. "Where's your housekeeper?"

"I told her to leave," Mom said as she shuffled across the marble floor in her slippers. "Want something to drink?"

Was she drunk? Was it her I smelled? What the hell?

"Soda is fine. I'm driving."

"I saw. That's your father's car."

"Was," I said and followed her into the kitchen.

She poured a shot of vodka into her tumbler, pulled out a Coke Zero from her fridge, and handed it to me.

"'Was'?" she asked, leaning against the marble countertop.

My shoulders tensed as I overcame my shock at her appearance and reality rushed in. She was a mess.

In the uncomfortable silence, we stared at each other.

"Why are you here?" she demanded.

"I . . . I . . ."

"Spit it out, Hadlee. As you can see, I'm busy."

My brows knitted together. She was busy? Doing what? Getting drunk?

My spine straightened, and I took a deep breath. "I just want to say I don't know what I would have done. If I'd been in your shoes."

"You've never been in my shoes. So, what?"

I bristled at her harsh words. Were we about to go down this path again?

No. I refused to take the bait. "If I'd had to make a decision to protect my daughter, like you did with me, I might have made the same one. I recognize you did the best you could in a horrible situation. Now that I'm grown, I can make my own choices, but I just wanted to tell you that." I paused, my focus dropping to my soda and then drifting back up to her face. "There's no way I can stay angry at you for doing what you thought was best. And, maybe it was. I don't know."

A flicker of emotion crossed her face as she gulped her drink. I wasn't sure if or how she would respond, but I'd said what I needed to. And I could leave knowing that I no longer hated her. I could let it go and take the opportunity to rebuild relationships as I moved forward. This was my life now, and one thing that I'd learned was it could change in an instant.

"He didn't do it," she whispered, tears in her eyes. "What have I done, Hadlee? I lost everything! I should have believed in him, stood by him. And I turned on you, too. I'm so sorry."

My feet stood rooted in place as I tried to wrap my head around what she'd just said. My mother had never apologized to me. Ever.

Shit. "I'm sorry, too, Mom. For everything. For Dad being in the wrong place at the wrong time, for our family splitting apart, for the choices you had to make during a difficult and scary time in your life."

Her body shuddered as she placed the glass on the counter.

"Mom," I said—no, it was more like a request. I took a few tentative steps and did something I hadn't done since Dad had left us. I hugged her. I wrapped this broken woman up in my arms and forgave her.

Maybe it was the booze that had softened her up. Maybe Kaisen was right and alcohol just gave us permission to show our true selves. Whatever the cause, this moment was something I'd never forget, and I silently hoped it was our turning point.

"Let me get you a tissue, and then let's get you cleaned up a little," I said and nodded toward her bedroom. I waited for her as she washed up and changed into something more presentable.

"Does this look okay?" she asked, stepping out of the bathroom in jeans and a light-blue short-sleeved sweater.

"That color is really good on you." I smiled, pausing for a beat. "I'd like you to meet someone." I took her hand.

"Now?" she asked, patting her hair.

"You look fine. I promise."

I led her into the living room. "Have a seat. And no more alcohol," I said, eyeing her. "I mean it."

I stepped into the bright spring air and walked up to the car.

"Hey," I said at his door.

His body jerked. "Huh?"

"You dozed off?"

"Nope." He quickly recovered. "I was just checking the inside of my eyelids."

"Come on." I grinned. "I want you to meet someone."

"Really?" he asked, unable to hide his surprise.

"Really."

We strolled into the house, our fingers intertwined. I steered him across the foyer and into the formal living room.

"Mom, I want you to meet Kaisen." I squeezed his hand for encouragement. He'd dealt with some awkward circumstances with my parents lately.

"Hello, Ms. Jameson." He stepped forward, shaking her hand.

"Hi! Nice to meet you." She shook it and then reached up, patting her hair.

"He's my boyfriend," I said proudly.

"Fiancé, actually," he corrected. "As of today." His smile lit up his entire face.

"Oh! Hadlee, I didn't know," she said, her voice trailing off as she turned to me.

"You do now, though. He's Cameron's son."

Her eyebrow arched, and her gaze returned to Kaisen's face. "Of course you are," she murmured. "You look like your mother."

He smiled softly. "That's what I'm told."

"Sit down, please," she said, never taking her eyes off him. "Did your dad tell you that your mom and I were best friends for years? We met through Jedd and Cameron, of course, but . . ." Her face softened as she appeared lost in thought.

"I didn't know. Dad never talked about her much. I think it was too difficult for him."

"I certainly understand," she said, wringing her fingers. "But Cindy and I had so much fun together. We would go to the movies when the boys were working on their cars or whatever other guy things they did," she said, laughing.

"I'd love to learn more about her, if you don't mind? If it's not too difficult for you? If you'd rather not, I can totally respect that."

"I loved your mom, Kaisen. Even after things in her life turned dark, I have wonderful memories of her. Why don't you two stay for dinner? Hadlee, maybe you and I can whip something up?"

Was she serious? Or was she up to something? I searched her face for any hint of deceit, but for the first time in years, I found none. Something had definitely happened to her. She wasn't the same woman I had kicked out of my house that awful night almost five months ago.

"Kaisen? Dinner?"

He nodded as he rubbed my knee. "I'd love to."

And for the next four hours, we heard stories about Mom and Cindy in happier times. I realized it was impossible, but I thought my heart was glowing by the time we left and made plans for next week.

The stars had come out and lit the sky; the full moon was gleaming. A cool breeze carried a hint of promise as we arrived home.

Forgiveness can be a funny thing. Never in my wildest dreams would I have imagined I'd see my dad again or give my mom a hug. But both things had happened on the same day.

Kaisen and I crawled into our bed well after midnight. I was exhausted, but my mind was racing a hundred miles an hour.

"You had a really big day today," he said, his fingers stroking my cheek.

"One for the books," I agreed, rolling over on my side and looking at him. "But you did, too. I had no idea our mothers were friends either. Hell, I had no idea my mother could be so much fun. She certainly wasn't the same person after Dad was charged." I sighed. "Did it help to hear about some of the happier times?"

"It was hard to hear about Mom at first, but then it was good. Really good. Maybe your mom will share more as we get to know each other."

"That would be nice." I groaned and rubbed my face. "It's late, and we're helping Kara and Syd move tomorrow," I mumbled.

"Yeah, we should try to get some sleep."

I pulled the blankets up and then snuggled down into them. Although spring was here, the nights were still cool.

"Thank you," I said, looking up at him.

"For?" He stroked my hair as he looked down at me and smiled.

"For giving me hope—and for loving me."

"And to think, this all started over that one package of coffee left on the grocery store shelf."

I slid my hands around his neck and kissed him.

"Hang on a second." He opened the drawer of his nightstand. "Here," he said, his expression serious.

"What is it?" I asked, sitting up.

"Your hand, please. I know the proposal went south, but hopefully, the ring will make up for it."

He flipped open the lid of the little box.

I gasped.

"You're the best part of me," he said, taking my finger and sliding the princess-cut engagement ring on my finger.

"Thank you for finding me," I whispered, "and for never letting me go."

Kaisen kissed me gently, and then we fell back into the sanctuary of our bed.

ABOUT THE AUTHOR

J.A. Owenby lives in the beautiful Pacific Northwest with her husband and cat.

She's a published author of six short stories, and she is currently working on her fifth full-length novel. She also runs her own business as a professional resume writer and interview coach—she helps people find jobs they love.

J.A. is an avid reader of thrillers, romance, new adult, and young adult novels. She loves music, movies, and good wine. And call her crazy, but she loves the rainy Pacific Northwest; she gets her best story ideas while listening to the rain pattering against the windows in front of the fireplace.

You can follow the progress of her upcoming novel on Facebook at www.facebook.com/JAOwenby and on Twitter @jaowenby.

Don't miss out on updates and giveaways at www.jaowenby.com.

Made in the USA
Monee, IL
13 February 2023